D1389583

NOYES, R.

RALPH NOYES

A Secret Property

F / 316550

Quartet Books
London Melbourne New York

First published by Quartet Books Limited 1985
A member of the Namara Group
27/29 Goodge Street, London W1P 1FD

Copyright © 1985 Ralph Noyes

British Library Cataloguing in Publication Data

Noyes, Ralph
A secret property.
I. Title
823'.914[F]   PR6064.08/

ISBN 0-7043-2486-5

Typeset by AKM Associates (UK) Ltd, Southall, Greater London
Printed and bound in Great Britain by
Mackays of Chatham Ltd, Kent

For
Roger F. Dunkley
fellow-craftsman

1
Entertaining Strangers

Whatever came at Jake on that November night in 1990 altered the course of history – his certainly, most other people's as well without much doubt.

Such things are easily said, of course. It just happened that in Jake's case they were true. Not that anybody knew it at the time, though . . .

In the autumn of 1990 there were other things on people's minds, most of them gloomy, one or two mysterious. The gloom collared the headlines, if only because doom sells more newspapers than happiness. The price of oil had trebled again in July. Employment was running at twenty per cent in Western countries. Russian tanks were massing in East Germany. The thousandth SS 25 had been deployed in Poland. The fifteenth round of disarmament talks in Geneva had just been called off. There was a Communist *coup* in Pakistan and a CIA one in Guatemala. Signs of senile dementia had begun to appear in the Marshal Hero of the Soviet Union, Comrade Zinsky, who had recently liquidated the majority of his civilian colleagues in the Politburo. Rocky McClusky – cow-punching, ex-tapdancing President of the USA – was striking terror into the hearts of Western allies by casual references, belched out between excessive bouts of bilberry pie, to a warning shot or two across Ruskie bows in central Europe.

To Jake, who sometimes scavenged newspapers to line his bed or to restart the fire in his grate, these worldly matters meant nothing. His eye was much more likely to be caught by the inside pages before the flames charred them or his stocky frame had creased them out of reading. By the disappearance of another million acres of rain forest, for example (Jake liked forests.) By the absence of any whale in Pacific waters since 1987. By the strange ring of light which had encircled a North Korean airliner on the last few hundred miles of its eccentric journey to Taiwan from Nagasaki. By the storm of ball-lightning which had nearly grounded an Aeroflot aircraft a fortnight later on its approach to Vladivostok. To Jake these things had the sound of prophecy; they reminded him of passages in the Good Book. It never crossed his mind that he, too, might have some part to play among strange events.

Jake was a no-man, a non-person. He lived in a no-man's-land in eastern Suffolk, inhabiting a shack which had escaped even the Census of 1982 and the quinquennial review of 1987. He existed on the records of no government department, he was unknown to tax-gatherers and social workers, he lacked even a National Insurance number, he was quite as obscure as any gypsy, far less visible than an illegal immigrant. He had no friends and no relations. His relations had been few and were now dead; friends, if he had ever had any, had gone away. Only a cat called 'Cat' and twenty homing-pigeons, numbered from 'One' to 'Twenty', made any pretence of knowing him. Jake was almost a non-entity, except to himself. He was the least likely of souls to be an 'instrument of destiny' (or however learned men would put it): such parts are said to be kept for the better-heeled and the less obscure. But Jake had been chosen. And those who had chosen him knew very well what they were doing. It suited their purposes that Jake would not be missed.

On that November night in 1990 Jake was gathering firewood in Rendlesham Forest in east Suffolk. The weather was cold and clear. The moon was full. Jake was padded against the frost with a waistcoat of straw (not too often changed, it has to be said; redolent of the farmyard he had filched it from and inclined to harbour insects). Tall trunks of pines stood up around him like Gothic pillars. Their canopy made vaulted arches high above him. In the sanctuary of this cathedral Jake went about his illicit business of bundling fallen branches into a wheelbarrow. He assisted the fall of others with a rusty saw. The vast moon, a hunter's moon, sent shafts of light into the great nave. It gleamed with radiance. It lacked only a spire to make it holy.

Jake went about his business tranquilly. Forestry officers would certainly have stopped him. Officials of the Suffolk Council would probably have dragged him before a magistrate. But he lived beyond the ken of these authorities, and he knew how to keep himself hidden. Only those ghosts from some military base towards the north – those 'phantoms', as he'd heard them called – ever came to haunt him. He would have been startled and very angry to know that the habits and patterns of his cautious life had been coolly studied for some time past, and that entities which watched him judged him very suitable for what they had in mind.

He pushed his wheelbarrow across the crackling carpet of the forest, collecting the burnable spoils which would presently keep him warm. At the edge of his vision, a hundred yards to his right, he became aware of something large and round, a glowing globe half hidden behind a thicket of holly. Jake gave it an indifferent glance. He was used to tricks of the moon; the moon was an old friend; he was used to trusting it, as he trusted Cat and the homing-pigeons. The globe of light in the undergrowth was soothing; only the sudden roar of phantoms somewhere above the ceiling of his cathedral caused him to put down the wheelbarrow and to shake his fist. 'Eff-fours', a farmhand had once told him, 'effing, bloody fours'; but 'phantoms' made a better joke of them and carried less risk of having to wash his mouth out for using bad language. Phantoms, indeed! Ghosts, perhaps, but very noisy ones! Poltergeists (if he'd known the word): thundering spirits which sometimes cracked his few remaining panes of glass.

The phantoms passed. They roared away to the south. The moon-globe remained, somewhere to Jake's right. It now began to pulse, turning a rosy red.

Jake's interest was caught. His old friend the moon had never behaved like this before. In any case, Moon was now well above the forest. Jake turned his weelbarrow towards the holly and trundled it up the northerly transept of his cathedral which lay between him and the brightening glow. The globe grew more fiery. It was more like Sun than Moon. It began to warm his face, even from fifty yards off, though not in a way that was altogether comforting. It felt more like the beginning of a scorch than the kind of cheerful hearth-fire he liked to warm his hands by. From behind his back Jake heard Cat yowling. Cat had followed him, as Cat often did.

Jake put down the barrow, puzzled. The globe began to pulse

more rapidly and grew still brighter. Cat yowled again on a higher note. Jake stood still.

And then they came. Two little spheres of greenish light, bobbing and bowling across the forest clearing. They seemed to be barbed with reddish hooks; sparks fell from them as they rolled and bounced. Jake backed away from these monstrosities.. They came to a halt a yard or two ahead of him. They had no eyes but he felt them 'watching' him. Behind his shoulder Cat had fallen into a frenzy; his mog voice had risen beyond yowling into bronchial panic. Jake felt like shouting, too, but found that his throat was frozen.

The little globes rolled forward. They were the size of footballs but the game they now began to play had nothing of sport to it. Each hooked itself to one of Jake's ragged trouser-legs like an outsized burr and began to scramble up him. Jake tried to shake them off. He kicked with his legs and beat at them with his fists. But he found himself half paralysed, and shaking with a kind of ague. They reached his chest, scrabbling at his undercoat of straw. One settled across his heart, the other climbed towards his face. They gave off an acrid smell – like the time he had thrown Flowers of Sulphur on to a bonfire to get rid of that useless remedy hoarded for fifty years as a gift from his mother ('brimstone' she'd called it when he was young, forcing it into him with black molasses).

The upper 'football' crawled across his mouth and nose, grappling his whiskers with its hooks. Jake tried to scream. Suffocating, he fell into the kind of hell-fire half-glow which sometimes came to him in dreams, reminding him of Calvinistic terrors preached at him sixty years before. Then all was blackness.

A long time later – his bones were frozen to the marrow and his old friend the moon was near to setting – Jake woke again. He was lying on his back, gazing up at the cathedral canopy of the pinewood. His face felt blistered and his legs were sore. His visitors had gone but the sulphurous smell of them still lingered on the air. He struggled to his feet.

Some yards behind him he found that there had been a murder in the cathedral. Cat was dead; Cat lay spread out face downwards, very flat, very empty, like a sad little hearthrug, his dark fur sparkling with frozen dew. His innards were gone. Something had dissected him with surgical precision. Weeping, Jake hearsed him homewards in the wheelbarrow and gave him Christian burial, reading aloud from the Good Book.

Later, lying cold and trembling on his straw mattress, Jake looked for comfort in the Good Book. It fell open at a favourite passage: 'Be not forgetful to entertain strangers; for thereby some have entertained angels unaware.' It was partly for the advent of such strangers that Jake made sure to keep a stock of unlawful firewood. He had always known that they would come.

In the morning Jake mounted his rusty bicycle and rode off towards the north. He had come to doubt that his visitors had been angels. His face was blotched and puffy, his legs covered with weals; and Cat lay in a cat's-cradle of damp earth under a cat's cross. 'Not angels,' thought Jake, 'but phantoms.' To the north lay the American airbase with its phantom-fiends. From its American commander, from the king of all those phantoms, Jake meant to seek redress. Unwontedly, against the instincts of a lifetime, to the interest of those who watched him, Jake was about to tangle with Authority. Weals and blotches mightn't have made him do so. Mere terror he would have grown used to. It was the killing of Cat that sent him up the road to Bentbridge. The killing of Cat was their first miscalculation. It altered the course of history.

Nine hundred miles to the east another man, called Lem, was also about to receive visitors though he did not yet know it.

He was talking to himself in English. English was one of his problems. French was another. He had no official reason for speaking either. It had got him into trouble – that and his tendency to see and hear things which he shouldn't.

'Eliot,' he was saying to himself aloud. 'A man called Eliot.' He creased his broad forehead in a frown and puckered his high cheekbones.

The warder standing in the corridor just beyond the grille in the cell-door caught the words without understanding them. He had no idea what Lem was saying. It was enough that Lem was again, for the third time in a month and despite his treatment, lapsing into some private languague of his own. It would set back his cure; the Comrade-Doctor had said so. The warder listened carefully, counting the words. He would presently report their precise number. He was a methodical man. He knew his duty.

'Eliot,' said Lem again. There had been a murder. A murder in some cathedral. The thought had come into his head a little while ago. 'Cathedral' was odd. There were no 'cathedrals' now, only State museums of an historical kind. His grandmother had once embarrassed him by kneeling in one of them at Lvov and muttering words to some authority other than the State. He had tried to hide her with his waterproof, smiling foolishly at the lady Comrade-Keeper.

But 'cathedral' it was. Lem sensed an image of tall columns, a vaulted roof, the moon beyond it, the body of a victim somewhere below it. A murder in a cathedral. Half-remembered lines of English came back to him. Written by a man called Eliot. Jack Eliot? Jake Eliot? Yake Eliot? His grasp of English consonants was shaky. 'Cathedral,' he said aloud, practising the language. 'Murder. Moonlight. Spectres.' The warder in the corridor kept count.

Lem half closed his eyes in the effort to see more clearly. They were eyes a little too big even for the round dome of the skull in which they were deeply set, just as his head was a little too big for his body, his body too big for the short legs. Standing, he had the look of a gnome. An amiable gnome. A gentle gnome. But a gnome now strained with some inner task as well as with traces of a recent illness. A gnome who had reasons for not being in the best of health.

Images drifted through his head. Spectres. Phantoms. Suddenly some words came back to him. A line by a man called Eliot (Jack? Jake?) foreshadowing the murder of some 'holy' man (some minister of the opiate of the people) by officers of the State in a tall and misty building. 'Since golden October declined into sombre November . . .'

Lem spoke the words aloud. He repeated 'sombre' several times, finding the sound pleasing. The warder had disappeared.

'Bar the door, bar the door,' murmured Lem to himself, remembering a moment of irony in the English play. 'The door is barred. We are safe. We are safe.'

The cell-door opened. The Comrade-Doctor entered, followed by a medical orderly. Lem was about to entertain visitors. They were no strangers to him.

The Comrade-Doctor was a small, round man with a gentle

expression who had been trained at the Serbski Institute of Forensic Psychiatry in Moscow. Now Deputy-Comrade-Commandant at the Special Psychiatric Hospital at Cherny-akhovsk in Lithuania, he had no doubts about what he was doing. He had seen many dissidents and other oddments of humanity at the Serbski Institute. He knew that they were mad. He was often privately moved by the wisdom and compassion of the State in recognizing their madness. It would have been so easy – so harsh, so misguided in the longer run – to treat them as responsible for their actions, to send them to some labour camp for five or six years. Instead, they were given the scientific mercies of advanced medicine. And they rarely came back again after their six months or year of treatment. The labour camps were full of people who had come back for the third or fourth time.

He puckered his forehead compassionately and gently shook his head. 'Lem, Lem,' he said with mild reproach.

Wrenched from his 'cathedral', Lem began to weep. He had entertained these visitors a number of times before. He knew what was coming. He made no effort to resist. He didn't want to be wrapped again in that hot, damp sheet and left to lie in choking claustrophobia for sixty minutes. The Comrade-Doctor had talked him out of his claustrophobia.

The orderly gave him the injection of Sulfazine. It scorched along his veins like liquid fire. In a while there would come the pains of his grandmother's Hell: the incessant trembling, the high fever, the agonizing ache in every limb, the glimpse of devils at the corners of the cell.

His visitors departed. They would leave him alone now for twenty-four hours. And then the Comrade-Doctor would come back and talk to him – quietly, compassionately – about his duties as a Soviet citizen, the need to be cured, the wisdom of the Mother State.

The ague began quite quickly. Lem got up and walked about the cell. He knew better than to lie down; every position was a misery; it was wiser to keep moving. The devils had not yet come. He began to wonder whether something could be done about the devils. They were 'real' enough. They were 'there'. They tormented him. They synchronized remarkably well with the painful spasms of the Sulfazine. They had the same sulphurous smell to them. Yet

7

they were not quite 'solid'. They could possibly be 'brought under control'.

Something beyond the bars of the cell-window caught his attention. He went and gazed out of it, grasping the cold metal with his trembling hands. It was the planet Venus. He knew the sky well enough to be certain of it.

The Comrade-Doctor had tried to tell him that it was the planet Venus which accounted for all those stories Lem had heard of through his Moscow friends about a great, orange, 'jellyfish-like' object seen over Petrozavodsk in September 1977, and again over Moscow in June 1980, and yet again near a spacecraft launching centre at Baikonour in central Asia two years later. 'It was the planet Venus,' said the Comrade-Doctor with gentle firmness when Lem told him about a 'vision', seen with his own eyes in the summer of 1988 on a lonely holiday some hundreds of miles to the north of Moscow.

Venus? It was certainly not Venus. It *could* just possibly have been the Aurora Borealis – except that Lem knew the Aurora Borealis quite as well as Venus when he saw it; except, also, that it formed, in vast outline, the features of an icon he had once seen in his grandmother's attic; except that it seemed to smile at him when he cried aloud in wonder. He had written to his English friends about this incident. It hardly seemed a *political* act. They had printed his letter (with one or two grammatical improvements) in the October issue of their obscure little English journal. In November Lem was arrested and taken to the Serbski Institute, where he met, for the first time, several other Soviet citizens with whom he had long been corresponding about absurdities of this kind. That had been two years ago, the November of 1988. In the following March he had been sent to Chernyakhovsk 'for rehabilitation'. It was now November again.

'When golden October declines into sombre November . . .' muttered Lem aloud, partly misquoting, knowing that he was no longer overheard.

He turned away from the window and stared at the cell-wall. The pains were beginning; the devils had not yet come. A little globe of light danced up and down on the dingy whitewash: an after-image of the planet Venus, probably. Lem tried to play with it, blinking his eyes. It seemed almost solid. He made an effort to change its shape. It seemed to grow a hook or two, pulsing in time with his heartbeat, threatening to become devilish. He closed his lids to exorcize it, and tried to think of other things. 'Eliot,' he murmured to himself, thinking of 'cathedrals', thinking of 'murder'.

From his turret window in the Ministry of Defence John Eliot leaned into the November air. Since last night, All-hallows Eve, the last day of October, the weather had turned sombre. Whitehall was misty. The towers of Westminster Abbey loomed sullen in the distance and the Horseguards clock, chiming a quarter to one, trembled on the air like the bell of a drowned cathedral.

Eliot closed the window and came back into his familiar fug. There was a draft answer to be done to some damned Parliamentary Question. The Air Force Minister was waiting for it. He too, like Eliot, would be munching dried-up sandwiches at his desk during the lunch break, preparing for Question Time at half-past two.

Eliot groped behind *Who's Who* for the bottle of gin he kept there to conceal it from the cleaning ladies. He slopped a couple of fingers into a glass and added lukewarm tonic. Why the hell hadn't ministers tried to postpone this bloody question? The chap tabling it belonged to their own party, for God's sake! Surely they could have nobbled him in a corridor and told him to belt up . . . Or to write a letter and wait for the anodyne reply . . . Or go on a fact-finding mission to Gibraltar . . .

He studied the order paper again: 'To ask the Secretary of State for Defence how many reports his department has received of Unidentified Flying Objects during the past twelve months and in how many cases a satisfactory explanation has been found.'

Eliot groaned. He reread the conscientious brief provided by his own division. There had been 763 reports since this bloody MP had tabled his last bloody question in November 1989. But seventeen of them were confidential reports made by Royal Air Force stations (who really ought to have known better) and a number of them were from overseas stations. These would have to be concealed, not by telling lies (which never paid), but by using a form of words which suavely overlooked them. 'The number of reports made by members of the *public* in the *United Kingdom* . . .'

The emphasis would be for the minister's information only. The background notes would say so. The version of the answer released to *Hansard* . . .

Eliot's door opened. His boss came in. Eliot suppressed his irritation and half got up. 'Aleister!' he said, sounding cordial. 'To what do I owe . . . ?' He left the jocularity floating. What the hell did Aleister want? He could have done without entertaining visitors at this point. It was a courtesy, of course. Aleister could have summoned him to his own bigger bit of carpet and his privileged view across the Thames. What was he up to?

'My dear fellow,' said Aleister.

John Eliot listened cautiously. 'Chap' would have been affable. 'Fellow' had a touch of reserve.

'You're going on leave on Friday? Tomorrow night, as ever is?'

'Yes,' said Eliot firmly. Aleister had authorized it – after talking him out of it twice. ('The draft White Paper, my dear chap . . . That row you're having with the Treasury about estimates . . .')

'You can do a job for us while you're up there. It *is* Suffolk, isn't it?'

Eliot hid his expression behind the lukewarm gin. For God's sake . . . ! He thought of a bird called Lucy; a snug ten days planned for a coaching inn at Ipswich; a break from the round of trying to talk his Air Force friends up the corridor out of their latest quarrel with the Navy.

'I want you to pay a call on a troublesome citizen.' said Aleister thoughtfully. He sat down with well-judged nonchalance on the edge of Eliot's desk. It was an act of *de haut en bas* without getting too near the *bas*, cordial but slightly arrogant. 'An awkward individual, it seems.'

He consulted a pencil note. It had to be said for Aleister that he never committed anything to a file until certain about his 'position'. Eliot admired his style.

'Name of Jake, I'm told. No surname, apparently. Camps in a bit of woodland in Suffolk. He's making himself a nuisance to our American chums at Bentbridge.'

'Chums' was nicely chosen, thought Eliot. It lay halfway between 'chaps' and 'fellows'. It expressed Aleister's modified rapture for their United States Air Force friends at the Suffolk base. 'What's happened this time?' he asked cautiously. The USAF were inclined to get tactless about the funny British ways of the local citizenry. Eliot had been up there several times to smooth over spots of bother which the resident RAF Wing Commander hadn't been able to handle. The poor chap was outgunned, of course. He was there only to preserve the fiction that Bentbridge remained the property of HMG, that the Americans were merely lodgers, that the USAF accepted a British finger on every trigger. In practice, the RAF chap, excellent though he was, spent most of his time trying to paper over cracks. The USAF Base Commander was a couple of ranks higher. He came from Texas. He had little patience with Limey susceptibilities. There was a war on, wasn't there?

'This Jake person,' said Aleister. 'A troublesome fellow, I fear. Claims to have seen a saucer. Says it's killed a friend of his. Thinks our American chums must have sent it.'

'A *what*?' said Eliot, glancing at the PQ folder on his desk.

'Unidentified Flying Whatsit,' said Aleister. 'Don't tell me you haven't read those hundreds of mad reports which keep crossing your desk. You've even had the nerve to refer one or two to *me*!'

Eliot remembered. Hundreds of reports. Thousands, to be exact. He usually uncluttered his desk by passing them smartly to the Meteorological Office and/or that building in Northumberland Avenue – once a posh hotel, now an outpost of intelligence 'friends' – taking their bland replies as the basis on which some junior chap in the division could send suave rejoinders to the lunatic public: old ladies who'd seen a 'flying hoop' over Whitby; crazed, ex-BOAC pilots, now clearly having the hot flushes, who'd been seeking sympathy for their persecution by a 'flying cross' in Dorset; even the occasional policeman who should have known better than to flog his Panda halfway across the moors to the north of Manchester in pursuit of a 'mystery helicopter' which had had no clearances from any Air Traffic Control Officer and which sometimes looped the loop at a couple of hundred miles an hour. Eliot began to wonder if he should have been taking these things more seriously. If Aleister was interested . . .?

'Why me?' he said neutrally. This Jake person – this 'individual', this 'citizen', this clearly undesirable 'element' – sounded more like a job for a police sergeant or some local GP who fancied his hand at home-made psychiatry.

11

'I'd like a report from somebody *sound*,' said Aleister.

'Sound' was difficult to resist. It was one of Aleister's highest compliments. Eliot wanly smiled.

'After all,' said Aleister, 'you were the chap . . .' ('chap' at last, thank God!) '. . . who went up to Anglia TV the other day to explain our position to the locals on that wee little station of yours on the east coast.'

John Eliot tried to look flattered. That wee little station on the coast of Suffolk was hardly 'his'. Even its precise purpose remained a bit obscure to him. Some information-gathering thing, it seemed, judging from the formal agreement with Washington (who were putting up most of the money), some bit of high-powered radar. The sort of thing best left to Def. Sci. He'd not needed to know too much. He had on the other hand done a fairly smooth publicity job on it. There'd been a note from the Secretary of State's office congratulating him on brainwashing the local populace into dumb acceptance of its hideous appearance and rumoured dangers to life and limb. Some clot of an assistant private secretary had sent this valuable piece of paper directly to him. It had cost Eliot half a morning to get it rerouted via the Permanent Secretary for the sake of getting some credit with the Old Man and (with luck) a dry little note of approval on his personal file. Did he really have to waste further time on it? 'Why not send Jenkins?' he asked, thinking of the Defence Scientist who'd proved such a pain in the neck about that wee little station. Mad Jenkins, menopausal Jenkins probably. Right up to the last moment Jenkins had continued to come up with wild scenarios, forecasting mayhem to local citizens from the vast power output of RAF Blandfordness, given absurd combinations of circumstances. Eliot had lost days getting him overruled. It would serve Jenkins right. It might even do him good. It would give him the chance to remove suspicions (reluctantly fostered by Eliot) that 'Jenkins has gone soft', perhaps even that 'Jenkins had better have his security clearance reviewed'.

'*Jenkins*?' said Aleister, rolling his eyes at Eliot's ceiling. 'That *scientist*? *Mon Dieu*, my dear fellow . . .' The lapse into French was ominous; he kept it for mild displeasure. 'I want a personal report from an *administrative* colleague. Somebody sound. *Not* for the file at this stage, of course.' He poured himself some of Eliot's gin.

'By Monday afternoon if you don't mind.' He studied Eliot's expression. 'I'm *so* sorry about your leave my dear . . . chap. You can pick it up a bit later. Have a fortnight in December. If we can spare you from the War Book Committee . . .'

'When did this thing happen?' said Eliot. It would be pointless to give way to self-pity. Fate had better be accepted.

'Some time during the night. The Base Commander rang me at eleven this morning.'

Eliot was astonished. What on earth was this panic on the part of a tough Texan who thought nothing of rolling his armoured personnel-carriers across local wheat fields and leaving it to the Brits to pick up the legal pieces weeks later? He was surprised that Aleister was taking it seriously. 'I'll do what I can on Saturday.'

'Day after tomorrow?' said Aleister. 'Too late. Give yourself a treat, my dear chap. Go on leave this afternoon. Have a good night's rest. Get on to it in the morning.'

'There's this PQ . . .'

Aleister gave him a quizzical glance. 'That stuff about Flying Objects? The Hon. Member wants his head examined. Give the damn thing to one of those expensive minions of yours.' He drained his gin and prepared to leave. 'You can't keep you name in front of ministers *all* the time! Give young whatsisname a chance.' He turned at the door and handed Eliot his pencilled piece of scrap paper. 'Just a jotting I've made. Chuck it away when you've read it. We'll decide what to put on the file when you've told me all on Monday.'

The Horseguards clock was chiming the hour. John Eliot opened his window again and stared glumly across Whitehall at the Cabinet Office. The afternoon was murky. The golden days of October had certainly gone. Somewhere to the left of the Banqueting Hall, in defiance of an electronic age, some weedy youth was selling the evening newspaper. He shouted into the mist at passers-by. For the first time in years John Eliot heard the cry of 'Read all abaht it!' The poor fellow must be needing money! There was something about a collision in space; the tangling of American and Russian vehicles. The President had been flown back to Washington from a golfing holiday. Marshal Zinsky had made an important statement in *Istvestia*. NATO had decided to bring forward its plans for a late-autumn exercise in West Germany.

Things were carrying on as usual, thought Eliot, closing the window. If only it weren't for that Jake person. And Aleister's ridiculous interest in him. He was a stranger that John Eliot could have done without.

Thursday 1 November 1990. A busy day for somebody or something. It was between half-past four and five in the afternoon in the Département of Lozères in southern France. A chilly, misty afternoon with the dusk falling. Dr Jean-Paul Bien-Aimé Foucault, distinguished physicist at the University of Grenoble, now seeking a few days of autumn to put his notes in order, drove his Citroën up a mountain road. His mind was on worldly matters – though matters which were also a little unworldly, perhaps, by the standards of a Jake or a Lem or a John Eliot. He was thinking about the trace of a new particle – something massive and mysterious – which had shown up in the closing days of October in the vast, new 'atom-smashing' particle-accelerator at CERN near Geneva. 'A "cathedral" of the modern age,' somebody had said of that concrete labyrinth, buried below a hillside, in which basic bits (alleged) of the (alleged) universe were hurled at each other with collossal energy to see what would happen to them. 'Cathedral' had not appealed to Dr Foucault. He kept piety for Sundays.

He swung round a dusky corner with his mind on the properties of the universe. And came to a skidding halt.

The thing on the road ahead of him was egg-shaped. It looked like an egg lying on its side. A big egg, to be sure: ten metres across, he reckoned, perhaps five metres high. It was three times as tall as the Citroën and six times its length from side to side. It straddled the mountain road which led up to the high ridge of the Cévennes. It blocked his path, extending a misty light into the chestnut trees on either side.

The first thing that struck him was its weirdness. He had seen no vehicle like it – if 'vehicle' it was. There was a low hum, almost beneath hearing. It made an odd reverberation which he had not heard before. The car was shaking with it. He began to open the car-door and then hesitated. The fine hairs on the backs of his hands had risen, and his scalp was prickling. Static electricity, perhaps? But it felt more like fear. The oddity ahead of him was *big*; it towered above him. It was also very strange. It gave off a greenish glow as well as that deep hum. He could now see that it had some window or portal towards its base and that it rested on stout, squat legs.

Dr Foucault had heard of such things. He had been opposed to them for years. He knew that they were figments of the imagination, a hobby of the freakish fringe, a means of enabling agencies of the French Government to grab scarce public money which Foucault believed – fiercely, bitterly, *scientifically* – would be far better devoted to other ends, his own faculty at Grenoble, for example. For months past he had been twitting the minister concerned, with all the vitriolic irony of a distinguished member of the French Academy, to close down that absurd outfit, GEPAN, and the little cell which controlled it from CNES. CNES itself could be tolerated. That *Centre National pour les Etudes Spatiaux*, that national centre for space studies, was needed simply as a means of keeping up the French end with those damned Anglo-Saxons, however frivolous its expensive rocketry might seem. But GEPAN . . .! Its very name was an insult to the intelligence: *Groupement pour les Etudes des Phenomènes Aéro-Spatiaux Non-Identifiés*, indeed! It was astonishing that the President had upheld its continued existence during the Cabinet rows about public spending in 1982 and again during the ecomomic crisis of 1988. (But what could you expect of a Socialist?) It was good to see that the minister concerned was now distinctly on the run. He had turned quite pale on seeing Dr Foucault at a recent reception.

A little pale himself, Dr Foucault fiddled with the door-handle. His instincts told him to stick within the comforting envelope of the little Citroën. It felt like a metal tent in which he could safely cower, like a safari tourist in strange jungles, until the beast outside had gone away again. Professional habit, on the other hand, told him to get out and have a closer look. In any case, who was to say whether that contemptible, that *cowering* minister hadn't hired some Hollywood director (some *Spielberg*, some wretched *Saxon*) to frighten the formidable Dr Foucault into dropping his sallies against that foolish Group For the Study of Unidentified Aerospace Phenomena? This was quite probably a put-up job. It was a movie set. He would complain about its cost to the Treasury. Shakily, if only because the car was shuddering, Dr Foucault

15

opened the car-door and climbed out on to the misty road. He prepared himself to meet ET and to give it the edge of his much-practised wit.

'Creatures' came from the 'vehicle'. One was man-shaped and man-sized. It wore a silvery suit and carried its flaxen hair to a little below shoulder-length. It looked gentle and not unfriendly. It occurred to him that poor Sainte Jeanne of Domrémy, that little Joan of Arc who had been abominably treated by Anglo-Saxons in 1431 and whose martyr-day Dr Foucault made a point of observing in his native Rouen, had claimed to speak with some entity of a similar kind, her 'St Michael', as she called him. Dr Foucault's patriotism was aroused.

The other two creatures were also man-shaped, that is to say they had two arms, two legs and a head on top. But they were half the size of Jean-Paul Foucault and their heads were not appealing – one-eyed, large-snouted, and – as he wrote in his diary later with Gallic precision – 'un très petit peu ménaçant'. They walked with a stiff gait like clockwork marionettes. From the 'face' of one of them sharp little 'metallic' sounds were being uttered; they sprang staccato from a lipless slit beneath the snout.

Clawlike hands seized Dr Foucault by the wrists. He had a moment in which to see – methodical scientist to the last – that his watch was flashing 16.49, eleven minutes to five on Thursday 1 November 1990. Then all became like a nightmare, though a nightmare suffered under heavy tranquillizers.

Silversuit spoke to him in a silvery voice. '*Je suis Michel*,' it seemed to say. Or perhaps, 'My name is Michael.' Or even something as commonplace – as *American* – as, 'I'm Mike.' Jean-Paul Foucault, having spent a couple of years at Cambridge, flattered himself that he was bilingual. In any case, the words seemed to come directly into his head.

'Michel?' he said (or thought he said). 'Michael?' (Was there some suspicion of wings at the creature's shoulders?)

Then he was lying on his back in some little cabin, enveloped in a greenish glow. Answering questions, it seemed. There were eyes above him.

Then he was lying on his back on a mountain road in the Cévennes. There were stars above him, the mist had cleared. His watch read 19.07. Two hours and eighteen minutes had . . .

elapsed? Disappeared? Been forced out of memory?

He climbed back into the Citroën and switched on the roof-light. In the driving mirror he saw that his face was 'sunburned'. It had turned copper-coloured and the skin was peeling. A touch of arthritis in his left hip which had troubled him for some months past seemed to have disappeared.

He drove on towards his planned weekend with the man whose job he aspired to: the retiring Professor of Physics at Grenoble, an Academician of renowned and pedantic rationality. Jean-Paul Bien-Aimé Foucault decided against mentioning the circumstances which had made him late. He turned over in his mind whether to report his experience to GEPAN, an organization for which he suddenly felt a degree less hostility than hitherto. On the whole, it seemed better not to do so. He had a professional reputation to maintain.

On the evening train to Ipswich John Eliot reread the pencil notes which Aleister had given him. They consisted mainly of a bad sketch, based on the Ordnance Survey, of an area of Rendlesham Forest to the south of RAF Bentbridge ('RAF' by the legal fiction of its resident Brit, otherwise an outpost of the United States at which a cigar-chewing Texan did more or less what he wanted).

There were two crosses on the map, one marked 'shack', the other marked 'incident'. Aleister seemed to have been very precisely informed.

Below the sketch were three words, scrawled in the 4B pencil which Aleister affected (mainly because it was easy to rub out): 'Us? Them? LGM?'

Eliot racked his mind for 'LGM'. Chewing a sandwich in the corridor, he remembered – from a bad bit of science fiction he had once read – what the initials meant.

Little Green Men. LGM. The name given by sceptical wits to those supposed visitors from outer space in which the freaky young believed. (Even some freaky oldies, when it came to it.) They had been bringing their 'saucers' to Earth for centuries – especially since a man called Kenneth Arnold had given the press that handy term 'saucer' in 1947. Flying over Mount Rainier in the State of Washington, Arnold had seen 'discs'. Flicking his eyes between Mount Rainier and Mount Adams, he reckoned that they were flying at well above a thousand miles per hour. The press had lapped it up. The 'saucer' industry had never since ceased to thrive. Later, a lunatic called Adamski (after Mount Adams, perhaps? – this whole mad field was filled with bad puns) had been 'abducted' by little green aliens, and taken to the planet Venus and back in a couple of hours, and given a 'blueprint' for Planet Earth . . .

Eliot stuffed Aleister's note back into his pocket, wondering what his boss was up to. It was hardly thinkable that Aleister believed in LGM. Perhaps the initials stood for something else.

He leaned against the corridor-window, staring into the November evening. An orange globe of light was pacing the train. It lay at some unjudgeable distance beyond the telegraph wires which rose and fell, rose and fell, as the train sped northwards. Even in the tunnel which they had now entered this unidentified object continued to haunt him. He was grimly amused to recognised it as the reflection of a reading-light in the first-class compartment behind his shoulder. Tomorrow he would exorcize another ghost in Rendlesham Forest. Later this evening he would enjoy the more solid comforts of the simulated, gas-fired, 'logs' in the Green Man Inn at Ipswich and the unsimulated ecstasies of a bird called Lucy.

The Sulfazine was coming to its peak. The devils were turning up.

Lem, not daring to sit down, leaned against the wall. He fixed his visitors with disco-ordinated eyes. Each of the phantoms was double. For that the Sulfazine could be blamed. But their shape was something else. Their shape was particular to him and them. They were, in some way, 'his'.

Lem had sometimes talked – covertly, discreetly, in canteen queues – to others who were 'on' Sulfazine. Their reports differed. Their visions were always abominable but they were never quite the same. 'Our devils are our own,' said Lem aloud. 'Our devils belong to us,' he added boldly.

The thing at the corner of his cell changed to a bird-eating spider – big enough to eat nightingales, Lem reckoned. Its fleshy legs, bristling with brown fur, tested the concrete floor. Its octagon of eyes swivelled, searching for prey. Up on the wall above it some thin grey tube of a creature writhed from the convenient hook on which Lem had once tried to hang himself during that first year at Chernyakhovsk. Presently, it would slip to the floor and blindly ooze its way towards him.

Shaking with the onset of fever, Lem stifled the impulse to cry out. Warders would come with that damp sheet if he did so. Better to choke on his own fear than to lie suffocating with his limbs swaddled in tightening linen.

The blind-worm dropped. The spider began its sidling scuttle towards his bare feet. A scream rose up Lem's throat but he choked it back, grinding his teeth. The effort bulged the veins in his domed forehead, his skull seemed bursting with it. Vivid colours flashed behind his eyelids – or a little in front of them. A little orange globe, tiny but fierce, burned before his eyes. It seemed to dart downwards towards the floor. There was a flash like lightning, sulphur-yellow and with a sulphur-smell.

Never before had Lem heard a spider scream. Or explode into wispy fragments of scorching tissue. Or drift about the cell turning into a grey ash which presently settled to the floor, changing to a viscous puddle and then evaporating without trace.

He turned his gaze to the long grey worm at his feet. Some frenzy was convulsing it. It writhed and twisted in a blind agony or rage. An orange glow suffused it. With his own limbs in the grip of the Sulfazine Lem hurled hatred towards the floor like a thunderbolt – and then pity. This poor sightless creature was no more to be blamed than he was! He reached down and picked it up.

But already it was inert. It hung in his hands like a piece of charred rope. Something had scorched beyond recognition whatever 'reality' this sad little 'devil' had recently possessed. As he watched it, it shrivelled and disappeared.

Later that night, the end of the first day of November 1990, other strangers, no less entertaining, came to other places about the world. They had been coming for a long time past; for centuries, some said.

Many were mere 'lights in the sky', those *Lumières Dans La Nuit* from which French UFO-buffs of a kind repugnant to

Dr Foucault took the initials for their eccentric organization, LDLN. Others came closer to Earth and appeared in other forms: a trace on radar, moving as swiftly as an Earth satellite but at no more than a thousand feet above the White Sands Proving Grounds in New Mexico; a glowing tetrahedron which swooped across a country road to the south of Stuttgart, stopping the Volkswagen driven by an elderly German couple and leaving them with a reddish irritation of the skin which lasted for several days; a multi-coloured hemisphere hovering above the field of a Spanish poultry farmer in Tarragona whose occupants – 'octopus-like creatures', he said, with several legs – whizzed their vehicle away into the sky at enormous speed on catching sight of him.

Other encounters were more direct, more personal. Like Jake's. Like Dr Foucault's. Like the Sulfazine-nightmares of a prisoner at Chernyakhovsk. Like the last half-hour of a certain Dr Faust or Faustus, dying at Wittenberg in mysterious circumstances in 1540.

Something came from the sea near Ponta Negra on the coast of Brazil with eyes which shone in the dark. It pointed a rod-shaped instrument at a young man and a girl, lying together on the beach, and compelled them to come, trembling and half paralysed, to a great cigar-shaped structure which rested among the sand dunes. There, they were 'closely examined', as the young man later put it. He had been forced to exercise his virility with a 'female of oriental features' who told him that she came from the Constellation of Orion, and that Planet Earth was in deadly peril. It did not surprise him that his girlfriend was subsequently found to be pregnant. He awaited the birth with great anxiety.

A Greek shepherd, tending flocks not far from Delphi, was set upon by two tiny creatures of ferocious force. Their heads were dome-shaped, their ears pointed. They had great white eyes, sunken and without eyelids, set above a nose which reached below the lower lip. Though less than three feet tall, they had broken his staff and bent his iron billhook before 'taking off' in the kind of 'flying saucer' he had once seen in a film in Athens.

On a farm near Le Roy, Kansas, terrified cattle fled from the descent of something in the moonlit sky above them. The empty hides of three of them were found on the following morning by a puzzled and angry farmer. It was no comfort to him that the same mysterious misfortune had befallen a herd of his grandfather's cattle on the same plot of land in 1897.

At a country house in Suffolk, not far from Rendlesham Forest, Gregorius Lampson, only son of an eccentric peer, conjured a vision of his own. Wiser than others to whom such things appeared, he stood within a pentacle, a five-pointed star, chalked on the bare floorboards of the Long Gallery. Just beyond this protective barrier there crouched and seemed to whimper some little greenish creature, trapped in a pulsing globe which hovered above the floor. 'Is it done?' said Lampson. The thing was silent. 'I'll send you back where you came from,' said Lampson amiably. The creature whimpered. It whispered in a little rasping voice like metal scraped against a windowpane. 'Done,' it seemed to say, and again, 'done', but with more malice than obedience. 'Have you brought what I told you?' said Lampson. Something dropped softly and bloodily to the floor outside the pentacle. 'I'm not falling for *that* trick,' said Lampson, smiling, 'throw it in.' The guts of Cat were tossed sullenly towards him; sparks spluttered above the black tallow candles at the corners of the pentacle as the oozy package crossed its boundary; there was a clap of miniature thunder. 'And the old man?' said Lampson, wrinkling his nose against the smell of sulphur. There was no answer. 'Ah, well,' said Lampson, shrugging, 'you'll have to try again. In a little while. He'll keep till we're ready.'

2
Equivocation of the Fiend

At thirty-five John Eliot had the stamp of success. Whitehall suited him. He had a keen eye for what was what and who was who. Promoted at an early age to take charge of a fiendishly busy division, lodged among the central staffs of the Ministry of Defence, he had already proved his worth. He had a suitable contempt for politicians, an admirable scepticism about what his military colleagues might be up to, the 'happiest of drafting styles', as Aleister had put it in that last confidential report which it had cost Eliot some trouble to catch an illicit glance at, a persuasive manner.

With an arm linked through his as they trod briskly across the crunching carpet of fallen pine-needles, Lucy Frensham wondered why she liked him. Perhaps for all those summer nights of a decade and a half ago when they had spent their long vacations from the trendy University of Sussex walking about Brighton beaches, making love in the very sh██████ of Palace Pier, talking away the small hours with the idea████ █bandon of undergraduates who have not yet been gru█bie█ █y ███ necessities of what is often called real life. Even then, th█re were ti█es when he made her uneasy. He was a little too quick at spotting which way the tides were running and swiftly changing course to swim with them. 'You'll lose your soul!' she sometimes said jocularly to him as they lay smoking after some bout of arms in the back room of his flatlet off Station Road and he – affectionate and assuaged, but never too long detached from his own concerns – coolly considered the prospects of his intended career.

The day was bright but cold. A trace of dead October gilded the sunshine but Lucy was glad of the thick overcoat and woollen scarf which had often kept her warm through the night watches at

Jodrell Bank. She had parked her car as far into Tangham Wood as the dirt road carried them. They were now walking south into a thickening stand of pines.

'Why?' she asked again, glancing at his thoughtful face. 'What exactly are we supposed to be doing?'

John Eliot, armed with a large-scale map as well as the precisely chosen clothes of a London gentleman choosing to show himself at home in the country without risking too close an identification with it, flicked open his shooting-stick and comfortably settled himself, one ankle casually crossed on the other. (He'll be getting pompous in a year or two, she thought – if they move him to the Cabinet Office, or that spell in No. 10 he keeps talking about. If he starts running to fat as well, I shall probably have to give him up!)

'Another few hundred yards,' said John Eliot, consulting the map, avoiding Lucy's question. 'I've brought you for the sake of your woman's intuition, my girl! Let's not muddle it with the facts.'

He folded the map, took bearings with a pocket compass and set off in a slightly new direction.

'I don't know why I put up with you!' said Lucy affectionately, linking arms again. Woman's intuition, indeed! She could make rings round him with the calculus! At Jodrell it wasn't intuition but sheer mathematical insight that paid her keep.

'We're monitoring that thing up there,' she said, holding her own. 'The Old Man has switched most of our resources to it since yesterday. He wasn't at all keen on letting me come down here a day early.' It really had been rather tiresome of John to summon her at half an hour's notice to join him on Thursday, the first, when they'd planned for a month past to meet on Friday, the second. 'Affairs of State,' he'd said on the telephone, jocularly self-important. 'I've got affairs of the Universe up here!' she'd complained. 'Yours will last longer,' he'd said. She'd come.

Instinctively, Lucy glanced up at the sky through the canopy of the pines – as though that extraordinary accident, not far above the stratosphere, could be seen with the naked eye. An American 'orbital platform' had somehow rammed the new Soviet SOYUZ-27. Five men had been killed instantly. Two others, one Russian, one American, were now making an unplanned space-walk, circling the Earth in wildly eccentric orbits which would shortly bring them into scorching contact with the atmosphere. A massive rescue operation was in train by the Americans (for their own man, of course). The great radio dish at Jodrell Bank had been taken off its scientific task of listening to what the tabloids called 'whispers from space' coming from thousands of billions of miles into the heart of the galaxy and pressed into something which seemed to the Grand Old Man who ran the place as local, as parochial, as *provincial* as mere coastguard service. He had fumed, grumbled and them complied, taking it out on everyone he could lay hands on to be unpleasant to. 'It's quite an "incident",' said Lucy casually, using 'incident' to keep her mind off the harsh fact that two young men, tumbling about the sky in suits as carefully chosen for their destiny as John Eliot's Jermyn Street tweed jacket, might shortly burst into the brief incandescence of shooting stars.

'Not *my* flap,' said Eliot shortly. Other divisions in the Ministry of Defence would have been sitting up all night with that one. A large clump of holly, a hundred yards to the left of them, had caught his eye. 'Holly Bush', said Aleister's pencil note, precise (though mysterious) even to its botanical detail.

They walked towards it. It glistened with morning dew trapped by the chill of the forest till well past the time at which the November sun should have steamed it off. Rounding this clump of greenery, they came face to face with unexpected facts. Three of them impinged at once on John Eliot's consciousness: a sergeant of the United States Air Force with a holstered gun at his left hip; a gouged out indentation in the earth from which ran two channels towards the south-east, ending abruptly at about fifty feet away; the low hum of a diesel engine.

The little tableau froze, two on the one side, three on the other. Which were the 'foreigners' and which the 'natives' might have been difficult to judge by outside observers (little green men from the constellation of Orion, for example). Lucy found that she felt like an intruder.

'Good morning,' said John Eliot. He politely doffed the stylish cap which complemented the rest of his outfit, sat down on the shooting-stick, took a swig from a hip flask, passed it to Lucy. It had to be said for him that he wasn't easily put out.

The sergeant came towards them with a little swagger, his hand dangling loosely by the holster. 'Pardon me, bud,' he said, fixing

Eliot with little hard-boiled eyes, 'if you wouldn't mind moving on
. . . ' He shifted a wad of something from one cheek to the other.
'Classified, you understand.'

Eliot cleared his throat and spat reflectively on to the damp
earth. 'In a piece of English woodland?' he said politely.

'Classified,' repeated the sergeant. He chewed for emphasis,
thrusting his jaw forward. 'Very high category.'

Through the trees to their right Lucy could now make out the
long low shape of an eight-wheeled transporter. It was the kind
sometimes seen these days on British roads shifting missiles on
deployment exercises. Her trained ear caught the sporadic crackle
of a geiger-counter.

Eliot got up and began to walk towards the vehicle. The
American stepped briskly in front of him his hand now visibly on
the butt of his revolver. 'I said APO, bud. Authorized Personnel
Only.'

Eliot half turned his head and raised an eyebrow at Lucy. She
saw that he was about to show off to his girlfriend and felt alarmed
but half amused. 'What makes them think that I'm not authorized?'
he said casually. He flashed a bit of pasteboard in a plastic wallet.
She had seen this talisman before. Its scarlet diagonals, criss-
crossed with yellow, overlaid the signature of the General
Commanding the US Forces in the UK. It gave Eliot – and very
few other British citizens – certain rights of entry to American
establishments. It went with his job. He valued it as much as his
new suite of Works Department furniture. He had told her once or
twice that not even Aleister carried one.

The sergeant's mouth fell open. This was no ordinary local
Limey. Christ, the Colonel might have warned him! His revolver-
hand abandoned the gun butt in favour of a perfunctory salute.
'You don't figure on my Detail Sheet . . .' he said doubtfully.

'My dear fellow,' said Eliot, picking with care from Aleister's
vocabulary, 'I've only just come up from London. Perhaps they
haven't told you.'

'The lady . . . sir . . .?'

'The lady is going for a walk,' said Eliot firmly. He handed Lucy
his map and Aleister's grubby piece of paper. 'You're going for a
walk,' he repeated. 'I'll meet you back at Ipswich. At the Large
Green Man. Some time this afternoon.' The hard-boiled official

had succumbed to something more buccaneering; perhaps that was why she still liked him. 'I,' he shot back across his shoulder, 'am going for a ride.'

He walked unhurriedly towards the transporter, followed by the USAF sergeant. Two other men came round from behind it, one carrying the geiger-counter, the other holding the kind of sterile, plastic sack in which goods of a certain kind of preciousness are best conveyed – moon-rock, pathological cultures, human remains when found in suspicious circumstances. A lump of something black, and perhaps charred, lay at the bottom of it.

Lucy Frensham watched as the ponderous vehicle drove slowly back along the track it had recently ground into the pine-scented aisles of Tangham Wood.

'What the hell are they up to?' said John Eliot, drinking the indifferent coffee of Wing Commander North.

He sat in the bleak little office of the RAF officer who was nominally in charge of the Bentbridge Base. Half a mile away across the runway and taxi-tracks some scores of USAF personnel were engaged in their daily task of overhauling the Phantoms of the USAF Fighter Wing. Their small, blue-suited figures clambered about the metal frames, testing, repairing, maintaining, repelling for a little longer the creeping mortalities which overtake aircraft as readily as men.

North shrugged. 'They tell me very little,' he confessed. 'But there was a hell of a flap in the small hours of yesterday morning. They scrambled half the fighter wing at about half-past midnight. They don't have to consult me about *that*, of course, but I could hear it even from my quarters at Bawdsey. It woke the kids up.' He moodily stirred his coffee. 'Then, at about one, Hoyt himself rang me . . .'

'The Base Commander?' said Eliot with interest. 'I thought he lived off-base at Ipswich.'

'He does. They'd hauled him in.'

'Some flap!'

'Not the first time,' said North. 'He was here three nights running about a month ago. Just after the launch of the new orbital station from Cape Kennedy. The one that's now tangled with SOYUZ-27. Something was up. But I wasn't told. 'No "need to know", of course.'

He joined Eliot at the window and stared glumly across the airfield. To the south of the fighter wing the perimeter fence of Hoyt's special compound, fifteen feet high and topped with barbed wire, sparkled in the November sunlight. It was a fortress within a fortress, a guarded enclosure lying deep within the already formidable defences of the Bentbridge base. It housed Cruise missiles, their transporters, their nuclear warheads, the 'protective' vehicles – heavily armed and armoured, cunningly wolfish in their sheep's clothing – which went with them on deployment. The compound also cocooned the vital piece of software which called itself Colonel Sherman Hoyt, together with one or two other 'functions' he commanded. Among these, as Eliot knew officially and Wing Commander North, with 'no need to know', merely knew, was a communications unit of the worldwide American Space Recovery Agency.

'I must say,' said North, 'that Whitehall's given them a pretty free hand.' He tugged at the handlebar moustache which officers of his newer generation were once more beginning to affect, perhaps because it recalled the gallant simplicities of half a century ago.

Eliot ducked the implied criticism. He had heard it often before from certain kinds of romantic Tory backbencher speaking with the same voice, though for different reasons, as doctrinaire militants on the other side of the House. Both front benches tacitly ignored them, knowing which side the national bread was now buttered. Competent officials like Eliot, swimming with the groundswell, knew better than to press too hard for 'triggers' or 'safety-catches' when settling agreements with transatlantic chums. 'What did Hoyt want from you?' he asked.

'Blanket cover,' said North. 'As usual!' he added bitterly. 'Said he had some 'top-immediate' operation to handle. Wanted to put some vehicles into the local countryside. He assumed I'd "cover" it – at once. Meaning there'd be a complaint up the line if I didn't, but that *I'd* have to cope with any offended yokels in the morning!'

'No reason given?'

'Classified', of course. Too sensitive for the blower. I said I'd come on over. He said not to bother. A quick nod on the phone from me would be good enough for him.'

'But you came?'

North gave him a reproachful look. 'The MOD still pays my wages – I presume. Of course I came. And naturally it was all over when I got here. They'd done what they wanted, "cover" or not. The Deputy Commander paid me off with a double Bourbon. In the Adjutant's office. *Outside* the compound.'

'Where was Hoyt?'

'Somewhere inside his barbed wire. There was quite a shindy going on. Lights, vehicles, every military policeman I've ever seen here. One of the transporters was going down the ramp into the underground servicing-bay. Some GI was having hysterics. I thought I saw a couple of the MPs doing him over pretty thoroughly in a corner.'

'And then?'

'Then nothing. The Dep. Comm. muttered something about a bit of "hardware" they'd had to "recover". Said he'd give me a run-down for the record later in the day – in case we had trouble with the local "kooks". That's his name for our fellow yeomanry up here. That was yesterday. I'm still waiting for the run-down.'

'Any trouble with the "kooks"?'

'Two calls from the Forestry people, one from the local rag. They'd seen lights in the sky or some such. We get a certain amount of UFO nonsense round here. Not too surprising when you think how often Hoyt puts up those Phantoms of his.'

'Nothing else?'

'Not a thing, mercifully. Our chums seem to have kept off the winter wheat this time.'

North went back to his desk and sat down. 'What brings Whitehall up here?' he asked. The tone implied that nobody told him anything and that he was getting fed up with it.

'Oh, business, business,' said Eliot cheerfully. 'What else should take anybody anywhere?' He forebore to mention that a USAF transporter had recently brought him here and that he had an interview with Colonel Hoyt in a quarter of an hour. North really had no need to know. 'Give my office a ring if anything crops up,' he said. He fingered with private satisfaction the hard edges of the piece of pasteboard lying in his pocket.

'Just one other thing,' said Wing Commander North as Eliot

prepared to leave. 'Some old tramp of a chap seems to have turned up at the south-west gate yesterday morning. I don't keep a man there; the estab doesn't run to it. I told our American chums to handle as they saw fit – unless it turned out to be Lord Lampson in disguise!'

'No read-out since?'

'Nothing they've told me,' said North. Few people told him anything, it seemed. But he had, as it happened, thought Eliot, told him all he now needed to know. It ought to be possible to settle Aleister's bit of business in the next half-hour or so and to get back to the comforts of LGM – Lucy at the Green Man – well before it was too late for the satisfactions of a mutton lunch and a drowsy afternoon in bed.

The great bible lay open at St Paul's Epistle to the Hebrews. Some late-Victorian imitator of Gustave Doré had illustrated the text with angelic visitors, strangers from outer space extravagantly winged with the pinions of gigantic doves. At their feet knelt an aged hermit seeking to entertain them with a bowl of bran.

Lucy stepped carefully across the mud floor. Kindling had been scattered on it in disarray. The fire it had been meant for lay cold and unlit in the crude hearth constructed of clay and broken bricks. The shack struck cold. Lucy gathered her overcoat about her.

There were traces of occupation but no sign of an occupant. Two ragged blankets lay on the straw bed, rumpled and half covering the bible. On a piece of board, propped on two piles of bricks, a dead rabbit lolled its head from a saucepan of cast iron. Other kitchen flotsam surrounded it, a rusty knife, three forks, a child's plastic jug decorated with Mickey Mouse, an earthenware saucer containing the drying remnants of the rabbit's heart and liver.

Lucy reread the sheet of pencilled paper which John's boss had given him. It was an odd mixture of the precise and the cryptic. 'Shack' and 'Holly Bush' were accurately marked on a tolerable sketch-map labelled 'Tangham Wood'. 'Incident' was shown with a cross, four hundred yards north-west of 'Shack'. It lay where she had recently seen two shallow channels gouged into the floor of

Tangham Wood and descending from 'Holly Bush'.

Below this sketch there were notes in smudged pencil. She took the paper to the large sheet of cracked and grimy glass which served the shack as a window and tried again to make sense of it in the wintry light which filtered down through the pine trees. It contained more questions than statements, and the statements were hardly illuminating.

'??? Loss of control ???' it began. Then, 'Temporary ??' A doodle followed, somewhat resembling a five-pointed star. On the next line were the words, 'Us? Them? LGM?' Then two or three sentences of rapid scrawl, heavily obliterated with 4B smudge. Then 'Witnessed? Chums upset. Better track him. *Unofficially*.'

She assumed that John had been told something more precise. But he'd kept it to himself.

She went back to the straw pallet on the floor and stared absently at the Epistle to the Hebrews. It reminded her of the pieties of her Wesleyan grandmother who had kept a declining village shop three decades before and who sometimes embarrassed her six-year-old assistant on Saturday afternoons by muddling tea with sugar but never for a moment forgetting the sonorities of St Paul for a customer who might profit by them. A familiar passage caught Lucy's eye. ' "Faith," ' (as her grandmother would sometimes say to a captive client, wrapping the wrong cheese at a mistaken price) ' " is the substance of things hoped for, the evidence of things not seen." '

Evidence of things not seen glittered from the hard earth at the side of the bed. Lucy stooped and picked it up. It was the cap of an expensive fountain-pen, half hidden by the edge of a blanket. Logic, rather than the woman's intuition for which John claimed to have brought her, suggested to Lucy that it had no place here. It could hardly have fallen to the ground much longer ago than the moment at which some 'witness' who had upset 'chums' seemed to have abandoned his bed and his bible for more urgent business. The gilt cap, perhaps even gold, scarcely belonged with the plastic jug and the poacher's spoils.

Making her way back to the car, Lucy passed a makeshift pigeon-loft in which a score of scrawny birds pattered disconsolate claws on its tin floor, thrusting their heads in ones and twos from the barred windows. She threw in a handful of grain from the sack below the loft and then – on impulse rather than logic – opened the loft-door, intuiting that the absent pigeon-master would not complain at their freedom to come and go while he remained away. They would hardly come to much harm. They looked like 'homers', they would not stray. Scarcely so much as a sparrow hawk was likely to descend upon them through the thick stand of pines. And in England there were no such things as bird-eating spiders – though why this last irrelevance had come to her Lucy was unsure.

'Hardware,' said John Eliot, drinking the Colonel's bourbon, 'I gather you had a bit of hardware to pick up.' He stared at his glass, carefully avoiding the scrutiny of the suave-suited civilian whom Hoyt had seen fit to have present. State Department? CIA? Perhaps merely some civilian egghead employed by the Pentagon.

Hoyt rocked on his heels. He had remained standing since Eliot's arrival. He was a smallish man, nearly as broad as tall. Sitting, he looked ridiculous (and knew it); standing, he kept something of the presence of a Texan cow-puncher. He fixed Eliot with eyes of periwinkle-blue, lodged among jowls of fat, and repeated the story which Eliot had already heard twice before in the past ten minutes. 'Unscheduled landing,' he said. 'No goddam hardware of ours.' He glanced at his civilian companion. 'Could have been a Commie plot . . .'

The civilian intervened. 'Friedman', he'd been introduced as, 'Conrad Friedman'. 'What the Colonel means,' he said, 'is that we've got nothing to hide from our friends and allies!' He gave Eliot a fresh-faced grin, keeping his hands hidden in the pockets of a jacket so elegantly casual that only a tailor operating out of Jermyn Street could possibly have sold it. Friedman must have been living in the UK.

'Hardware,' repeated Eliot. He extended his glass to be refilled. The whisky was sharpening his perceptions. ('You're losing your soul,' Lucy sometimes jocularly told him, 'but the spirits will keep you going.') 'Your chaps picked up a bit of hardware earlier this morning. What else have you found?'

Friedman and Hoyt exchanged glances. 'Now, look –' began the Colonel. Friedman broke in. 'We want to take you into our full confidence.' He smiled engagingly. Only a nest of crows' feet around the eyes belied his look of a fresh-faced college boy. 'We've gotten some evidence . . . Something out of the routine . . .'

'Come off it!' said Eliot, emboldened by Bourbon, smiling broadly to show that he meant no offence. 'You're testing something up here. Something you haven't told us about. You should have done, of course. But, never mind! Give me the facts and I'll smooth it over.'

Outside Hoyt's window a military policeman went to and fro, keeping the Colonel's peace. Beyond him, through the meshes of the compound's wire enclosure, the legal fiction of the Royal Air Force Station, Bentbridge, glittered under the November noon.

'We're testing nothing you guys don't know about,' said Conrad Friedman firmly.

'Space gear?' said Eliot.

Colonel Hoyt chewed on the butt of his damp cheroot. 'In a goddam pinewood?'

Conrad Friedman pulled his chair a little closer to Eliot's. 'I want to take you into our confidence,' he said smoothly. He patted Eliot's knee. 'What's turned up is the biggest thing in history!' He smiled with freshman frankness. 'We've been suspecting it for a couple of decades. Now we've got it.' He studied Eliot's expression. 'You won't believe this . . .'

'On Fridays,' said Eliot, 'I believe almost anything . . . Even if only to get away for the weekend.'

'They've landed,' said Friedman. 'Not for the first time. You should see what we've got at Wright Patterson . . . But this is the best one yet. Hardware. Specimens. Software.'

'Software?' said Eliot.

'Bodies,' said Colonel Hoyt with military frankness. 'We've got 'em on ice.'

A silence ensued, respectful of the dead.

'Can I see this . . . software?' said Eliot, fingering the piece of pasteboard in his pocket.

Hoyt coughed. Friedman widened his young man's, old man's eyes to their frankest. 'There's an autopsy going on,' he said. 'Under *the* most sterile conditions! God knows what they could have brought with them . . . from "out there". Ever seen a movie called *The Andromeda Strain*?'

'I don't mind putting on a plastic nightgown,' said Eliot. He offered his glass for a third Bourbon. 'Don't forget,' he added, lying, 'that I'm up here with Buchanan's authority.' Not true, of course. He was up here to talk to an undesirable element called Jake. It was only by chance that he'd stumbled into the chums. But Aleister could hardly mind.

'Mr Aleister Buchanan,' said Hoyt, rocking on his heels. 'Shall I put a call through?' He returned to his desk and put his hand on the green telephone which nested among the others. It was the one with the scrambler, the right instrument for top-secret calls.

Bluff called, thought Eliot. Better not press it. Better get back to Aleister first. He changed his tack. 'I've got to put in a report, of course.'

'Of course,' said Friedman.

'And you want me to say that you've had visitors? From Outer Space?'

'You're goddam right,' said Colonel Hoyt.

'Little Green Men?'

Friedman withdrew well-manicured hands from the jacket-pockets and studied the backs of them. 'Greyish-yellow,' he said, not looking at Eliot. 'Three and a half feet tall. Like others we've had traces of. But these are the best specimens yet.'

'When are we going to be privileged to have a look at them?'

There was a brief silence. 'Just as soon as we've got them quarantined,' said Friedman. He glanced at Hoyt. 'I'm giving London a full run-down,' said Hoyt. 'I'm writing to Mr Buchanan.'

'OK,' said Eliot. 'I'll brief him.' He swirled the whisky in its glass, considering his tactics. 'No chance of a look? While I happen to be on the spot . . .?'

'As of now . . .' said Friedman. He left the sentence dangling.

'OK,' said Eliot cheerfully. The position was now quite clear to him. The American chums had been up to something which they wanted to keep hidden ('under wraps', they'd say) until ready to take Limey colleagues into confidence. They'd better be pressed. And soon. Even in these latter days it wasn't quite good enough for American friends to play free and easy with British airspace and a bit of British woodland. 'I'm told,' he said, 'that you've had a call from some old tramp of a fellow. I'm trying to track him. We don't want our gallant allies bothered with British eccentrics!'

The speed of Hoyt's response surprised him. Hoyt picked up a telephone – black, unscrambled, totally without security – and gave crisp instructions to his secretary. 'We've got him in sick bay,' he explained.

'A British citizen?' said Eliot. He tried to sound outraged, but the Bourbon had now mellowed him. 'You can't hold a Brit cit in custody.'

'Very sick,' said Friedman. 'He can go whenever he wants to. But tell him to stay put. He's getting the best we can give him.' He gave Eliot a frank and boyish grin. 'It'll be better for his health if he stays with us for a while.'

The sick bay lay well outside Hoyt's special compound. It was lodged in the heart of the administrative complex of the fighter wing, halfway across the airfield. Whatever went on there was clearly not thought to need the security of barbed wire. It struck Eliot that Hoyt hadn't so much as bothered to give him an escort. Something must have caused him to lose the sudden interest he seemed to have been displaying to Aleister a bare twenty-four hours before in a troublesome British element.

'What's he got?' said Eliot to the young intern conducting him along a corridor.

The shoulders politely shrugged under the close crew-cut. 'Senility, maybe. Malnutrition. We're running some tests.'

'What's this I hear about an autopsy?'

The young man looked at him with open astonishment. '*Autopsy*? The old fellow's crazy. A sick guy, we reckon. But nowhere near dead.'

'No, I mean inside the compound.'

Eliot received the same baffled look. 'We haven't had a death since I was posted. Fine record, these Phantom guys. Fine commander, the Colonel.'

So what was Friedman's talk about an autopsy? An autopsy on what? LGM? The crew of some US capsule jettisoned back from space? John Eliot suspended judgement. The immediate problem was some British 'element', some foolish old man who was making himself a nuisance. 'Where is he?' he asked. The young intern looked at him uneasily. 'In one of our private wards.'

Eliot was conducted along the corridors, losing his bearings. Presently he came to a door behind whose formidable locks he discovered the offending citizen, huddled in solitary confinement in a clean, white, comfortable room. The intern left them. 'We're keeping the old boy on his own,' he whispered at the door. 'You'll find out why.'

Jake stared at Eliot out of wide, rheumy eyes. There were bandages at his hands and face, not altogether concealing a puffy, purplish discoloration. 'Was it *you*, then, that done for old Pussy Cat?' said the elderly, cracked voice. Eliot detected as much sorrow as anger. He shook his head.

'They gimme a bath,' said the old man reproachfully. He clenched and unclenched the bandaged hands. 'But they ain't going to wash me brains, mate!'

'What happened to Pussy Cat?' said Eliot gently.

The story came in rambling jerks and starts. It was interrupted by rheumy tears, by references to the Book of Revelation, by the identification of Colonel Hoyt with the Whore of Babylon, by memories of sulphur and the sound of devil-phantoms. A picture formed in Eliot's mind of some damned bit of USAF 'hardware', some undeclared 'device' under secret test, plunging out of control into Tangham Wood (the phrase '??? Loss of control ???' in Aleister's pencil notes briefly troubled him), shedding two propulsion units which then bounced across the forest-floor, gouging two channels, disgorging sulphurous fluids, killing a cat, scalding an old man's face and hands. There was a potential case for damages . . .

'Don't tell me it was them Green Men, mate!' shouted Jake, convulsed with sudden rage.

'How did Green Men get into this?' asked Eliot, surprised.

'Them!' shouted Jake. He wheezed and hawked, spitting without much accuracy at the bedside spittoon. 'They keep telling me Green Men, mate! From up there!' He shook a bandaged hand at the ceiling. 'They tell me it was Green Men what done for Pussy Cat!'

Did they, indeed? It seemed very clumsy of them! It would hardly make a defence in law. Eliot was half moved to anger himself, but the cautious official in him thought better than to show it. 'Who knows?' he said carefully. It could be extremely awkward politically – perhaps in defence terms, also – if Jake now took his injuries to a British court. Aleister would expect some suaver outcome than *that* ... Devils of his own began to whisper to John Eliot that a crazed old tramp with no surname and very little language need not be taken too seriously. They would see that he was all right ... Eliot would attend to it personally. A hundred quid or so ...? In the meantime he was in good medical care. His symptoms might well disappear. Some neighbouring unit, some good-looking WRAF girl, could be instructed to offer Jake a bright new Pussy Cat at the next open day. It would make a cosy picture for the local rag.

Eliot got up to go. 'Get me *out*, mate!' wheezed the old man, weeping rheumy tears.

'You must stay,' said Eliot with gentle firmness. 'Just for the time being. You're in good hands.'

'I got *pigeons* ...'

But pigeons were outside Eliot's brief. There was no mention of pigeons in that note of Aleister's.

He cadged a lift back to Ipswich in the Colonel's staff car, satisfied with the information he had picked up. He looked forward to committing a minor breach of the Official Secrets Act in Lucy's delectable bed. She would be entertained by the story. She might even have a thought or two to contribute.

He was quite ruffled, on arriving at the Green Man, to find that she was not there.

There was a note for him, lodged in their boldly declared joint pigeon-hole of 'Eliot/Frensham'. 'Developments!' it read. 'I think I've got on to something interesting. I'll ring you. Luv, L.'

He disconsolately tried the reception desk.

'There was a letter for madam.'

'From ...?'

'I really can't say, sir.'

Eliot went back to his room – *their* room – and gave way to a few moments of sullen self-pity. Really, she might have had some consideration. He needed this leave. He needed her. She was rather good in bed. He could have done with it. What in hell was she up to?

He saw that most of her make-up was still on the bedside table. He judged, out of male folklore, that she wouldn't remain separated from it for too long. She would be back in an hour or two. He lay on the double bed with his arms behind his head, enjoying the prospect of a jokily buccaneering row and wondering what capital could be made for it from the glittering top of an expensive fountain-pen – a *man's* fountain-pen without a doubt – which lay among the bottles of female magic.

Some hours passed.

At half-past six he decided to teach her a lesson. He packed his suitcase and took a taxi to the station, leaving a curt little note about 'urgent stuff in Whitehall'.

It was perfectly true when he came to think of it. Aleister would be impressed with his self-sacrifice.

The sacrifice of a black cock. Its blood was spilt on the altar cloth beneath some trumpery of an inverted crucifix. Looking more closely, Lucy saw that this little victim was no real Bird of Dawning, merely some scrawny pigeon, dusky and unkempt, which had followed her from an old man's pigeon-loft. She tried to weep, contemptuous and disgusted, but her eyelids were gummed together, her mouth refused to pucker.

'What do you see?' commanded someone's voice at the back of her head.

'Nothing, nothing, nothing,' she croaked, forcing the words across a dry tongue, choking back some filthy taste at its parched roots. It was true, it was true. She had seen nothing, nothing whatever. Her eyes were tightly closed.

The voice cackled. 'You'd make a good trance-medium, luvvy! Nobody ever told you thàt?'

The 'a' of 'that' was drawled. It was a 'thaaat' of Wiltshire, of the country around Salisbury Plain. It was not the pert little 'that' of Home Counties' BBC.

'You'd be in touch with t'other side in no time!' said the old woman's voice. There was something of relish to it.

Lucy kept her eyes screwed up. She had held them tightly closed for some hours past. She had seen no 'sacrifice'; it could only have been a dream. 'I'm an astrophysicist,' she stumbled out, clumsily shaping the syllables of this tongue-twister, still possessed by the spirits they'd pressed upon her under the cold vault of Lampson's

37

chilly refectory. 'An astrophiz,' she repeated, 'a phiz . . . a phiz . . .'
The alcohol, or something else, administered some hours ago, half
paralysed her tongue and eyelids. Only at the back of her mind did
some black cock, some darkly feathered cock-robin, some dingy
pigeon, bleed to death. ' "I," said the sparrow, "with my bow and
arrow . . ." ' Some sparrow hawk, some furry-legged monstrosity,
devoured its prey.

'Lucy,' counterpointed some other voice. 'Lucy Fr . . . Lucy
Fr. . .'

It stammered in jest, a male voice pretending to copy her own
confusions. 'Lucy Fr . . . Or Lucifer! Did you come to bring us
light?'

She heard voices laughing. 'Lucifer,' she thought. Lucifer, the
fallen angel. Lucifer, who brings light. Lucifer, the Son of the
Morning. Lucifer, the Prince of Darkness. 'Light and darkness!'
she said, trying to smile. She attempted 'paradox', but gave it up.
'I'm an astrophizzz. . .' she repeated. 'I'm a scientist,' she thought.
'I operate with radiant energy.' The human retina saw very little of
it – merely some limited range of Angströms. The great dish at
Jodrell Bank was more perceptive. Sometimes it saw men spinning
to their deaths.

'Open your eyes,' commanded Lampson's voice.

Lucy forced her eyes half open. Nothing of the visible spectrum
had fallen upon them for some hours past, only the rosy glow – not
far above the infra-red and totally without resolving power –
which filtered through the flesh of the closed lids.

She looked around. The Long Gallery was candlelit. The little
tallow flames burned smokey and vertical in the still air. No
'sacrifice' was visible. It lay merely in the mind's eye.

In the east, across the unlit fields towards the sea, the Ness
lighthouse flashed its warning at the precise interval of forty
seconds. In the middle distance some little farmhouse, its windows
still uncurtained, gleamed with an innocent domestic radiance.
Ten miles to the west (the pine wood of Rendlesham lying in
between) the ship-burial of Sutton Hoo exposed its timbers to the
desecration of twentieth-century man. To the south-west lay
Manningtree, birthplace of one Matthew Hopkins, Witchfinder
General, who had hunted to their painful death more witches than
any other man who had ever lived to the west of the Low

Countries. Within a stone's throw of this zealous spirit might be found the epicentre of the great earthquake of 1884 which had toppled steeples across half of England, left a 'black and stinking' sea off the coast of Essex, produced 'lights in the sky'.

'What do you see?' said the male voice, the voice of Gregorius Mansfield Lampson, the voice of the 'Hon. G.M. Lampson' whose scribbled note on the back of his pretentious piece of pasteboard had brought her to this little destiny, the voice of the man whose expensive, capless fountain-pen she had glimpsed among a pile of papers in his study.

Lucy looked around. There were a dozen people in the Long Gallery. She had met them before at that ill-fated lunch. Lampson she knew at once: his eyes were pale-blue, his hair as white as an old man's; he was an albino, poor chap. (She could hardly blame him for it!) She knew the old woman to her left, though the name escaped her. She recognized a man called Oleg, some mournful Slav, introduced as an émigré, an escapee from foreign horrors, a friend of Solzhenitsyn's, he'd said. But it was the girl crouching awkwardly by her side to whom she turned – somebody called Julie with a surname as plain as Smith, a touch of the ordinary and wholesome among this weird bunch she'd fallen into some hours ago. She took the girl's hand, surprised to find that her own was trembling.

'What do you think you saw?' repeated Lampson. Lucy noticed that his hair, as white as the winter stalks of Moonflower, came down nearly to his shoulders. That and the wide, pale eyes in the oval of a Botticelli face gave him the look of a pallid St Michael.

'Tell us,' he insisted. The voice was too light and musical to be trusted. A 'white' voice. An 'albino' voice.

'Leave her alone,' said Julie Smith.

The man Oleg came and stood over her. He was a little pig of a man with sad eyes, vastly enlarged by pebble glasses. He stared down at her, mournful and owlish. 'You talked in your sleep,' he said. 'You had a dream. Tell us again.'

Lucy half rose, found that she was staggering, clutched at Julie Smith for support, sat down again. 'You've poisoned me!' she said angrily. 'What did you put in my drink?' She glared round at the other faces, dimly lit by the dozen candles standing on the long oak table.

'We've all drunk from the same bowl, luvvy!' said the old woman with the Wiltshire drawl. There was a rustle of approval around the table. A laugh. A murmur of unpleasant mirth.

'I want to use your telephone,' said Lucy, turning to Lampson. Across his shoulder, through the westward window of the Long Gallery, the Ness lighthouse blinked its routine message. A little to the north of it, the radio masts of RAF Blandfordness – that 'wee little station' of John's as he sometimes called it, pursuing a private joke – were caught by the November moon. 'I want to make a call,' she said, fumbling in her purse for the dignity of some coin with which to pay off this over-familiar stranger.

'I've telephoned already,' said Lampson pleasantly. 'Your gentleman friend has gone back to London. No message, I'm afraid.'

'I think we'd better go,' said Julie Smith. She helped Lucy to her feet.

The squat little Russian barred their way. 'Not yet, if you please.' He rocked on his heels, turning his large eyes from one to the other.

'If you please, of course,' said Lampson, courteous and musical.

Somebody blew out the candles on the long table. The Long Gallery fell into darkness. It was punctuated ten seconds later by the Ness light. Forty more seconds went past. The flash came again, a brief and rational gleam of sanity. A moaning chant was started by some kaftanned man, bearded and beaded, who sat at the head of the massive board. Lucy was propelled forward. 'Lucy Fer!' said Lampson's voice at her elbow.

Above the table something had begun to form, a little bluish globe which pulsed and slowly grew in size. 'Are we guarded?' said somebody's voice on a shrill note of anxiety. The Ness light flashed again, strobing the company into frozen action. Lucy saw that there were thirteen of them, counting herself and Lampson. Lampson remained standing, his white hair aureoled for a millisecond by the distant lighthouse.

'We're *not* guarded!' shrieked a woman's voice. The globe above the table pulsed and grew. In the half minute of darkness still remaining before the next flash from the Ness it expanded to twice its size, humming and crackling, seeming to drop molten light upon the table in beads of electric blue. Lucy heard chairs shoved

40

back, garments rustling as people turned away. Instinctively, she threw up an arm against her face.

The Ness flash came and went. The globe in the Long Gallery exploded into incandescence. People screamed. Even through the merciful veil of her long sleeves Lucy was conscious of the scorching blast of a furnace. Glancing sideways, she saw that Lampson had turned his back. He seemed to be laughing. Julie Smith was crying aloud, her eyes wide and staring, her hands extended with the fingers as open and useless as a wicket fence against nuclear blast. A smell of burned sulphur was drifting about the room.

Lucy stumbled towards the door, dragging the girl with her. 'I'm blind! I'm blind!' moaned Julie. They fell down the stone stairs. Above them, a door had opened. Feet came in pursuit. They staggered across the unlit hall, fumbled with the bolts and chains of its great doors, found themselves among dank laurels under the risen moon.

With trembling hands Lucy struggled with the car keys. She dropped them to the gravel, hearing voices behind her. The lights in the hall had come on. Figures were silhouetted against the yellow rectangle of the porch. Feet crunched on the gravel. 'You can't escape us!' shouted some woman's voice.

Lucy scrabbled among the chippings at her feet, found the keys, held one hand with the other to stop it shaking, opened the car-door, stumbled into the driving seat. She began to drive off, and then remembered Julie . . . suffered a flush of shame for allowing craven fear to come uppermost; wrenched open the passenger door; dragged in the half-blinded girl.

Running feet were almost upon them. They skidded off along the drive, spraying gravel behind them. Half a mile down the road Lucy remembered to pull shut the rattling passenger-door. Leaning across Julie, she saw that the girl's face was scorched from temple to chin with a purplish burn like a birthmark. 'I can't see,' said Julie, whimpering.

They'd better find a doctor. Some elderly, benevolent GP, some silver-haired old father figure who would be delighted to be dragged into his surgery at half-past seven in the evening to treat a case of witchcraft. But the moonlit road was bare and desolate.

She drove on towards Ipswich. There must be some general

hospital, some friendly casualty department. (Why the hell had John chosen to frig off back to London?)

Two miles out of Ipswich she caught the lights of another car behind her. It signalled with its headlights, a swift, suave Porsche rapidly overtaking the little Renault. Lucy stamped on the accelerator. The car behind came on remorselessly, its headlights glaring.

On the outskirts of Ipswich, speeding along a tree-lined avenue, the Renault was overtaken. The Porsche drew alongside, screaming a warning fanfare. Lucy was forced to the verge, braking and skidding. A tree loomed ahead. Trapped between the Porsche and darkness, she swung the wheel. The Renault tumbled into a ditch, spinning over and over. Stars and moonlight spiralled into darkness as the windscreen began to shatter. Lucy's last thought was of the two men, a thousand miles above them, spinning into the vortex of their own destiny.

3
The Insane Root

Wishing to know something is not the same as being allowed to know it. Whitehall, for example, sets a stern boundary between the two, and patrols it with codes and safeguards. A mere appetite for facts, even if backed with some show of 'relevance to business in hand', is not a sufficient passport. The lowliest of custodians is entitled to stop the highest of personages at this frontier unless they carry clear proof of a 'need to know'. And the household gods of government departments have defined the shibboleths, the pieces of paper, the cards of identity, without which no visa will be issued. There are times when it seems as though those other gods who operate in the wider world may be acting on similar principles.

Having travelled, dined and composed his mind to the framing of an interesting report (which would certainly redound to his credit), John Eliot returned to his bachelor apartment at the edge of Covent Garden and put through a telephone call to the Green Man at Ipswich. A glass or two of wine had mellowed him towards forgiveness. He was ready to be jocularly friendly to a disconsolate Lucy, propped solitary among soft pillows on a double bed, even to promise his early return.

She was not there. 'We really can't say, sir,' said the reception desk. Something like a smirk was audible across the seventy miles of telephone line. Eliot was glad he had not tipped the man. 'Tell her to ring me when she comes in,' he said, choosing 'tell' rather than 'ask'.

Having failed to establish his Need to Know where Lucy was, Eliot dialled another number, the frustration of one phone call tending to beget another by sheer momentum. It was the home number of an Air Commodore with whom he sometimes transacted business – a useful chap, a knowledgeable chap, whose job straddled some uneasy boundary between the Air Staff and military intelligence on the subject of space research and development. He might know, if anybody did, what bit of hardware the Americans seemed to have lost in Rendlesham Forest. A laconic chat, cautiously using a codeword or two, might possibly dig out the information. It would look rather well to Aleister if the report he received on Monday morning contained not only a shrewd assessment of USAF activities at Bentbridge but evidence of selfless research into 'background' during the weekend.

There was no answer. Eliot allowed the phone to ring for a couple of dozen times before slamming it down in irritation. (For God's sake, was *everybody* swanning off for Saturday except himself?)

He poured himself a gin and tonic, allowing it to fuddle him towards a degree of brassiness. Aleister might as well have proof positive that he was back in London, doing the State some service. He dialled Aleister's home number.

Mrs Buchanan answered. There was a sound of guests somewhere in the background.

'Do we really have to bother him?' she said plaintively.

'I'm so sorry. A weeny bit urgent. But it won't keep him long.'

'If it was anybody but you, Mr Eliot . . .' she said, sighing. Eliot snapped up and pocketed the implied compliment, smiling with the boyish courtesy which he judged she would have fallen for if present. 'I'll ask him to take it in the study,' she said grudgingly. 'Do make it quick, Mr Eliot. He's got some important guests. American *and* Russian, as it happens.'

Eliot had no time to digest this unlikely news before Aleister was on the line.

'I'm back,' said Eliot cheerfully.

'Back?'

'Some fairly hot stuff to tell you. From the "chums" . . .'

There was a pause of some seconds. 'Chums . . .' said Aleister neutrally.

'At that place of ours. Near my leave address.'

There was an even longer pause. 'My dear . . . fellow,' said Aleister, 'I didn't ask you to get in touch with any chums.'

John Eliot was a little taken aback. 'I've seen our "citizen".'

44

'That's what I told you to do.'

'Told'? He began to feel ruffled. 'Ask' would have been more suitable; civilians in the Ministry of Defence made a point of avoiding anything which smacked of military forms. 'He was with the chums. They've taken him into . . . protective care.'

The silence was so long this time that Eliot began to bang his earpiece, suspecting a fault. 'I think you and I had better meet tomorrow,' he shouted. 'Shall I come down to you? Or do you want us to meet in your office?'

He heard Aleister laugh, and felt briefly reassured. 'My dear chap, it'll keep till Monday. If I were you, I'd go straight back up to . . . that country pub of yours . . . and have a relaxed weekend with your lady friend.'

'I thought this was urgent,' said Eliot, thinking of his spoiled leave, trying to keep the reproach out of his voice.

'It'll keep, it'll keep,' said Aleister breezily. 'Monday will do. Now I really must get back to my guests . . .'

The phone was replaced before Eliot could think of anything else to say. He considered redialling, but thought better of it. It had been a mistake to ring at all; Aleister was clearly having some relaxed weekend of his own; he would have to be nobbled with a written report.

Eliot began to frame one. He sat up till half-past two in the morning, trying to do so. But the narrative seemed strangely bald. He fell asleep and dreamed of Conrad Friedman and Colonel Hoyt. The one had the look of a suave St Michael, the other of a squat, gnomish, Texan bullfrog. He would have liked to swap notes with Lucy. (Where the hell had she frigged off to?)

'You're bright and early, sir,' said the doorman at the Richmond Terrace entrance to the Ministry of Defence.

Eliot scrawled his name on the long list of weekend unfortunates who had been dragged back to the Kremlin-like towers on the south side of Whitehall, glancing at the names above his own. (Poor Chapman! Clobbered because of HMG's sudden interest in some little Caribbean island which nobody had heard of until yesterday. Poor Fenner! Trying to catch up with the Treasury's latest assault on the Sketch Estimates.)

He let himself into his own eyrie, lodged in a turret at the north-east corner of the building, and wondered what he should do next. He hauled his secretary's heavy typewriter on to his pseudo-mahogany desk and began to type (more potently, he hoped, than his little portable permitted) the news for Aleister that chums at Bentbridge were clearly testing an uncovenanted 'vehicle' but had decided to make up an unlikely cover story. At half-past ten, craving the morning coffee which the indefatigable Beryl would, by now, have brought him if this hadn't been one of her two days off, he went down restlessly to the fourth floor, knowing that the Defence Intelligence people (on whom the sun never set) would be manning that strange outfit, even on a Saturday. A little wheedling would probably produce a shot of caffeine.

A trace of diffidence (though none of his friends would have believed it) caused him to introduce himself as 'Buchanan'. Aleister's name would certainly be better known to them than his own. He had very little 'need to know' anything about the fussily guarded peculiarities of Def. Int.

The pleasant kid of a WRAF girl (her sergeant's stripes looked so new that they could only have been put up a few days earlier) gave him a shy, confident smile. She remembered the name of Mr Buchanan. Papers were frequently sent up and down to his office. She had, in any case, been briefed about 'senior civilian colleagues'; she knew they were touchy; her womanly heart was sympathetic to them; she pitied them for their lack of a uniform. Poor Mr Buchanan would have been something like an Air Marshal if only they'd allowed him the necessary blue stripes and the double row of scrambled egg.

'You want the PROSPERO file again,' she said, proud of this competence. Mr Buchanan's office had been on about PROSPERO all week. 'Which part this time, sir?'

'Actually,' said Eliot, hearing a devil at his elbow, 'I could do with a cup of coffee.' He gave her the masculine smile which experience showed did wonders with womankind. 'But I wouldn't mind another look at PROSPERO.'

'PROSPERO'? The name meant nothing to him. How in hell did the coding clerks come to think of these outlandish titles? He was certainly not 'cleared' for PROSPERO. The simplest challenge to prove his identity would floor him at once.

46

'Which part?' said the girl again.

Eliot made rapid calculations. The latest part of the file would probably have the most up-to-date information. He had no 'need to know', of course . . . But she'd offered it on a plate. He stifled qualms. If Aleister had been calling for PROSPERO in the past few days, it might have something to do with the flurry at Bentbridge. It was almost his duty to find out. It might make his proposed report still more commendable. 'The latest part,' he said.

'Part Three,' said the WRAF knowledgeably. 'It's the only part your office haven't asked for this week.'

She went and fetched it, slamming the grilled doors behind her and firmly locking them to show that she knew her duty. Presently she came back and asked for a receipt, getting the forged signature of 'A. Buchanan'. She poured hot water from a battered kettle on to instant coffee and added condensed milk. 'If you wouldn't mind giving fifteen p to the tea club. . .' She was delighted to receive fifty.

Eliot climbed back up the stairs, slopping coffee into the saucer with one hand, clutching a file called PROSPERO with the other. He settled down to read it, conscious of sin but assuaging it with good excuses.

He was disappointed to find that INTFILE 1327/3: TOP SECRET – PROSPERO contained nothing but a list of names and organizations, facing a 'Remarks' column in which the remarks were few and unilluminating. It was a weird list, a tally for the most part, it seemed, of cranks and freaks whose interest lay in harmless absurdities – 'PARASEARCHERS OF BRISTOL, THE (Membership now 14, still declining)', 'MUFOP (Midlands UFO Phenomena)', 'FRIENDS OF AVEBURY, SOCIETY OF (SOFA)'; 'METAPHYSICALS OF WOOD GREEN, THE (but accepts out-of-London members – trace)'; 'SHEFFIELD TIBETANS FOR A BETTER BRITAIN'; 'STARWATCH (seems to have penetrated the British Astronomical Association but concerned mainly with "extraterrestrial contact")'; 'SOCIETY FOR THE PROPAGATION OF SPACE WISDOM'; 'BORION (Buddhists of Orion)'.

Glancing over the forty or fifty pages which the file contained, Eliot found a preponderance of groups whose interest lay in Little Green Men. Others – a minority, but still a large one – were 'psychics' of one sort or another (a coven of middle-class devil-

47

worshippers in Orpington; spiritualist chapels; a society for examining 'The Unexplained'). One or two foreign organizations were listed. Eliot remembered, from desultory conversations with his space-oriented Air Staff acquaintance, the name of GEPAN, that foolish offshoot of CNES, the French space agency, which spent French money solemnly looking for traces of radiation where lavender-farmers in Provence claimed to have been plagued by gnomes descending in mushroom-shaped objects from outer space. In the Remarks column opposite GEPAN was the obscure comment, 'Useful! But under threat. Foucault could be a nuisance.'

Eliot sat back, irritable and disappointed. He had broken the rules for nothing. But he was also puzzled. Intelligence 'friends' did, of course, have a duty to keep an eye on subversive groups. But this lot hardly looked subversive. Why, in any case, should *Defence* Intelligence be taking an interest? It was the sort of thing they might cheerfully have left to MI5 – assuming it was worth bothering with it at all.

The list also seemed oddly random. What was 'LAMPSON, Viscount' doing between 'LANCASTER GROUP FOR AERIAL MYSTERIES' and 'LDLN (*Lumières dans la Nuit* – amateur French UFO group)'? Why was his younger son listed immediately below him – 'LAMPSON, Gregorius Mansfield, The Hon.' – with the remark, 'Dangerous; but a possible asset for PROSPERO'?

Idly, Eliot noted that the Lampsons, Viscount and Hon., were listed as living at 'Lantern House, Nr. Sudbourne, Suffolk'. He smiled at the little coincidence of having passed within a mile or two of them the day before while tramping through Rendlesham Forest. He thought fondly of Lucy for a moment, tempted to take Aleister's advice and to go back to his lady friend for what now remained of the weekend.

Then memory returned.

Lampson. His mad lordship. 'The Suffolk Wonder'. The old chap who tabled ridiculous questions in the House of Lords. One of Their Lordships' saucer-freaks, who belonged to the all-party group on UFOs, using the taxpayer's money and the time of busy officials in the pursuit of LGM.

LGM. They were looming absurdly large. Even the initials of 'LAMPSON, Gregorius Mansfield' spelt LGM! (the Hon. being omitted). 'Us? Them? LGM?' had said Aleister's note. That elderly undesirable called Jake had wittered something about them. Conrad Friedman had boyishly mentioned them. Most of a file called PROSPERO seemed to be obsessively concerned with them – or with others who were.

Eliot went thoughtfully to lunch, downed a gin or two in St Stephen's Tavern, returned fortified, telephoned the registry of Def. Int., demanded parts one and two of INTFILE 1327.

The friendly WRAF had gone off duty. A gruff male voice confronted him. It demanded, politely but firmly, the rigmaroles which the girl had set aside – his Defence Identity Card, a cross-check with the list of those entitled to see PROSPERO papers. Eliot had some difficulty even in returning his forbidden Part Three without raising awkward questions. There was no possibility of laying hands on earlier parts.

He downed tools for the day. His report could wait till Sunday. He walked back to his flat in Covent Garden, making a detour along Charing Cross Road. There was a bookshop on his mind. He had often passed it on lunchtime perambulations, occasionally glancing inside with amused distaste at the gullibilities it served. It was an ill-kept barn of a place, a warehouse of shoddy dreams, untidily stacked with pulp science fiction, tales of the weird and other-wordly, horror comics, badly printed guides to the telling of fortunes by one cheap trick or another, insights into ancient wisdoms, instructions for the effortless mastery of demons or dowsing, blueprints for outstanding gains in cosmic understanding without so much as a bad 'O'-level pass in elementary physics.

Eliot went self-consciously into this murky underworld and found a shelf marked 'UFOs'. He stood, well-tailored and recently shaven, among unaccustomed fellow citizens whose clothes and hair seemed to him well fitted to their choice of reading. Furtively and at random, he picked a dozen books and took them to the cash desk.

'Keen Eyed They Were And From Afar,' said the cockney black, watching Eliot hesitate over the addressing of his cheque. 'What?' said Eliot in the tone he used with waiters. He was rapidly sized up. 'Name of the shop, mate. KETWAFA will do.' Eliot shrugged and complied. KETWAFA was no worse than PROSPERO. It was clearly a day for codes and acronyms.

Furtively carrying his intellectual pornography along Litchfield Street, Eliot was relieved to find himself still in the world of the rational and solid. An evening headline told him that the American space-castaway was already dead, frazzled to a shooting star somewhere above India. His momentary glory had caused rumours of heavenly intervention in a troubled north-eastern province which had been having some bloody differences of view with the central government. Astrologers had told the people that it meant they were in the right. The Indian Prime Minister had sent troops to restore the calm of rationality. The Russians were said to be mounting a massive, though covert, rescue operation for their own doomed traveller. They would claim a triumph if they found him. They would deny that they had even tried if they happened to fail.

Eliot bought the paper and wrapped his books in it to hide their aberration from the rational eye of his porter.

Aleister Buchanan poured another brandy for his guests. He had been softening them up since Friday evening. It was something of an achievement to have captured them both together. He had been working with the Foreign Office on it all week.

'Cognac?' he said across his shoulder to Oleg Birkov, remembering the austerities of Birkov's mother-State, hoping to mellow Birkov into indiscretion by the judicious application of bourgeois vices. He diluted Birkov's brandy with vodka – odourless, tasteless truth-drug of the Soviet Union – hoping that Oleg would fail to notice it. He decided not to try the same trick with Conrad Friedman's drink. Friedman was half a friend . . . He might, in any case, notice the deception; he was an old CIA hand. Of Birkov Aleister was still unclear whether he belonged to the KGB or had merely been planted by them. (The inefficiency of M15 was almost unbelievable some days!) But the vodka trick might be worth trying.

Birkov took the drink, drank heartily, put it down, stared at it thoughtfully through the pebble lenses. His round, black eyes seemed almost cheerful. 'We have made some progress, Mr Buchanan. Thanks to your hospitality.'

'We have an agreement on broad principles, I hope.'

Friedman leaned back in his chair, nodding. Silver cuff-links flashed from beneath his jacket sleeves. Somebody had probably told him that gold would be ostentatious.

Birkov looked sly. 'Your good lady is doubtless running the tape-recorder in the dining-room!' He came as near to twinkling with good humour as his gnome's eyes made possible.

'Margery?' said Buchanan, startled. 'For heaven's sake, my dear fellow!' A senior official hardly expected his wife to do that sort of thing. 'I've got a secretary installed in the spare bedroom,' he added, knowing that Birkov was probably aware of this already. 'You, I presume, are using your usual methods.' The furniture van across the road had been there since Friday afternoon with an almost contemptuous lack of concealment. At predictable intervals its crew took turns to go to meals.

'Naturally,' said Birkov, shrugging. 'We would all wish to have the same record of this important – this historic – meeting.'

Buchanan forebore to ask what methods Friedman might be using. A mini-transmitter concealed in a gold filling, probably. American gadgetry was touchingly ingenious. The Russians looked like peasants in comparison. 'I'll get the record typed for us to have a look at in the next half-hour or so. I suggest you then take it back to your . . . usual addresses. We can meet here for lunch tomorrow to draw up documents for our governments.'

Friedman said, 'Check,' then added, 'Just to recap, we've agreed – subject to ratification . . .'

'Subject to a draft treaty within thirty days,' interjected Birkov.

'Check,' said Friedman affably. 'We've agreed – subject to conditions – on a free, frank and comradely exchange of information. We've settled the channels. We've agreed to lean on the French to come in . . .'

'A crucial matter,' said Birkov loudly, doubtless for the sake of his furniture van. 'My government will be surprised that they were not here.'

Buchanan sighed, exchanging a glance with Friedman. 'You can leave us to handle the French, Oleg.'

'Fourthly,' continued Friedman, 'we've agreed to set up a joint scientific group to check out incidents. *Wherever* they happen to occur. Fifthly, we've agreed on a total security blackout . . .'

Buchanan cut him short. 'It'll all be in the record, Conrad. In

51

impeccable language, I may say. The lad upstairs has had some Cabinet Office training.' He nodded at Birkov. 'We'll get out a suggested Russian version at the same time.'

'I likewise,' said Birkov drily. His furniture-removers would certainly include a skilled linguist as well as the electronics men. He took a swig from his glass, frowning. 'Mutual trust is essential in these matters.'

'Sure, sure,' said Friedman with a wide-eyed smile.

'That's why our recommended documents will include all those suspicious checks across frontiers!' said Buchanan, unable to resist the irony. He added, more soberly, 'It's already taken a good deal of trust merely to arrange this meeting.' It had, in fact, been common fear and common bafflement. But 'trust' would sound more worthy in the furniture van and the upstairs bedroom.

Birkov stood up. He was five feet four, but seemed nearly as broad as tall. Silhouetted against the window and the distant view of Blackheath, he had the presence of an ugly little Minotaur. He glared impassively ahead of him. 'Then why are you cheating us, Mr Buchanan?'

Lucy knew that she must be dead. The great White Light of Tibetan Buddhism lay upon her half-open eyelids. She knew that this was the first vision of the departed soul. Soon there would come demons, some in the guise of tempters, some with the duty of torturers, intent on driving the freed spirit back towards rebirth.

A tempter-torturer came, a young man white-clad, aureoled by the white radiance. He gently forced some liquid between her lips, raising her bandaged head with his free head. The ache of it caused her to cry out.

'Whoa there, lady!' said the cool, young, American voice.

She brought him into focus. Competent, concerned eyes studied her from under the crew-cut. Behind him, slung from a stand, the plastic bag of a saline drip drained slowly towards her bandaged wrist. It was night; the curtains were drawn. 'How long?' she said, memory returned. She screwed up her eyes, trying to steady the Renault as it tumbled into starlit nothingness. Panic rose up her throat but refused to blossom into the scream it demanded. She seemed to be under heavy sedation.

'It's Saturday,' said the young orderly.

A day. A whole day had passed. Irrelevant tears welled up. (Whatever this stuff was they'd given her, it seemed to have side-effects!) 'He must be dead, then,' she said abruptly.

'Dead?'

'That shipwrecked sailor of yours.' She had an image of a dazzling white suit catherine-wheeling out of black space into dazzling death. She *knew* that he was dead. The tears brimmed over and trickled down her cheeks. A thermometer was slipped into her mouth. 'Your name . . . ?' she mumbled round it.

'Mel,' he said, smiling.

'I *knew* it was Lem,' she mumbled, closing her eyes again.

'Mel,' he repeated.

LEM. MEL. Little syllables without meaning. They made anagrams of each other. They formed ELM if you twisted them, the wood from which men made coffins. They also made acronyms. Little Extraterrestrial Men! Mephistopheles Ex-Lucifer!

She giggled round the thermometer, shutting out memories of some bad joke about Lucifer.

He withdrew the little glass tube, studied it for moment, shook it back to normal. 'You'll live,' he said, medically jocular.

'Where am I?'

He was silent for a moment. 'In good hands.'

'No, *where*?'

'In quarantine, lady.'

'Quarantine' had a strange sound to it. Its syllables jostled in her drugged mind. They kept LEMs in quarantine, she seemed to remember. 'Little Extraterrestrial Men!' she said aloud.

'What?'

'Little Green Men! Little Green Men from Outer Space!' Perhaps they came and went less painfully than white-suited *Homo sapiens*.

'You Brits!' he said shaking his head. 'I don't know where you get it from.'

Abruptly, she thought of Julie. 'Julie,' she said, wide-eyed, struggling to sit up, gasping with the discomfort of it.

Julie lay in the second bed of this two-bedded ward. She seemed to be deeply unconscious and was breathing slowly. The right side of her face was marked with a fiery burn, overlaid by some daub of a yellowish ointment. The memory came back to Lucy of a distant lighthouse seen through an east window; of a glowing globe much closer at hand. She remembered, now, some face at the globe's centre, pallid and fleshy, gross as a toad's flesh. Its frog's eyes stared at her, dispassionately malevolent.

'Julie!' she cried aloud.

'You'd better let her rest,' said the young man. He turned on silent rubber soles and went to the ward-door.

'Where are we?' she shouted after him, struggling to sit fully upright.

'In good hands, lady. In quarantine.'

He went out, shutting the door behind him. She heard the key turn in the lock.

Common fear. Common bafflement. An unprecedented accident in space. Other puzzling events which straddled frontiers. The feeling that something had got out of control in recent months. It was these things which had driven the three governments to permit this highly unconventional meeting in the Blackheath living-room of a senior British official. The French might have been collared as well if there'd been time. They, too, were having their troubles according to M16. But they could be brought in later (kicking and screaming with Gallic chauvinism, no doubt) if confronted with a solid agreement among the Big Two and the Little Anglo-Saxon Third. But a tripartite agreement was essential first.

Keeping the dismay out of his voice, Aleister Buchanan merely said, with the polite rictus of a dry smile, 'Cheating you, Oleg? In what way are we cheating you?'

Birkov rocked on his heels. He drained the remainder of his vodka-laced brandy and put down the glass. It seemed to have left him disturbingly sober. 'It was the understanding of my government,' he said loudly, 'that we would frankly list – without commitment at this stage; simply as a token of our good faith in advance of the setting up of a joint scientific commission – every experimental establishment, every government source of information.'

'We have, Oleg, we have,' said Buchanan, maintaining the smile.

'Sure,' said Friedman, studying his fingernails.

Birkov stared ahead between the two of them. 'What experiments are the British Government conducting in Suffolk?'

Buchanan tapped the sheaf of manuscript notes in front of him. They were, at this very moment, being rendered into typescript in the upstairs bedroom. 'I've already told you, Oleg. It'll be in the record. We have a little research going on at RAF Blandfordness. Out on the coast there.' He glanced at Friedman.

Friedman nodded. He felt proprietorial about 'RAF' Blandfordness. His own government had put up most of the money. That 'RAF' bit was handy cover. 'Sure,' he said. 'Blandfordness. Your technical guys can have a look at it. When we've set up that joint commission. Just as soon as we can take a peek at that little outfit of yours at Plesetsk.'

Birkov shook his head. The magnified, dark eyes looked melancholy. 'I mean Lantern House, Mr Buchanan. I mean the home of that privileged member of the British establishment, Viscount Lampson.' He took off his glasses. Without them his eyes dwindled to little black currants of hostility.

'What's never understood outside this country,' said Buchanan jocularly, buying time, 'is that the House of Lords is a harmless eccentricity. Mainly for the tourist trade. If anything's going on at Lord Lampson's place, it's probably no worse than a mangy lion or two and a bad cafeteria. It's certainly nothing which HMG has been consulted about.'

'Why have you sent underlings of yours to Lantern House, Mr Buchanan? No longer ago than yesterday.'

Buchanan got up and went to the window, turning his back on the other two to conceal unease and anger. What the hell had Eliot been up to? Perhaps he should have listened more carefully to Eliot's call on Friday night. Across his shoulder he said neutrally, uncertain what Birkov knew, 'Lantern House is not a government establishment. Nobody has been up there on any instruction of mine.' Both of these statements were, as it happened, true. Buchanan liked to stick to the truth when possible; it was often the least risky of the available options.

Birkov remained silent. His suspicion was almost tangible. Buchanan came back from the window and splashed himself a large glass of soda water. He would have liked time to make urgent private enquiries but knew that it couldn't be spared. A committee of the Cabinet – a small group of senior ministers meeting without the knowledge of Cabinet colleagues – expected his report by midday on Monday. They would want the outlines of a tripartite agreement. He couldn't allow it to be wrecked at this stage by Russian paranoia.

'I take it,' he said, feeling the ground with caution, 'that you've put some agent of your own into Lantern House.' Birkov remained impassive. 'If you have,' continued Buchanan, 'you certainly know a damn sight more than *I* do about the carryings-on of the effete British aristocracy!' He waited for a comment from Birkov but got none. Glancing at Friedman, he received nothing but a polite smile. 'I'll make you a concession,' he said boldly to Birkov. 'You can put Lantern House on the list of British locations to be looked at by the joint commission.' He sipped thoughtfully, making rapid calculations. 'I hope you've taken in what sort of a gesture I'm making you. We've no powers over British citizens – not even members of our mad peerage! We shall have to make . . . special arrangements.'

'We have the greatest confidence in you, Mr Buchanan,' said Birkov, unsmiling.

It was only when Birkov had left and his furniture van had moved slowly off that Buchanan found himself forced into a direct lie. He stood with Friedman in his well-stocked cellar, picking a claret for the 'ratification lunch' which he had planned for the following day, the Sunday before his intended report to the few selected ministers. 'A St Emilion, I think,' he said casually, studying the ruby glow by the light of a candle.

'I know for a fact,' said Friedman, 'that you're on to this guy, Lampson.'

Buchanan kept his eye to the bottle, assiduously looking for sediment. 'We know nothing about him,' he said, lying; confident in the lie, certain that the lie could not be detected; thinking of the PROSPERO file.

Friedman snickered. 'We've picked up those two agents of yours.'

Buchanan was glad of the dim light. It concealed his bafflement and his increasing rage against Eliot. 'What do you mean by "picked up"?'

'Oh, just some medical care,' said Friedman casually. 'One of them's got some interesting symptoms. What the hell *were* you Brits up to in Tangham Wood the other night? It's giving that dim-wit Colonel of ours the hot flushes. Second "saucer" scare he's had in a month.'

'Blandfordness, perhaps?' said Buchanan, feeling his way.

'We've checked.'

'Then it's some damned accident of yours,' said Buchanan angrily.

Friedman boyishly wrinkled the pouches beneath his eyes. 'We're *allies*, old man! What have we got to hide? Either of us?' He picked up a bottle at random from Buchanan's stock. It was a St Julien, cobwebbed with age. Pricier than Buchanan's St Emilion, he reckoned. 'Another little old saint!' he said. He held it up to the flame of the candle. 'Hoyt picked up some radiation in that pine wood of yours. Not to mention some animal remains. If they *were* "animal" . . . A very small heart. A very small liver. Hoyt's talking about LGM. I'm not discouraging him.'

'Us? Them? LGM?' thought Buchanan, remembering some notes he had been foolish enough to give Eliot. Aloud he said, 'Who are these people you're holding?' He could afford to be bold; Eliot was back in London.

Friedman tucked his cobwebbed saint under one arm and consulted notes. 'Some chick called Julie Smith. Another called Lucy . . .' He brought his piece of paper closer to the candle. 'Lucy Frensham. Some egghead lady you're keeping at that joint of yours at Jodrell.'

Buchanan was relieved to find that he knew neither name. 'We're "keeping" nobody at Jodrell Bank. Jodrell belongs to Manchester University. It's engaged in pure research. Radio astronomy.' He eyed his bottle of St Julien with anxiety. It was the last of the 1959s. He was saving it for his now nearly visible knighthood. 'The trouble with you intelligence fellows is that you sometimes have more imagination than common sense.'

Friedman gave him an engaging grin, tightly gripping the venerable claret. 'What a coincidence!' he said cheerfully. 'The Frensham chick tells us she's the sleeping partner of that Mr Eliot of yours.' He shook his head. 'Some days I think you Brits have given up marriage altogether.'

They climbed back up the cellar-steps. The last of the 1959s went with them. Coldly furious, Buchanan attempted nonchalance. 'Those Lampsons,' he said, shrugging. 'I can't think why Oleg's so interested in them. The old man makes himself a bit of a nuisance to us in the House of Lords. He's a "saucer-freak" or some such. His Hon. son is a mere devil-worshipper – or so I'm told. Our decadent British lordships have a long and dishonourable tradition in that kind of nonsense.'

'Ah, well,' said Friedman amiably, 'we'll find out, I guess.' They came to the insulating door which Buchanan used to keep his wines at the right temperature. ' "Devils", old man?' He glanced at the bottle he was carrying. 'Saints,' he added thoughtfully. 'Devils and saints. Could be just what the research boys now need!'

Angels and devils haunted the dreams of John Eliot. Fair-haired creatures with a suspicion of wings; squat, loathsome entities with a smell of sulphur. Ariels and Calibans. Familiars of some powerful PROSPERO. Snatches came to him of the books he had been reading, of others he might once have read, evocative phrases, numinous sentences, which resonated at some level of the imagination which he was not used to treading – 'a partially formed event . . .'; 'bedevilled by angels . . .'; 'the earth hath bubbles as the water has . . .' He was possessed by images of cloven pine, a cloven hoof; of scurrying demons out of a Bosch triptych; of beautiful and evil flowers growing from an insane root.

He woke at half-past three in the morning, drenched in sweat, cursing himself for the folly of a night cap of double brandy, thrown down on toasted cheese. He was not used to nightmares. They followed the kind of logic which had no place in official argument. He was accustomed to keeping his head clear for more sober realities: the case for (or against) some 'modernization' of nuclear warheads, against (or for) the further development of chemical weapons, pro (or contra) the precautionary stockpiling of napalm. Sulphurous dreams could do nothing but confuse these dispassionate urgencies.

Resigned to wakefulness, he drafted, by hand, his report for Aleister Buchanan on 'The Bentbridge Incident'. In one or two passages he drew, with dry wit, on his recent reading in the lunatic fringe of devils and saucers. They would gird Aleister's loins against the kind of nonsense which he now seemed likely to receive from Colonel Hoyt. They would show Aleister that his trust in John Eliot's thoroughness was not misplaced.

Picking among the celebrated cases, Eliot chose three, arranging them, with official dispassion, in the order of their supposed 'closeness' of encounter: the sighting of many aerial lights performing impossible manoeuvres above Cook Strait, New Zealand, in the December of 1978 (they had, it seemed, deceived even a bunch of hard-headed journalists and the experienced crew of the Air New Zealand Argosy which was conveying them between Wellington and Christchurch); communication, by the waving of hands and other visual signals, between an Anglican priest and the man-like 'crew' of certain 'vehicles' hovering near a mission station in Papua in 1959 (thirty-eight other witnesses had been present and twenty-five of them had signed a written deposition); entities – four feet high, with vast eyes and pointed ears, illuminated by some inner glow – encountered face to face, after the 'landing' of a 'bright object', by members of a large family living on a farm near Kelly-Hopkinsville, Kentucky, in 1955 (they had suffered ostracism for ever after for their foolishness in reporting these matters to the United States Air Force and to local authorities).

In listing these testimonies to human gullibility, Eliot stressed that they did duty for many thousands of similar reports – a sorry catalogue of fraud, folly or misperception. He had picked them, he said, to show the current poverty of the USAF imagination. Did they really suppose that well-grounded British officials would take some fairy tale of a similar character as adequate cover for uncovenanted tests of a device which had landed in Tangham Wood? The Ministry of Defence had better be prepared to receive some farrago of this kind and to deal with it pretty sharply.

He passed over, because they blunted the point of his argument (and also made him uneasy), one or two cases which lay closer to hand: objects in the sky above Suffolk in 1956, moving at impossible speeds, detected by military radar at the USAF bases at RAF Bentwaters and RAF Lakenheath, pursued by an RAF aircraft which had found itself dazzled by an aerobatic display which defied known physical laws; a monstrous egg-shaped glow which put out of action two cars driving between Avon and Sopley, inland of Bournemouth, in November 1967, caused one passenger to be taken to a nearby hospital in a state of profound shock, brought a Ministry of Defence official hot-foot to interview witnesses, put the authorities to the cost of resurfacing two hundred feet of road. Eliot was relieved that these incidents were so far before his time that he felt no obligation to comment on them or even to mention them.

Sleepless but stimulated, he went back to the Ministry of Defence at half-past eight on the Sunday morning and spent a couple of hours putting his report into readable form on the office typewriter. At eleven he went down to Aleister Buchanan's suite and 'posted' the report through the slit of Aleister's security-safe. He returned to his office, relieved of a burden, confident of official gratitude for a job well done. At eleven-twenty, as he was about to leave for Covent Garden and a quiet Sunday, his telephone rang. 'I've read that stuff of yours,' said Aleister's voice. 'You'd better come and have a word.' He went back down to Aleister's place, ready to receive praise, framing the modest disclaimers which would make light of the effort he had been put to while at the same time leaving Aleister in no doubt about its personal cost.

'I'm suspending you from duty,' said Buchanan.

He stood at the window with his back to Eliot. Beyond him, the Thames gleamed sullenly in the misty November light. A long way off the bubble of St Paul's Cathedral loomed above the waterscape.

'You've got a right of appeal, of course.' Buchanan paused. 'But I don't advise you to use it.'

Eliot could merely say, 'Why?', finding his mouth dry with astonishment and anxiety.

'I'm told,' said Buchanan, 'that you commandeered a file yesterday which you've no right of access to. I'm told that you forged my signature to get it.'

'PROSPERO . . . ?'

'I don't advise you to use that word again. The word itself is classified. SECRET, as it happens. You're very near to a criminal offence, my dear fellow. We shall have to think about it.'

'I've only been doing what you asked . . .' began Eliot, blustering.

A train of barges went down the Thames, carrying the detritus of a city towards some unknown destination. Its tug hooted. Buchanan's window was briefly intersected by it. Half a minute passed in silence.

'I didn't instruct you,' said Buchanan, 'to get among our chums at Bentbridge. Or to put some doxy of yours into places where the stupid bitch has no business. Or to get her picked up and shoved into sick quarters at Bentbridge.'

'Lucy . . . ?' said Eliot. The sheer, coarse brutality of Aleister's language left him bewilderd. It was out of character. It indicated rage and perhaps alarm. He thought for a moment. 'What does "suspended" mean?'

'It means,' said Buchanan, keeping his face to the window (not once during this interview had he looked at Eliot, not once would he do so), 'it means that you'd better get back to that apartment of yours and wait for instructions.' He seemed to be studying the expanse of river beyond his glass vista. 'It means that the Old Man – in his soggy mercy – will probably be posting you to the Lands Organization or the Claims Commission or the department's auditors – or any other bloody place where you can't do further damage to the national interest.'

'What have I done?' said Eliot.

But to that question it would be some time yet before he knew the answer. For the moment one appalling fact had displaced all others, that Lucy – incomprehensibly, alarmingly – was lying in a sickbed within the confines of an American airbase where a bare forty-eight hours before, he had heard crazy talk of an autopsy. He was surprised to find how much he missed her. This sudden discovery – tiny by planetary standards – displaced even the front-page news in the Sunday newspaper he bought on the way back to Covent Garden.

'RUSSIAN ASTRONAUT RECOVERED. SOVIETS CLAIM SPACE VICTORY.'

Eliot twisted the paper to the back page, pursuing this main-page Sunday sensational, postponing for the moment the rather more soothing story of a vicar's shame which the inside pages promised him.

'Russians allege American plans for War in space,' continued the Sunday tabloid's Man in Moscow. There was talk of withdrawing the Russian Ambassador from Washington. Troops and tanks were massing on both sides of the border between the two Germanys. A stiff note was being prepared by the President's advisers.

These diplomatic niceties kept Eliot engaged till he found himself turning the key in the door of his comfortable apartment in Covent Garden. He let himself in, tipped the newspaper into the waste-disposal unit, confronted the titles of the books he had lost his money to the day before. In sudden disgust he threw them into the waste-paper basket. Their triviality appalled him. What relevance had 'discs' and goblins to the stark brutalities of the real world? What light could be shed by mere 'lights in the sky' on present fears and horrible imaginings?

The last of his discarded titles stared at him from the tasteful white cylinder at the corner of his living-room where he dumped rubbish destined for destruction. Lying above the dozen others he had bought only the day before in a mood of aberration or conscientiousness, it flashed its absurd message at him in letters as tall as the headlines of his newspaper. '*Let's Hope They're Friendly*,' it said.

4
Mavericks

In a tent on a ridge near Warminster Julius Ben Caesar Schultz tucked in his toes against the persistent dew. He had come here to see flying saucers. Warminster was famous for them. But his enthusiasm, like his cash, was now nearly exhausted. He had already got up five times since dusk in the gaudy hope of seeing visions, only to find that they were merely sky-rockets let off by the eccentric British in the town below the ridge. The previous three weeks had been just as disappointing.

Down in Warminster the British were using gunpowder to mark some odd little moment in their history. On 5 November 1605 (pre-Gregorian calendar) a certain Guy, or Guido, Fawkes had tried to blow up the Houses of Parliament at a moment when the King was visiting them. He had been using the latest in technology, but had been caught out by the security guard. The British now marked the occasion by setting fire to gunpowder. By 1990 this gesture had become as cosy as witchcraft or apple pie. Newer technologies hung in the night sky a thousand miles above Warminster Ridge. Peoples, rather than kings, were threatened by them. Security guards (of a newer kind) were said to track them. Squibs and Roman candles had dwindled into innocence. They seemed a controllable kind of terror. Perhaps that was why they were still used.

In the triangle of night sky at the end of the narrow tent, somewhere beyond the end of Julius B.C. Schultz's bootless feet, another globe of light exploded. He groaned, casting a self-pitying arm across his eyes. His dollars were nearly exhausted; his visa was running out; he had wasted three weeks in fruitless effort; even his socks and underwear would now be in a terminal condition had it not been for Julie Smith. Julie had proved the only compensation for this expensive odyssey. 'Phenomena' had proved elusive. He hadn't seen so much as a Daylight Disc, let alone an Encounter of even the First Kind – that mere perception that 'something' had 'landed', at far too great a distance to permit intercourse with ambassadors from Venus, but with promising indications that this consummation might be hoped for. There hadn't been a 'phenomenon' worth noting – apart from Julie. Julie (he had to admit it) had turned out 'phenomenal'. These British girls . . . He smiled soggily in the darkness, reckoning that his dollars had maybe proved good value. She even washed his socks. Her mysterious absence for five days on end had proved the point. A faint effluvium of unwashed socks now lingered beneath the fly-sheets.

The tent-flap stirred. A dark figure groped its way towards him. An entity . . . ? A visitant . . . ? He sat up in hopeful terror.

'Julius,' said Julie's voice.

'Hi, Girl!' he said joyfully. Something in her voice – it seemed hoarse and tremulous – caused him to shine his torch. It caught her face. Even with the near-extinguished battery he glimpsed an angry blotch of scarlet which ran down from brow to chin. 'For gosh sakes . . .'

'Put out that bloody thing!' she whispered sharply. He dropped it to the grass beside him.

In the darkness she clasped his calves, her shoulders shaking. Julius faintly moaned: this had been so often the first step towards phenomenal encounters. 'Julie,' he muttered, groping for the torch again.

'Get up, you slob,' she said, urgently, affectionately. He could hear the affection even through the rasping, shaking voice. But what was wrong with the girl?

'Lights,' she croaked. 'Lantern lights.'

'Goddam pyrotechnics!' said Julius bitterly.

'No,' she said, 'No!' She tugged at him to get up. 'For God's sake remember what I'm saying.'

He unfolded himself from the camp bed, struggled into his boots, jack-knifed on to the hillside. Julie clung to him in the darkness. She seemed to be glancing wildly about. 'Lantern lights,' she mumbled again. 'Get those words into your head, you oaf!' She suddenly stood stock-still, staring across his shoulder towards the north.

'Lights?' he said stupidly – and then saw them. Two tiny brilliant globes hanging side by side a little above ground level in a lane which skirted the northern flank of the ridge. Even from half a mile away through the hedgerow they dazzled like the headlights of a car which had been turned to search for them. A faint, metallic hum hung in the air, eddied by the night breeze. Now that a first Encounter seemed upon him, Julius disliked the look of it. It far too closely resembled the eyes of a great beast about to spring.

Julie tugged him sharply in the other direction. He followed, unprotesting. Behind him the hum mounted to a sudden distant roar. Something rasped and screeched like a grinding of gears.

They ran down the slope together towards a piece of woodland, five hundred yards away. Julie croaked and gabbled incomprehensible nonsense to him. An address. A telephone number. A word like 'Prospero'. She made him repeat them, gasping and panting as they ran.

'Don't say "Prospero" unless you have to,' she gasped out. 'Only if they won't listen to you.'

'When . . .? How . . . ?'

'If anything happens to me.'

They stumbled their way across a muddy streamlet and came to the spinney.

'For chrissakes what should happen?'

She stood still at the edge of the thicket, catching her breath. 'Tell them Men in White – but I got away. Then tell them . . .' She hesitated.

'Men in Black?' he said hopefully, dredging up an archetype from the saucer myth.

She thought for a moment. 'Say . . . aliens,' she said.

She pushed on forward through the dead brambles. He tried to follow. She pushed him gently, fiercely, back. 'Get on, you slob! Get to that address I've told you. With any luck I'll be there first. But we can't risk it.' She disappeared into the woodland.

Julius stood still, stunned and bewildered. Peering after Julie, he thought he could see a distant glow somewhere on the edge of the thicket. The far-off lights of Warminster, maybe? Some Limey bonfire on the edge of town? And then he heard that deep hum again, and somewhere, a long way off, sounds like the trampling of dead branches and a muffled cry.

With a beating heart he stumbled into the wood, his boots squelching in the November mud. Branches whipped across his face. An owl shrieked close at hand. Lights suddenly flamed into incandescence through the canopy of leafless trees above him. A sulphurous smell drifted on the air.

He came to a clearing, silvered by the newly risen moon. 'Julie!' he shouted among the leafless shrubs around the open space, unsheathing his large jack-knife.

Silence. A smell of sulphur.

Aided by the moon and his pocket torch, he thought he could make out indentations in the boggy ground – gouges where the fins or landing-pods of some 'vehicle' might have rested. He made out other marks like little hoofs. Semi-circular marks with a raised cone of earth in the centre of each. They looked like the footprints of something cloven. And there, suddenly, was one of Julie's shoes – sensible shoes, low-heeled, comfortable – lying with its heel upturned.

For a quarter of an hour he stumbled in and out of the surrounding undergrowth, calling her name with a shrill, hoarse voice. Brambles whipped across his forehead. Blood trickled down one side of his face. He wiped it with a muddy hand. Then he remembered that there were messages to be delivered – if anything should happen to her. 'Lantern lights'; 'Men in White'; 'Prospero'.

Muddy and bloody, distracted and distressed, an alien with a near-expired visa, clutching an open jack-knife in his hand, Julius Ben Caesar Schultz stumbled his way to Warminster among bursting rockets and the shrapnel of Roman candles. He found the local police station. He poured out his story.

There was this English chick, yeah? She was a real honey, yeah? She'd gone away last week. Some other guy, maybe? He was broad-minded about that sort of thing. She'd come back, hadn't she? He didn't give a shit what she'd been up to. But she'd come back beaten up, he'd guess. By Christ, he'd tear that bastard limb from limb! Then she'd gone away again. Kidnapped! Fucking aliens, too! He'd cut them to pieces if he found them! That's what the knife was for. Well, for chrissakes, of *course* that's what the knife was for! What the fuck else, mate? And he had to use their telephone. No, *not* for a bloody solicitor. What the fuck did he need a solicitor for? No, he didn't know who they were. The

Psychic Circle, maybe (Ha, Ha). The British CIA, for all he knew. But *urgent*, mate, *urgent*. Maybe she'd die if he didn't. Maybe she was dead already.

'Dead already, sir?' They looked at his bloody face. They took his bloody jack-knife into custody. They recorded statements. He signed them without looking at them. They were, on the whole, rather polite. He compared them favourably with the Kentucky Sheriff's men on a civil-rights march in 1985, not to mention some seal-cullers he'd tangled with the following year. It was only at half-past two the following morning as he clung to the bars of his cell, shouting the venerable words of 'We Shall Overcome', that a mean sergeant punched him in the chest and followed through with a kick to the groin. It seemed to him fairly mild when he thought about the kinds of thing which went on in Russian mental hospitals and the prisons of El Salvador.

Lem went north.

He travelled on a train in the company of two men sent from Moscow. From the cut of their suits – Western, expensive – he judged that they must be KGB: that, and the uneasy respect which was paid to them at railway stations. They had comandeered a whole compartment to themselves and him. Meals were brought to them from the restaurant car, wonderful meals, fulfilling meals, meals such as he hadn't eaten for half a lifetime. They brought back with nostalgia the meals given to a hungry boy from his father's patch of backyard in the Ukraine – until that day in the middle fifties when his father had been taken away for ever for the bourgeois deviation of selling cabbages at a profit to housewives in Lvov.

'You have talents, comrade,' they said to him from time to time. Nobody had said so before, least of all at Chernyakhovsk. 'The Party expects much of you.' He disliked that bit, it had often been the prelude to unpleasantnesses of one kind or another. 'You have a role to play in the historic struggle of the masses against the forces of bourgeois-imperialsim.' Lem was damned if he could see what. (Well, 'damned' was shoving it a bit. It was the sort of language his pious grandmother had used. 'In need of the Party's guidance' was probably less risky.) But he uneasily tucked away the implied compliment, noting that he was still in custody, even though more comfortable for the time being.

They had been saying things of this kind to him – windy things, things which were not very down to earth – ever since that strange moment, no more than a day and a half ago, when the Comrade-Doctor had let them into his cell. The Comrade-Doctor had seemed uneasy, as though he had overlooked some duty or been late in meeting it. The men in black had treated the Comrade-Doctor with less than respect. 'Have you studied the directives, comrade? Have you read them with the attention the Party expects?'

The Comrade-Doctor, wearing a fixed smile on his pale, round face, had fluttered his pudgy hands. 'We couldn't be certain sooner, comrades . . . Pretence is very easy in such matters . . . We had no wish to trouble important comrades from Moscow . . .'

He had received nothing but a blank, bleak look with no trace of a smile. Only to Lem had the visitors creased their faces into some sort of greeting.

They travelled north. They ate. They slept. Through the half-shuttered windows Lem saw, at a railway station they stopped at, that they had reached the latitude of Moscow, though somewhat to the west of it. Night came, and with it a meal fit for Tsars, brought by comrade-attendants who showed with their expressionless, averted faces that they would take care to remember nothing.

They bedded down on comfortable bunks. Lem was politely handcuffed to his (to the detriment of his wish to make water during the small hours). His companions took it in turns to sleep, unstrapping holstered pistols from beneath their well-cut jackets.

As the late-November dawn was coming up across the icy threshold of Siberia Lem saw the Aurora Borealis. It shimmered across half the sky in a tremulous curtain of mauves and greens, a serendipity of the planet he happened to be living on. An unlooked-for thing which he found mysterious and moving. It seemed to have little to do with the unkind carryings-on of the species he belonged to. It was merely – or so they said – an interchange between the 'solar wind' (that stream of charged particles flowing from the sun) and the earth's magnetic field. It had no will or mind. It merely happened. It seemed to possess far less mind or will than the sharp, observant eyes of the KGB attendant who had kept himself awake in order to be sure that Lem did not intend to avoid his duty to the masses by escape, or premature death or mere descent into withdrawal. Lem gave him a cheerful morning smile.

Some hours later, at Plesetsk – the same Plesetsk near which he had once seen some face of glory or of terror staring down at him from the lambent sky with searching and melancholy eyes – Lem met a man who had come back from outer space, an astronaut, a Hero of the Soviet Union, a two-legged entity who had been thrust by the force of chemical propellants wildly beyond the gravity-well of the cosy world he had grown up in.

This astronautic hero lay on a bed in a white ward. His courage had been placed beyond doubt on many occasions. He had been decorated by two successive Secretaries of the Party at the unanimous request of the Soviet Praesidium. He had saved a life in space. He had proved his manhood by begetting three herolets and a heroleen upon a busty and thoroughly reliable young woman from Kuybyshev who had been strongly recommended to him by the local Party. He had recently figured in the world's headlines: he was the only survivor of an inexplicable collision in space between Russian and American vehicles. The cost of bringing him back to earth would deprive some tens of thousands of loyal citizens for at least two years to come of their hoped-for ration of the plainest kind of shoe.

He lay on his back among the pillows and trembled. He gestured with a shaking, bandaged hand towards the ceiling. Lem knew that the conversation was being recorded. He hoped that the Comrade-Hero did, as well.

'Out there . . .' said the Comrade-Hero, shaking with a kind of palsy. 'Out there . . . Sometimes . . .'

'Yes?' said Lem helpfully, wishing he knew how to cut off the crafty little microphone concealed in the skirting-board.

'Sometimes there are *ghosts . . . devils . . .*' A sobbing rasp came up the throat of the Comrade-Hero.

Lem nodded sympathetically. He knew it well. He seemed to have known it for a long time. 'Spiders, too?' he asked with compassion.

But it was the wrong question for that particular moment. Tactless, it seemed. The Hero-Astronaut of the Soviet Union lay on his back sobbing like a small child till uniformed attendants came and gave him the rubber-soled release of some injected soporific.

Lem was glad that it did not seem to be Sulfazine.

The little, twisted corpse lay face upwards under a sheet of toughened glass. The steel walls of its coffin closely imprisoned it. Staring down at the hairless, rounded head and the tormented limbs, Jean-Paul Foucault was torn between pity and disgust.

'How long?' he asked.

The French Air Force officer at his elbow hesitated for a moment. 'Three years ago. We picked it up at Oloron.'

'Oloron Sainte-Marie?'

His companion nodded.

'Why haven't you made it public?'

The officer shrugged. 'Would *you* want to make that public?'

Shuddering with the cold of the place, Dr Foucault forced himself to study the little entity more closely. It was barely four feet from heel to skull. Its greenish-yellowish flesh clung to the bones. Whoever had brought it here to be preserved against decay by the Siberian temperature within the casket had stripped it of clothes. Between the legs it was sexless or, at the best, grossly undersexed. There was the merest suspicion of some mound or slit which suggested gender but left it quite ambiguous. All the energies of its creation had gone into the vastly disproportionate head. The head lolled, foolish in death, extending the tip of a tiny, leathery tongue from the lipless gash which served it as a mouth.

'I would make anything public which was a scientific fact,' said Foucault, shuddering. He had in his time made public – that is to say, published – many facts which, if laymen understood them, might terrify them to death. The ghostly flowering of new particles from collisions of elementary matter in the chilly labyrinths of CERN. The solid certainty that solid substance was nothing but the interplay of a myriad of wraith-motes, engaged in some eternal dance. The hints dropped by Nature, when under torture, that time might be reversible, that even space was a mere figment of the life-process of men and other animals.

'I would always publish the truth,' he said. 'Nobody has the right to conceal facts.' Not even the fact of some hydrocephalous dwarf, supposedly from regions beyond the Earth, whose head was hideously gashed by the incidents of its death near Oloron Sainte-Marie in the shadow of the Pyrenees.

'Remember that you're under oath,' said his companion. 'The President, himself, has decided that nothing should be released about these matters for the time being.'

Why, then, were they showing *him* these things? Foucault wondered. Didn't they know that he had a reputation for speaking his mind? Had they never heard of the scientific conscience? Keeping his gaze fixed to the tiny, alien corpse, avoiding the eye of his companion, he consulted his conscience and began to reach conclusions.

The scientific conscience can often be as much of a nuisance as the religious kind. Foucault's had driven him, as ruthlessly as any need to seek weekday confession before taking the sacraments on a Sunday, to go to Paris on the Saturday following his close encounter in the Hautes Cévennes and to hunt out the headquarters of GEPAN. He had stood before its door in the rue de la Tombe-Issoire, glancing furtively to left and right, hating the ethical necessity which impelled him, hoping that no gutter journalist would detect him (*him*, Dr Foucault, *the* Dr Foucault) in the act of yielding to superstition, as the 'yellow' press would undoubtedly put it. Half against his hope, he had been let into their shabby offices and allowed to tell his story. They had listened with the same concerned but neutral benevolence as his doctor showed him from time to time when Foucault consulted him about his arthritic hip – now 'miraculously' cured, it seemed. They had made notes. They had asked him to sign them. He reluctantly granted them a degree of bureaucratic efficiency. Twenty-four hours later, shortly after attending Mass in the somewhat vulgar setting of Nôtre Dame, he had been telephoned at his Paris *pied-à-terre* by CNES, the space agency to which, as he knew, GEPAN was attached. CNES had pressed him cordially to witness 'something of importance' at a military airbase not far from Paris. Now, on the Monday, he stood in its chilly vault – converted from a former, and much-celebrated wine cellar – and thought about what he should do next.

'I'd like to have a closer look,' he said, staring down into the cryogenic casket. Something about the flesh of the creature left him uneasy. 'Can we open the . . . coffin?'

The officer shook his head. 'It would disintegrate at once. We're as far down to absolute zero as we can get. It's the only way of keeping the specimen intact.'

'Has there been an autopsy?'

The officer was clearly relieved. He had been briefed for this question. 'Of course! In 1987. A few hours before we put it into deep-freeze.' He groped in a pocket of his jacket and handed Foucault the crisp new copy of some sizeable document. Foucault glanced over it, picked up a word or two ('boron', 'silicon', 'calcium', 'magnesium'), looked again at the specimen below the plate-glass cover, wondered what scientific honesty required of him.

' "Angel's Hair", as well?' he asked, studying the little tangle of tubes or threads – as complex as any spider's web – which lay at the bottom of the frozen casket. He had heard of 'Angel's Hair'. It has been falling for centuries past, acording to the weird reports he'd reluctantly committed himself to study over the weekend. In the twentieth century it had fallen at Oloron Sainte-Marie in the October of 1952, the same Oloron – innocent and rural – as had witnessed in 1987 the capture (or 'recovery') of the little green corpse which now lay beneath his scrutiny; it had also fallen at Gaillac ten days later, not much more than a hundred and fifty kilometres to the north-east. Hundreds of witnesses had seen it at both places.

Angel's Hair. There had been reports of it for a millenium. It seemed like gossamer, said the witnesses. It drifted from the sky in long, wispy strands which soon dissolved into a jelly-like mass. The superstitious called it 'Devil's Jelly'. The unsuperstitious were inclined to rush it as quickly as possible to the laboratory of some local and preferably sceptical chemist. It never survived for long. But once or twice it had survived long enough to reveal traces of boron, silicon, calcium, magnesium . . . It seemed very like the gluey, rubbery substance which some called 'ectoplasm'. A hundred years before, in the nineteenth century, many a good man and true (some with the highest of scientific credentials) had pondered hard on 'ectoplasm'. Ectoplasm emerged from every orifice (even the least mentionable) of gifted 'mediums'. It took strange forms, sometimes as protozoan as a jellyfish or a vast amoeba, sometimes approaching human shape. There was something plastic about it, long before plastics had been invented. It seemed as mouldable as clay, though what force moulded it remained uncertain (the human imagination? Spirits of the dead? Other entities from beyond the daylight world?) It very readily made 'partially formed events' – and then snatched them back into whatever limbo they had come from.

'Angel's Hair' and ectoplasm. They both had the look of some amorphous substance which was all too ready to flow into grotesque forms. Assuming one believed in either of them.

Dr Foucault studied the 'Angel's Hair' at the foot of the steel coffin and the dwarfish figure whose texture so closely resembled it. The one might well have been 'moulded' from the other, as surely indeed as the metamorphosis which had caused Professor Charles Richet, distinguished pathologist teaching at the University of Paris in the 1890s and winning the Nobel prize some years later (a Frenchman, it had to be said, no mere damned Anglo-Saxon), to speak of the 'liquid or pasty jelly which emerges from the mouth or breast of Marthe' (his favourite medium) 'and which organizes itself by degrees, acquiring the shape of a face or limb'.

It would be very easy to believe that 'Angel's Hair' or ectoplasm had somehow contrived to take the form of the little hydrocele beneath the plate-glass cover – if it weren't so evident that both had been fabricated from foam rubber.

Dr Foucault gravely nodded, accepted the supposed 'autopsy', handed back his temporary pass (signed by no less than some secretary in the President's office) and returned to Paris in a ferment of the scientific conscience.

The grossness of the fraud left him surprised. But what surprised him more was the apparent wish of the authorities to convince him that some little yellowish-green entity had come from a distant constellation to the town of Oloron in 1987 for purposes not yet declared. Did they expect him to make it public, knowing his reputation for the truth? Or were they serious in binding him to secrecy? What were their motives? What did they want of him? Regardless of that, what should he now do?

It seemed more like a political problem than a scientific one. Only as the train was waiting in the suburb of St Denis, a little to the north-east of the Gard du Nord, did the real conundrum cross the troubled mind of Dr Foucault (accomplished conjurer with the weirdnesses of sub-atomic forces).

By what distasteful miracle had somebody contrived to form, in the vulgar disneyfication of foam rubber, a remarkably close approximation to the little entities which had detained him in the Hautes Cévennes two days before?

Entities pursued John Eliot. They came from the compound of Colonel Hoyt, sirens shrieking, headlights at full power. He stamped on the accelerator and raced across the airfield towards the east. Behind him, the lights of the Bentbridge sick-quarters cast shadows of the hangars of Fighter Wing halfway across the tarmac.

He headed back to the RAF guard room at the main entrance. They had let him in. They knew him well. They would let him out again.

They didn't.

The crash-barrier was lowered. The guard room blazed with light. Three RAF policemen stood in his way.

He braked to a halt, wondering whether to fall back on British calm, claiming – for God's sake! – the immunity of a British official on this piece of British territory.

Behind him, the USAF vehicles came up with a wail of sirens. Brakes squealed. Dull-green uniforms – a dozen of them – leapt out and began to run towards him.

For God's sake, why? In the name of heaven, what for? Rage and bewilderment kept him briefly helpless. For the mere kidnap of a British citizen? (She lay on the back seat, wrapped in a stolen USAF blanket.) For stealing a USAF staff car? Well, maybe . . .

He began to open the car-door, ready to pass off this fracas with British phlegm, confident in his rights, happy to return their stolen property (excluding his baggage on the back seat).

A bullet whined past his head into the darkness beyond the crash-barrier. He had no time to be astounded that they were ready to kill . . . ready to murder. . . Reflexes of the most primitive kind now gripped him. Given a gun, he might even have returned their fire. He slammed the door shut and jerked the car forward with a screech of half-engaged gears.

Two of the RAF policemen leapt for the bonnet of the car and tried to grasp it. His compatriots! His fellow citizens who had admitted his striped pasteboard with grave respect a bare twenty minutes before!

He slammed into the barrier, heard it crunch, saw a headlight shatter into fragments, turned on to the main road and swerved wildly south. He gained two hundred yards before the vehicles behind him had got on the move again.

He came to crossroads, turned left, switched off all lights, sped swiftly east. It had to be said for Colonel Hoyt that his car was tough and speedy.

His pursuers were somewhere behind him. He hadn't yet shaken them off. Two miles further on, to the left of the road, he saw some great house or mansion, some outpost of that discreet gentry which still contrived to own half of England. The orange glow of some upper window showed that they were still about. He braked at the laurel-clad entrance to its winding drive and began to turn into it.

Lucy, swathed in a stolen blanket, gripped his shoulders from the back seat. 'Lantern House!' she shouted at him. 'For God's sake, not Lantern House!'

Silently cursing this womanish nonsense but yielding to its vehemence – she sounded near to hysteria – he drove on eastwards towards the coast. Somewhere soon they must find sanctuary. Lights hung in the night sky behind him, reflected from the military furies who pursued him. Against the cover of low cloud they formed domes and discs in the November darkness. Lucy gabbled into his ear some weird tale about Lantern House that he had no time to attend to.

Sanctuary . . . Where could he find it? A thought came to him.

On the coast, still ten miles off, a lighthouse flashed. At intervals of forty seconds its beam completed one cycle of a circle. Unidirectional, sharply focused by the parabolic mirror placed behind its lantern-light, the beam flashed messages to the four corners of the world. Seaward, it told mariners to sheer away eastward from the pebble-bank of the Ness and the sandbars which lay offshore. Inland, its flash was wasted – except to worried souls who wanted some routine explanation of the strange lights which had been seen above Suffolk in recent days, except to a man fleeing from the powers which followed on his heels.

Eliot pointed his car towards the coastal lantern-house, finding that the road went that way, too. Somewhere to the north of this beacon lay RAF Blandfordness, covered by darkness, since the moon had not yet risen (the moon was pursuing some cycle of its own since it had shone upon the near-sacrifice of Jake). Blandfordness lay in obscurity. But John knew where to find it. It was a 'cathedral' of the modern age, an artefact which went as far beyond the suburban villas – and the comprehension – of the populace which had met its cost (or the British part of it) as any megalith or henge-monument must have seemed to the peasant farmers of the neolithic age. It was, in a certain sense, a temple, at least in being mysterious. It would give him shelter. Its resident priesthood knew him well. It, too, like Bentbridge, was nominally a British station. He knew its RAF controllers. He had been up to see them a number of times. He had done a good publicity job for them in the face of local hostility to its unappealing masts and concrete outlines, not to mention local fears of its technocratic witchcraft.

The road bent north a little inland of the lighthouse. He took the curve, then braked to a halt and listened. Away to the west across the marshy landscape, the high-pitched hum of the other vehicles could still be heard. But they seemed to be growing fainter as the seconds passed. With any luck, his pursuers were going north along the inland route, knowing that the coast road led nowhere except to Blandfordness and that their quarry would not be so foolish as to trap himself in a cul-de-sac.

Craftily foolish, John Eliot drove slowly and quietly along the remaining mile of road. He remembered the local row when the Ministry of Defence had announced its plans for building it. He had helped to smooth over that spot of bother, talking with the same suave charm to naturalists troubled about the fate of the nearby bird sanctuary as he employed with politicians, with air marshals, with troublesome journalists and – when the chance offered – with women.

Lucy leant across from the back seat and put an arm round his shoulder. 'You're in trouble, chum,' she said softly. 'You seem to have put your foot in it.'

'We're both in trouble.'

His own was clear enough – breach of security, forgery of a signature, kidnap, theft of a car. (Getting her out of the place had been like a bad B-movie of the kind he avoided.) But what had *she* done to interest them? Radio astronomy? Knowing him . . .?

He rested his unshaven chin against her hand, surprised by the unaccustomed feel of the day-old bristle. Not for years had he failed to shave before breakfast.

To his right the derelict bird sanctuary lay sullen and deserted, a land-locked lake of salt and marsh, trapped between the road and the pebble bar of the Ness. Two years before he had heard curlews here. But the sedge had now withered. The cement lorries had come, Blandfordness had put up its towers. No birds now sang.

Palely loitering, he stopped the car, glad not to be alone. Turning round, he kissed Lucy fiercely, unsuavely.

Across country, behind her shoulder, he thought he could see the lights of another vehicle. An orange glow hung above the inland, marshy fields to the south-west. It moved at fantastic speed.

Trapped in his cul-de-sac, he jerked the car into motion again and drove the remaining few hundred yards to the unpromising sanctuary of Blandfordness.

Jake, like Lem, was impelled northwards towards the region of the aurora. Unlike Lem, he was not escorted.

Strange events had overtaken him. There had been a great flurry in the warm, white place where he lay in uneasy comfort. Lights all over the place, people running, some shouting, doors opening, doors left unlocked.

Pigeons had been on Jake's mind since Friday, his homing-pigeons, numbered from Mr One to Mr Twenty. They were trapped in their loft, he remembered. What would become of them? They would be needing grain – the grain which the Lord permitted him to pick up from the rich-man's-tables of granaries around local farms. They would be needing water – water from the local stream, for which not even the Lord's permission was necessary but which pigeons, barred against dangers in their comfortable prison, could hardly get for themselves.

Jake had stumbled his way among strange buildings, in the

chaos of shouts and flashing lights, drawn by a glare at the other side of the airfield. Entering a vast shed of a place, he had found it filled with winged creatures, half covered with tarpaulins. He failed to recognize them as Phantoms, that newer breed of supersonic interceptor which, in 1989, had taken the same name as its F-4 predecessor of the late 1950s. If he had been told so, he would have scorned the information. These things were neither phantom nor alive. They were merely tinny. They had nothing of the grace of pigeons, little that could be called ghostly except their hooded silence. Grain and water would have been wasted on them, exorcism would not have shifted them.

He made his way across the tarmac and the great concrete road from which, had he known it, the Phantoms thrust themselves skyward on pillars of the precious oils laid down in the Carboniferous phase of the Earth's history, the same road or loft to which they homed back again when their unghostly tasks were done.

At the far edge of the airfield he came to a broken crash-barrier and a lighted guard room, briefly empty of its custodians. It looked like the same guard room he had wheeled his way through three days before, seeking vengeance for the death of Cat.

But it wasn't.

Stumbling forward into the liberty of the public road, he saw the flash of the Ness lighthouse and knew that he must be facing coastwise – eastish as men said. He guessed, being a man to whom compass bearings were unintelligible but directions obvious, that his pigeons lay to the south, the position shown by the little finger of his right hand.

Except that, miraculously, his pigeons were here. . .

Wings fluttered about him in the patch of light shed by the deserted guard room. The birds settled on his tattered clothes. Deprived of his straw padding, which the white-suited crew-cuts had, in their wisdom, taken away and burned, Jake looked more like a scarecrow than a man. Crows he might have scared, but his pigeons felt at home. At Jake's shoulders there was suddenly somewhat more than a mere suspicion of wings. Half a dozen of his birds clambered about the upper part of his scarecrow jacket. Their pinions, nervously half-extended, gave him the look of a grubbily plumed St Michael whose great aerofoils had not yet been fully unfolded. Three clung to his waist, flapping their wings to keep their balance. The rest scurried about his feet in inane circles, nodding their heads like wooden toys.

Jake peered upwards through his eyebrows to Mr Seventeen, now perching on the top of his head. Mr Seventeen was a favourite, though he took care not to let the others know it. Mr Seventeen had white plumage, marked with curlicues of palest grey. Dr Foucault might have said that these feathery extravaganzas resembled the eruptions of some exotic particle, wrenched from violent and close encounter between nucleons a hundred feet below the Swiss-Franco meadows of CERN, the *Conseil Européen pour la Recherche Nucléaire*. But to Jake, an ignorant man, they looked like frost-feathers on a windowpane.

Reaching up, Jake stroked the nervous feet of Mr Seventeen. Mr Seventeen shot abruptly skywards like a November rocket or an apparition of the Blessed Virgin Mary snatched into Assumption. The other pigeons followed. They wheeled in a feathery cloud above Jake's head, then headed northwards.

Something drew Jake northwards, too. Freed from the need of feeding his pigeons, knowing, with a grief gruffly felt, that Cat was dead (that Cat had played some part which belonged to a larger story), sensing that he shouldn't go back to his shack, feeling – without understanding why – some tug or resonance towards that part of the world where Sun and Moon never rose or set, Jake turned in the direction of his left thumb and went widdershins towards the Northern Lights. Coal trucks and uncovenanted gaps among mail bags in passenger trains would have to convey him; a lorry driver or two would have to take pity on an old, roadside tramp; many footsore miles would have to be trudged on feet not too well protected against the raw chill of November nights. But he needed to get there (wherever 'there' might be). And he would, too – however many times his rheumaticky bones were obliged to take their chance in roadside ditches.

Standing in the on-site quarters of Air Commodore Crowley, British Joint Commander of RAF Blandfordness, John Eliot hunted for plausible explanations. Lucy, wrapped in her overcoat and woollen scarf, concealing with difficulty the mere hospital gown in which he had rescued her, now waited in the security wing, politely detained by men in black. Eliot wanted her with him. They were both on the run, now. 'Geoffrey, we're in trouble,' he said experimentally. Lucy had no pass; she was a woman without qualities.

Geoffrey Crowley gave him an uneasy glance. They were old colleagues. Eliot had proved wonderful 'cover' for Blandfordness. But security was security.

'We've come up in one hell of a rush from London,' said Eliot. 'She's a . . . scientific colleague. We didn't have time to get her a pass.' He studied Crowley's expression and judged it expedient to put on a show of irritation. 'Goddamit, Geoffrey! You're not going to stick on a mere bit of paperwork. You've got my own clearance!' (Aleister Buchanan, in his rage and haste, had failed to withdraw it!)

Crowley avoided his eye. 'Why didn't you warn us you were coming?'

'Security, for Christ's sake!' Security was always a useful god to take the name in vain of; the mere mention of it was sometimes enough to excuse the grossest breaches of it. Eliot stared through the window, searching for the furies on the coast road. 'We're being followed. You'd better brace your chaps to resist boarders.'

Crowley joined him at the window. 'Followed?' he said flatly.

'KGB,' said Eliot, ad-libbing. 'Following us from London. Masquerading as Americans, we think. You'll have them here in the next three minutes, putting on corny Texan accents and telling you I've pinched a car from Bentbridge.'

They scanned the southerly countryside. Something lay across the road, half a mile away towards the lighthouse. It cast an orange glow and pulsed in the November darkness. It was stationary and formless.

'I take it you know,' said Crowley neutrally, 'that I had some instructions from Buchanan this afternoon.'

'Of course,' said Eliot, playing for time. Instructions? What instructions?

'They've been confirmed from the American side. My gallant colleague here has got the same marching orders as mine.'

'Of course.'

Crowley turned and looked him full in the face. 'Then, what's this crap, John, about KGB?'

The thing on the cul-de-sac road had begun to edge forwards. It illuminated the dying sedge and the bleak marshland to either side of it. Now that it had drawn nearer, it could be seen as a rectangular shape, thirty feet across the front, by a hundred feet on the side. Windows or portholes were visible. Behind them, there was a supicion of figures.

Eliot stared without comprehension, hiding signs of fear. This was certainly no USAF pursuer. He could almost have wished it had been. Crowley's indifference to it was nearly as weird as the thing itself. A deep vibration shook the room, something like infra-sound, almost beneath hearing. It semed to penetrate his skull. His vision was growing blurred. A double image of Crowley flickered across his field of view and pulled down metal blinds across the window.

'We know as well as you do that the Russians are on to us', said Crowley impatiently. 'They won't have followed you up here to prove it again. They've known about Blandfordness for months.'

The room had grown abruptly calm again. Nothing could now be heard except some pulsing throb deep within the concrete corridors of the establishment.

'Why are you up here?' said Crowley. He poured Eliot a gin. 'Come to see our "warm-up"?' He studied Eliot's half-averted face. 'Friedman's up here, too. Talking to my American chum. But you know that, of course.'

Eliot nodded, glad that poker was a game he understood.

'I hope to God that Friedman's giving our gallant Joint Commander the same marching orders as mine! What the hell do we do with our dual key if the PM and the President are sending us different messages?'

Eliot moistened his parched mouth with the gin and nodded again. He glanced towards the shuttered windows, remembering the monstrosity beyond them. 'We need a car, Geoffrey. The Frensham girl and I. Something less spectacular than that Cadillac of Hoyt's. We're on our way to . . .' To where? Somewhere. Anywhere. Out of range of all authorities. Beyond the ken of goblins, flying saucers, murder . . . Sherwood Forest crossed his mind. He came near to giggling.

'I think I'd better ring Buchanan,' said Crowley woodenly. He went to his desk and picked up the telephone.

'For God's sake don't do that!' said Eliot. He glanced around the room, wondering what he could hit Crowley with which would stun him without killing him. The half-heard throb of some powerful machinery within Blandfordness reminded him that he (and Lucy) were trapped in a fortress. 'You *must* know why I'm up here. It's urgent, Geoffrey. It's vital.' A word came to him, recently seen, not yet understood. He staked his last chips on it, hoping for at least an Ace. 'PROSPERO,' he said. 'I'm up here because of "Prospero". You know that Aleister can't say *that* to you on an open phone.'

Crowley put down the telephone. He sat on the edge of his desk, cradling his cheeks in clenched fists. 'For Christ's sake, why couldn't you have said so before?' He got up and began to walk about the room. 'So, what hand does the Cabinet want me to play up here?' He went to the shuttered window turning his back on Eliot. 'I suppose I've got to keep the American chums thinking we're shoulder to shoulder?'

Eliot nodded. It seemed the only plausible response.

'So, we're to go on with our preparations?'

'Yes.'

'Can I assume that any instruction I get from Buchanan – authenticated with the right codeword, of course – is to be acted on?'

'Of course.'

'But he *won't* be confirming the same orders as our gallant American chum gets?'

Eliot twirled his glass, leaving the question implicitly (in-explicably!) answered.

'And we'll just leave it to you at PROSPERO?'

'What else?'

Crowley drained his own gin and poured stiff follow-ons for both of them. 'It's going to be quite a hand to play.'

'Of course. That's what you're here *for*, Geoffrey!' Drink and a modicum of information had made Eliot bold.

'You know,' said Crowley jocularly, 'I'm going to want a knighthood out of this – if not a life peerage.'

'I'll make a recommendation.'

Crowley leaned forward and pulled up the metal blinds again. Eliot braced himself against hysteria, determined to imitate

Crowley's nonchalance in the face of the absurd and monstrous. But the thing on the road had gone. There was nothing now except a flurry of blue uniforms, some USAF, some RAF, scurrying about some task in the blaze of a searchlight mounted on the back of an armoured vehicle. A smell of something sulphurous drifted through the half-open casement.

'Thank God for the lighthouse,' said Crowley, shrugging. 'It gives us a cover story when we need one.'

They gazed together across the south-west landscape. The moon was just visible, grazing the eastern horizon. The flash of the Ness light came and went.

'You know we've been having this interference up here?'

Eliot dumbly nodded.

'Something's been "bleeding off" the power. Towards the south-west. It's quite upset our American colleague!'

Towards the south-west Eliot could remember nothing but an old man's shack and the clicking of a geiger-counter three days before.

'But I gather from Buchanan that you clever chaps in Whitehall have done something about it.'

Eliot judged that silence was the least troublesome form of agreement.

'Now, then,' said Crowley briskly, 'we'd better find you something which will get you up to Loch Keisgaig without breaking down.' He searched his efficient, military memory. 'Something unobtrusive?'

'If possible.'

Crowley picked up his telephone. 'I've got this little "banger". Ten-hundredweight van. No markings. Glasgow registration number.' He waited to be congratulated. Eliot mumbled his thanks.

Much later, parked in a side road to the south of Lincoln under the risen moon, John Eliot made desperate love to Lucy Frensham, unshaved, unwashed and among greasy tarpaulins on the hard floor of the van. It was his least suave, his most unguarded, action for many years, an animal need for comfort and shelter in a world which had grown abruptly strange.

Towards dawn, hunting among tattered maps, they discovered that Loch Keisgaig lay a little below Cape Wrath at the northernmost point of Scotland. It seemed as suitable a place as any to be heading for.

Under the same dawn Gregorius Mansfield Lampson, seeking to perfect new kinds of murder in the Long Gallery of Lantern House, was unexpectedly attended by three men in black. They took him away, politely handcuffed, in a large black car. He left behind him a black cockerel whose throat would shortly have been cut, together with some gelatinous trivialities which the well-informed might possibly have recognized as the eye of a newt, the toe of a frog, the fillet of a fenny snake, the root of some poor hemlock, digged in the dark, the finger of a birth-strangled babe.

5
Webs and Networks

'Are you trying to tell us,' said the Minister Without Portfolio, 'that the Russians are not prepared to initial the agreement?' He pointedly turned a shoulder towards Buchanan and the other officials clustered at the end of the mahogany table and addressed the chair. 'I thought, Prime Minister, that Mr Buchanan had given us every reason for optimism at our last meeting.' The other ministerial heads nodded. The Prime Minister remained impassive. Her coiffure had now reached the point at which any sudden movement of the head might prove disastrous to the image constructed by her advisers.

Aleister Buchanan shifted uneasily in his seat. He glanced at the Government Chief Scientist but got no comfort: 'Beezie' was not going to lift a finger to get him out of present difficulties. At his left, the Head of MI5 maintained a suave smile above his discreetly chosen tie. The Chief of the Defence Staff kept himself to his gaunt and naval persona, determined to distrust anything which was not seaborne.

They sat upstairs in the 'secure' committee room of No. 10. Its cosy chintzes had been chosen by Lady Dorothy Macmillan some thirty years before. None of her successors, single or married, had quite had the nerve to change them. Their comfortable flounces concealed bug-proof walls which were also strengthened against explosives.

Buchanan consulted notes, considered his tactics, cleared his throat. 'There are problems, Prime Minister . . .'

'There are *always* problems, Mr Buchanan.' Her voice shifted a little towards the party political. 'My government is here to solve them.' She paused and put the knife in. 'We *had* hoped that officials might assist us.'

Ah, well . . . One had long grown used to this sort of thing. On the whole, she bullied him rather less than most of his Whitehall colleagues. Better be incisive, though . . . He had once heard her putting down a rather distinguished Foreign Secretary merely because the poor chap was trying to explain a complex matter instead of offering her the kind of simplicities which she was capable of understanding. Better avoid the word 'problem', too; it tended to over-excite her. Problems were not objects which she lightly brooked.

'The first point, Prime Minister,' ('point' was relatively safe) 'is that one of our agents has been picked up by the other side.' The Head of MI5 politely nodded. 'Name of Julie Smith,' added Buchanan. Not that the name would mean a damn thing to anyone present; but she might as well have the brief glory of a mention in the minutes of a Cabinet Committee; she would probably not survive for long the attentions which the KGB were now doubtless giving her.

'The point about this . . . incident . . . is that Miss Smith was the agent we put into Lantern House to keep an eye on the Lampsons. The "other side" possibly now know more than we do about Lantern House. They may be thinking it's an establishment of ours. It may have put them off signing an agreement.'

The Head of MI5 ('A', as he now preferred to call himself, the rest of the alphabet having been recently exhausted), examined his fingernails, which were splendidly groomed. 'Prime Minister,' he said smoothly. He spoke partly with a catlike grace, partly with the assurance of a man who had certainly attended educational establishments which were somewhat more expensive than the Prime Minister's family had aspired to. 'Prime Minister . . . We, too, have been doing our "picking up". We have under interrogation at the moment a United States citizen who appears to have been having a sexual liaison with Miss Smith. A certain Schultz, assuming there's no question of an alias. He has told us a great deal.' He smiled cordially at Buchanan. '*So* sorry not to have been able to tell you before this meeting!'

'The shit!' thought Buchanan privately. It was not the first time that 'A' had upstaged him in front of ministers without warning. Aloud he said, 'We, too, Prime Minister, are acting with all speed. Last night we arrested Lord Lampson's son. We're asking Special

Branch to do their best with him.' He was glad to see that 'A' showed signs of discomfort. 'I think we can take it that the Americans will not yet know anything about PROSPERO – assuming MI5 have been acting with their usual efficiency.' He smiled cordially at 'A', detecting that MI5 had not yet heard of his own swift action in getting the younger Lampson into custody.

The Defence Secretary shuffled his papers. Beyond his shoulder Buchanan could see the Horseguards Parade. Some piece of ceremonial was being conducted on its broad, blank square. It brought a flavour of the eighteenth century to their twentieth-century distresses. It crossed Buchanan's mind that perhaps the British had been prematurely retarded at about the time of Pitt the Younger.

'Prime Minister,' said the Defence Secretary with a boyish smile (he had been to the same tailor as the Head of M15 and knew how to use its slightly campish cut to keep on the right side of his political mistress), 'I'm a little out of my depth. Could we ask the Secretary to the Cabinet to sum up our discussion so far?'

The Prime Minister smiled bleakly at the Secretary to the Cabinet.

'The note I propose to make, Prime Minister – not, of course, for circulation to your Cabinet colleagues generally until I have your instructions – runs as follows.' The Secretary to the Cabinet drily coughed, conscious that his drafting style was impeccable. ' "At their twenty-seventh meeting, the committee noted that an agreement between HMG, the Soviet Union and the United States appeared imminent but that temporary difficulties had arisen as the result of special enquiries currently being conducted by agents of the Soviet Union and by British agencies." '

'Meaning,' said the Minister Without Portfolio, who tended to be down to earth, 'that the Russians have picked up one of *ours*; that we have failed to pick up anyone of *theirs*; and that the MOD and MI5 are holding two people who may or may not be of much use to us.'

Officials at the far end of the Prime Minister's table stirred uneasily. Buchanan decided that it lay with him to grasp these several nettles. If he played his hand right, it might even make him look competent. Tailoring his prose to the kind of thing which even the ageing Secretary to the Cabinet might be expected to record with accuracy, he chanced his arm on a summary. Ministers would probably fail to understand it, but at least he would have done his best.

'Prime Minister . . .'

She cautiously inclined her head.

'May I summarize, for the benefit of the committee, the position we have now reached?'

He saw that she was relieved. She could do with a summary. She would give him time. Only later would she put him down in order to keep up some 'end' of her own. In the intervening period he might possibly have the chance to convey to these several politicians – these elected representatives of the people – the urgency of the events they were dealing with. After that, she and her bevy of 'kitchen Cabineteers' would have to take whatever decisions they thought fit. He hoped they would be the right ones.

'Prime Minister . . .'

She came near to nodding.

'Three years ago the committee gave us substantial funds for setting up a secret facility in the northern part of the UK for the speediest development of PROSPERO. Our scientific colleagues tell us that it is now very nearly ready for full-scale operation.'

The Defence Secretary inclined his head. The Government Chief Scientist blandly smiled.

'Secondly . . .' Buchanan glanced around, 'we have collaborated with United States colleagues in establishing a prototype station on the coast of Suffolk which makes use of this British invention but – as usual – gives *them* much of the apparent control of it.' He paused. 'This has kept our American friends fairly happy, but has left us in the lead. The Suffolk station is never likely to have more than nuisance value, either to ourselves or the Other Side. And we – the committee will remember – have a dual key at Blandfordness; we can inhibit the operations there if we have to – and fairly unobtrusively.' (How he had fought for that double key! How woodenly – how ironly, how ironically – the Prime Minister had opposed this vital precaution! For all her supposed chauvinism, she often acted like the mere lap-dog to transatlantic cowboys.)

No one dissented.

Buchanan cautiously continued. 'The Russians now seem quite near to reaching our own level of operation. It may only be a matter of weeks before they do – assuming MI6 are fully up to date in what they tell us.'

The Head of MI5 stared ahead of him without expression. M16 was no business of his.

'What about the French?' said the Minister Without Portfolio, asking, as usual, the bluff and awkward question.

Buchanan silently thanked him. He had taken the precaution of speaking only that morning to 'friends' in Paris. The French were far too close for comfort, but they had been momentarily confused by the maverick conscience of some French physicist who was about to publish papers, not only in the scientific Press but also, it seemed, in *Le Figaro*. Pursuing this awkward Dr Foucault (or whoever he was) would probably set back the French by a few vital days. 'We've got the French under control, Prime Minister. I'll put in a written report to the committee by close of play today.' He saw that she was impressed. She had never liked the French; they had too many farmers, for one thing, while she, herself, had always been at the retail end of that particular business. 'What do you recommend, Mr Buchanan?' she asked him. She had often found this a useful ploy when out of her depth.

Buchanan braced himself. It looked like being his bravest hour for some time past. He was about to say something which might be unpopular. He had repressed tendencies of this sort for at least a quarter of a century. (How else should he have got where he was?) But a crucial moment had arrived; even Buchanan felt it. Everything had better now be staked on the curious poker hand they were all playing. Russian troops had already made an experimental foray across the boundaries between the two Germanys at half-past four that morning; even the Blackheath residence of a prospective KCB might not escape that holocaust if the 'balloon' went up.

'An agreement with the Russians not to use this . . . new capability . . . for defence purposes is now vital.'

The committee glumly assented.

'It is no use expecting the French or the Americans to secure this; they're too far behind.'

There were signs of agreement, modulated according to their hair styles and personal convictions.

'So, we'd better put on a show of strength,' said Buchanan,

appealing to the Prime Minister's patriotic simplicities. I'd like the committee's approval to authorize Loch Keisgaig to make a series of . . . demonstrations. As quickly as possible. With enough force to impress the Other Side – not to mention our gallant allies.'

'With an *untested* facility?' said the Foreign Secretary.

Buchanan glanced at the Chief Scientist. There had, as it happened, been a test or two – without the approval of Ministers. 'Beezie' had been a party to them. One of them at least had gone seriously wrong. He counted on 'Beezie' to keep his mouth shut. 'Risks will have to be taken, Prime Minister. There is far too much at stake.'

The committee argued for a quarter of an hour. He had thought they would. But 'show of strength' and 'enough force' had penetrated to the Boadicea within the Prime Minister's breast. She rounded on her Wets and spent an enjoyable moment or two savaging them. It had to be said for her that she was often quite as ill-mannered to senior ministers as to civil servants. 'But *my* finger must remain on the button, Mr Buchanan.'

He gave a deferential nod. If there were time, he would certainly consult her about the details of the Loch Keisgaig operations – if only to shift the burden of responsibility from himself. But there might not be time . . . The SOYUZ 27 'event' had happened with appalling speed.

'What about RAF Blandfordness?' asked the Chief of the Defence Staff. He faintly emphasized 'RAF'. As a naval officer, he felt some distaste for this junior service.

'We must use our dual key,' said Buchanan boldly. 'We must stop them doing anything which might go off at . . .' He found himself approaching 'half-cock' and decided that the Prime Minister wouldn't like it. 'We must inhibit any half-baked steps.' He saw that she liked 'half-baked'. 'If the committee approves . . .' Glancing around him, he noted that the committee had, as usual, given itself up to Her *diktat*. '. . . I'll instruct our own man at Blandfordness to make sure that nothing happens from Suffolk which will get in the way of Keisgaig.'

'Why not use Blandfordness to help us with Operation DISINFORM?' said 'A'. Buchanan cursed himself for not having got in first. 'I was about to recommend that, Prime Minister,' he said.

A further few minutes passed, permitting time for everybody around the table to put himself on record. The Secretary to the Cabinet had a way of making even the most foolish of comments sound sensible when the draft minutes were circulated. Buchanan sat back and mopped his round, red face with a silk handkerchief. (Why did they always over-stoke the boilers at No. 10?) He had won his points: PROSPERO to be given full steam ahead; Operation DISINFORM to be mounted. There remained only a few pin-pricks to be suffered.

'The committee should know,' said 'A' suavely, 'that a Ministry of Defence official, a certain John Eliot – on the staff of Mr Buchanan, we understand – is causing serious problems. He seems to have had illegal access to PROSPERO papers. He has seriously embarrassed us at RAF Bentbridge. He has witnessed "phenomena" at Blandfordness. He may well be heading for the PROSPERO station, together with some female.'

Well, really! 'A' was certainly efficient, but he might have sorted this out with colleagues before troubling ministers!

'I would like the approval of the committee for . . . special steps to deal with Mr Eliot and his . . . companion.'

'Do what you see fit in the public interest,' said the Prime Minister. 'We leave it to your discretion.'

Buchanan knew what she meant. It was the same message as Henry II had given to his four knights when Thomas à Becket had turned out to be too 'turbulent' a priest. It meant, 'kill him if necessary – but don't expect me to admit that I said so.' Pity about Eliot; he had quite liked the chap. Pity about MI5's Miss Julie Smith, for that matter. But she, at least, must have known what she was joining.

There remained two awkward questions. The Defence Secretary asked one of them, nodding uncomfortably in Buchanan's direction, knowing that Buchanan should have briefed him. 'Why have we pulled in Lord Lampson's son?'

Buchanan was not yet ready to answer this question. The Hon. G.M. Lampson was still under interrogation. 'Security, Minister.' It was a word which excused almost anything. 'I've explained to the committee that Lantern House has upset the Other Side.' It had upset their own side, too! 'I'll report tomorrow.' With any luck, Lampson would 'crack' overnight.

It lay with the Minister Without Portfolio to ask the last of his appalling questions. 'Can Mr Buchanan – can any other official round this table – tell us what caused the space disaster to SOYUZ 27 and its American counterpart?' His long, sharp nose jabbed at the Prime Minister. 'There are rumours which link it with PROSPERO.'

Rumours? For God's sake, what rumours? He glanced at 'Beezie'. But the Chief Scientist was carefully avoiding his eye. Buchanan cleared his throat. 'We've no evidence of any such thing, Prime Minister. But we're following up a strand or two . . . I'll report again.'

Strands . . .

Strand upon strand, it seemed according to what he'd been told so far by scientific colleagues. It was clearly time for Operation DISINFORM – not least for the disinformation of Her Majesty's ministers while anxious officials tried to find out what had gone wrong.

Strands.

Strand upon strand.

'It *spins*!' whimpered the Cosmonaut-Hero of the Soviet Union, now lying under heavy sedation. 'The planet *spins*!'

Well, yes . . . Lem couldn't feel terribly impressed with this information. Galileo had said so, even an ancient Greek or two had said so. Church authorities had tried to hush up this embarrassing fact, but Marxism-Leninism had embraced it. The Earth turned on its axis. Quite probably Stalin had once said so.

'It spins,' said the Cosmonaut-Hero, lying on his back between white sheets. 'It spins like a spider!'

To Lem this made much better sense than any Newtonian platitudes. He played about with the idea in English, exercising his shaky grasp of that interesting language. Here at Plesetsk they seemed less inclined to punish him for this deviation than at Chernyakhovsk; there had been no talk yet of Sulfazine, or tight swaddling sheets, or solitary confinement. By the Party standards to which he had become accustomed, they were treating him rather well.

He had always guessed that the planet span . . . spinned. (The form of the verb escaped him.) He remembered the great spider on the wall of his cell at Chernyakhovsk and the ropy strands of its incipient web. He remembered letters exchanged with Moscow 'saucerfriends' about falls of a substance which Western colleagues called 'Angel's Hair'. There had been rumours of it quite near Plesetsk, and again on the shores of Lake Baikal. 'It looks like a partially formed event,' somebody had written to him. 'It has the appearance of a substance which has not yet been moulded by Historical Necessity.' This particular letter continued with learned remarks about the need to bring the several 'unidentified phenomena' with which they were dealing within the framework of Dialectical Materialism. They were somewhat beyond Lem's grasp; the best he could make of them was the private joke that a bit of 'dialectical materialization' would not come amiss if they were to get to grips with this elusive stuff. It looked like a tough kind of spider's web but always evaporated within hours of being found. Another comrade, a humourless little electrician who lived in Novosibirsk and was active in the local Party, had suggested that calling this substance 'Angel's Hair' smacked of bourgeois deviation. Angels had been abolished. 'Lenin's Hair' might be more suitable. After the arrest of the group the authorities seemed to have found this comment unamusing. They suspected it of *lèse-majesté*.

The planet spun . . . spinned . . . Well certainly *something* did. Experimenting with his English, Lem remembered a curious saying he had once seen on the sleeve of a Western record during a holiday in Prague. It had passed into the language of North American white settlers shortly before they had succeeded in nearly wiping out the Indian tribe from which it came. 'Near to the Day of Purification,' it ran, 'there will be cobwebs spun back and forth in the sky.'

'Cobwebs,' said Lem aloud in English. 'Cobwebs,' he said again in Russian.

The word raised a groaning sob from his captive audience. And then the story came. The little microphone in the skirting-board had been waiting for it for several days. Lem was later to be congratulated on dragging it forth. But for him, scarcely listening to the words, it hardly had to be groped for thread by thread, it leapt into his mind with the force of a forgotten legend now suddenly remembered.

A web was woven in the sky. A great lattice of ropy strands. A textured trap as remorseless as the tough golden net in which Hephaestus, smithy-craftsman to the gods of Olympus, forger of Zeus's thunderbolts, had snared the goddess of love and the god of war, Ares and Aphrodite, at the moment of their adultery, crushing them together in a far more terrible embrace than any they had intended. A meshwork, stickier and springier than Hephaestus's now lay in the sky drawing the two craft together in a copulation of death . . .

The space captain lying on the trolley-bed cried aloud. The agony of his terror scorched Lem's mind. Lem fell back from legend into fact, into the kinds of sober terror which could be picked up from newspapers.

On 7 October 1990, SOYUZ-27 had been launched from a station in central Asia. Its great, dark cylinder had been thrust up against the tug of the planet on pillars of groaning fire. It carried a crew of eight, the largest ever to be clawed up the sides of the gravity-well by brute force into the black vacuum beyond the stratosphere. It was armed with a number of 'experiments'. They were, according to *Pravda*, 'peaceful and scientific' but at the same time well designed to demonstrate to the forces of bourgeois-imperialism that the peace-loving masses were not to be terrorized by technocratic blackmail. It was the latest in a series of Russian 'killer-satellites'.

'I was to make a demonstration,' whispered the Cosmonaut-Hero. 'I was to hunt down a NATO communications satellite and to blast it out of existence by laserfire. Comrade-Marshal Zinsky would publicly regret this accident. At the same moment I was to destroy, by means of a ten-megaton nuclear space-mine, an intercontinental ballistic missile launched on a harmless trajectory from our own side. It would show our invulnerability to revenge.' He turned his sweat-streaked face to Lem and smiled with a moment of proud and peaceful joy. If all had gone to plan, these glorious pyrotechnics would have marked a great moment in the onward march of Historical Necessity, and he, the Cosmonaut-Hero, would have been its instrument. It would have been – had all gone well – a day of purification.

Lem saw strands of nuclear debris drifting towards the strato-sphere, mingling with the solar wind, projecting an auroral fire into the rarish air at a hundred thousand feet, falling towards the upturned face of the world. He remembered another saying of those half-forgotten Indians, whose conception of the inverted bowl above them could hardly have gone much further than the soaring eagles whose feathers they prized as ornaments of bravery. 'One day,' they said (having perhaps been visited by a god or a demon long ago), 'one day, a container of ashes might be thrown down from the sky which could burn the land and boil the oceans.'

On 8 October 1990, an American 'killer satellite' had been launched from Cape Kennedy. It carried, somewhat more economically than SOYUZ-27, a crew of seven. It, too, was armed with peace-loving devices. It knew very well what SOYUZ-27 was up to. The Central Intelligence Agency of the United States would have felt offended in its manhood if it had not succeeded – at the cost of a life or two and some well-judged brutalities behind locked doors – in ferreting out what the Other Side intended. MICKEY-III, cosily named for a culture-hero of the North American continent, knew what it had to do. It craftily stalked its enemy on a parallel orbit, listening, probing, employing the latest in anti-privacy, ready at a micro-second's notice to 'put out' the Russian laser by newer wizardries of the most secret sort. At the right moment it would detonate (by electronic miracles kept well concealed) the space-mine carried by the Russian vehicle, swerving at once into the emergency orbit which would prevent anything too kamikaze for its personnel. NASA was a humane organization: it meant its crew-cut crew to return safely to the bosom of its families and to smile cheerfully on television.

Lem saw strands of nuclear debris drifting towards the stratosphere. He saw the upturned face of the world.

'We knew all this, of course,' said the Cosmonaut-Hero in a shaking voice. 'Our comrades on the committee of State Security know how to probe the entrails of those bourgeois hyaenas!'

SOYUZ-27 went about the planet on cunning orbits which sometimes came near to grazing the atmosphere and sometimes took it vastly beyond the realm of the geo-stationary communications satellite, lying at a mere twenty-three thousand miles above the earth, for which it intended laser-death. MICKEY-III coyly pursued it. Once, they spoke to each other on an 'open' frequency, ironically casual, moved by the camaraderie of skilful enemies. 'We see you, comrade,' said the Russian captain, playfully shifting his laser through an angle not quite menacing enough to provoke counter-measures. 'Up yours, bud!' said the fresh-faced American commander, keeping his finger near the 'detonate' button, but contenting himself with jettisoning into the path of SOYUZ-27 the latest plastic bagful of United States waste products.

On 12 October SOYUZ-27 saw that MICKEY-III was in trouble. Something wispy had wrapped itself around the solar panels, growing hour by hour into a gossamer ball. It served them right, thought the Russian captain, for recent dirty tricks. But his optical telescope and a radar-probe suggested that something odder than the mere necessities of human biochemistry was fouling up his opponent's source of power. He jubilantly called his base control on ultra-secret code and reported the matter. It meant nothing to them; it even seemed to worry them; but it chimed with reports reaching them by signals intelligence of a major flap in the American communications system. A gabbling panic had over-taken the Space Recovery Agency, even as far afield as one of its minor outposts in the English county of Suffolk, a place called Bentbridge. The bourgeois radar-telescope at Jodrell Bank had dropped its research programme, swivelling its Cyclops eye towards MICKEY-III.

'We could do it now, comrades,' said the Russian captain urgently in ultra-code. 'They will be low on power. They will be helpless to retaliate.' He gave orders to his crew, preparing his own electronic miracle of remote detonation. SOYUZ-27 was no less well-equipped than MICKEY-III; and MICKEY-III, like SOYUZ-27, carried a weapon whose force was to be measured in megatons.

The face of the world stared blindly upwards at the containers of ashes far above it. Lem looked skywards through its sightless eyes, feeling the skin of the planet wrinkle and its oceans prepare themselves for boiling.

It was Comrade-Marshal Zinsky who chose, for the time being, to save the world. He did so because the President of the United States had taken time out from a cattle-breeding weekend in the Western White House to have a friendly word on the hot line. 'Hi there, Ivan,' said Rocky McClusky. 'Ivan' was as near as he ever got to 'Dzhugashvili'; he left it to the translation-boys to put the frills in. 'We're on Red Alert at my end. And when I say "Red", feller, I mean "Red" – and no offence meant.' The background noise of a bull in rut gave force to his words but proved untranslatable. There were, said Rocky Mac, some seventy thousand nukes now rarin to go. A thousand of them were targeted on Moscow. Suppose no more than a hundred of these homing-pigeons fluttered their way to the onion domes above Red Square? Or ten . . .? Or even five . . .? 'Just one goddam nuke, Ivan . . .' Dzhugashvili Zinksy denied thoughts of laying so much as a grappling-hook on MICKEY-III. He said that he had, however, ordered a White Alert of all nuclear systems of the peace-loving peoples (white being, for him, a dangerous colour): that an important autumn exercise would be taking place in East Germany: that they had better keep in touch, regardless of the phone bill. It was the nearest he had come in fifty years to making a joke. But, for the moment, the joke was an agreement to do nothing rash.

Lem heard somebody or something, somewhere, expiring a vast breath as though in relief or laughter.

'It left them on the fourteenth,' whispered the Cosmonaut-Hero, staring at the ceiling with unseeing eyes. 'That substance clinging to them . . . That space-weed . . .' Sweat ran down his face with the memory of it. 'It *dissolved*, comrade. It boiled away.' Lem, already knowing the end of the story, sweated with him.

For sixteen further days SOYUZ-27 and MICKEY-III pursued each other about the world. Fingers were poised above their detonation triggers. Below them, a golden October weathered out the time towards winter darkness. Fruit ripened, leaves prepared to fall, the planet made ready to accept the first mantle of hoar frost across its northern shoulders, troops and missiles were deployed forward among the autumn woods. Rocky McClusky and Dzhugashvili Zinksy spoke often together on a line between Moscow and Washington which was sometimes hot, sometimes lukewarm, and sometimes downright chilly. They conversed like old acquaintances sharing a common illness which often made them testy but for the most part left them baffled. They were elderly men without much intelligence, each in the grip of the complex bureaucracies they nominally controlled, both of them haunted by the prospect of a megadeath within milliseconds which was passing beyond their control.

On the eve of sombre November the inevitable misjudgement took place. Sooner or later it was bound to happen. Some minor fault in a retro-rocket in MICKEY-III swerved it off orbit on a course which SOYUZ-27 took to be menacing. SOYUZ-27 swung its laser. The American commander lifted the safety-catch on his detonation-trigger. Messages were gabbled back and forth along control channels. 'If we don't, they will ... If they do, we can't ...'

And then it came. Sprouting in a microsecond out of nowhere. A vast meshwork of ropy strands. A great net encompassing both vehicles, sticky as cobwebs, springy as Angel's Hair. Hair of the Angel of Death smothered them in darkness. They were crushed together, came to a deadly coupling, split like ripe pods, spilling their contents.

Two young Americans, unlucky enough to be wearing space-suits, survived for three days, destined to be frazzled above Northern India. The Cosmonaut-Hero, swaddled in the command capsule which guarded him day and night, was swept into space as tightly wrapped in steel as any political lunatic in the winding-sheets of Chernyakhovsk. For the rest blood boiled, lungs burst, arteries exploded with merciful swiftness.

Tumbling in a mad orbit about the world, the Cosmonaut-Hero was accompanied by visions. Some small green creature, crouched in a transparent bubble, floated alongside him and watched him with froglike eyes. It seemed to be munching on the entrails of a Comrade-Sergeant. A spidery thing with seven legs scuttled back and forth across the toughened glass of his space-visor. Even in the silence of space he could hear it giggling. Presently, as he grew feverish with thirst, a Lady of Mercy, flicking an adder's tongue between pale lips, poured water just beyond his grasp from a silver chalice.

It was all as Lem had always known it must be. He left the Cosmonaut-Hero to howl himself into oblivion and crept back to his comfortable quarters, foreseeing the tasks to come.

Gregorius Mansfield Lampson – 'LAMPSON, G.M.' as he figured in the PROSPERO file, 'L., G.M.' for short – stared with his pale eyes at Aleister Buchanan. The long, white hair, nearly to shoulder length, framed the gaze and focused it. It struck Buchanan that Lampson's eyelids had not moved for some minutes past. He faced without flinching the two hundred watts of the desk lamp which some minion of A's had placed there a while before to assist the enquiries in which Buchanan and the Government Chief Scientist were now engaged. The brilliant light, close enough to be painful, left Lampson undisturbed. The retinas behind the pale-blue irises glowed rosy-red with it; they seemed to cast back with an augmented force the lambent energy falling upon them.

Buchanan turned his head aside. Even protected by the darkness outside the dazzling pool of lamplight, he found that Lampson's unwinking stare gave him the sensation of falling down a gravity-well or tunnel towards things best left unseen. He glanced at Bruno Zadig, lounging in the easy chair beside him; 'Beezie', too, was avoiding that weird laser-look.

They sat in a room on the top storey of A's little Mayfair palace. Even at two o'clock in the morning the sounds of traffic rose up from Park Lane, filtered by thick walls and heavy draperies. Lampson had now been without food and water for the better part of a day. He was lightly shackled to his chair, denied even the comforts of relieving nature. Two hundred watts of electric light had been thrusting their hot brilliance at him since shortly before midnight. He should, by now, be near to talking. But it was his two interrogators, comfortably at ease with their coffee and whisky and expensive sandwiches, who felt themselves under pressure.

' "Lantern lights",' said Buchanan, staring fixedly between his pudgy knees, avoiding Lampson's eyes. 'We've had that message. It's come back to us through channels of our own.' A certain Julius Schultz, whisked up to London by Special Branch from a police station in Wiltshire as soon as he'd had the dangerous good sense to mention 'aliens' and PROSPERO and 'men in white', had told them so. 'Lantern lights. We know what that means.'

Lampson kept silent. Buchanan took care not to look at him.

'It means,' said Bruno Zadig, making a cat's-cradle of his bony fingers and peering into the hollow it left between his hands, 'it means that we know a great deal about Lantern House. We know that you have . . . faculties . . . powers. We have watched your abilities with interest.' As an ex-Czech physicist who had had the energy and skill to rise to high level in the British government service, BZ prided himself on the wide palette of his synonyms. He spoke better English than many of the half-illiterate government scientists whose work he oversaw. Some days he reminded himself of Joseph Conrad. 'It means that we are very well informed about you.'

'It means,' said Buchanan, mopping his damp cheeks with a foppish handkerchief, 'that we know what sort of "light" you're tampering with at Lantern House.' (Would that they did!)

'We also know,' said Zadig, flexing his fingers, cracking a knuckle with a sharp snap, 'that you are not quite as powerful as you think you are. You have been trading upon a much larger source of power which happens to belong to Her Majesty's Government.'

Lampson softly laughed. 'Have your brought me here to present the bill for a little stolen electricity?'

Glancing up at him, Buchanan was briefly giddied by the lidless stare. He toyed with the idea of sending for one of A's experts in discomfort. There were always two of them on duty roster, waiting to perform patriotic tasks. They knew how to be intolerable to A's clientele without leaving the kind of trace which might have over-excited magistrates. It would be simple enough to leave Lampson to them for a quarter of an hour. He and 'Beezie' could take their whisky into the adjoining, soundproof room. He found cruelty somewhat embarrassing. As a boy, he had never tormented anything much larger than a butterfly.

'What are your motives?' said Zadig. 'What put you up to that little adventure in Tangham Wood the other night?'

Lampson rocked with mirth. Cautiously studying him, Buchanan saw that his eyes were at last closed. He had screwed them up in the ecstasy of some private joke. ' "*Motives*"!' he spluttered, rocking back and forth within the limits of the straps which bound him to the chair. 'What were the motives of Moses, Mozart, Maimonides, Mesmer . . .?' He choked on his inward enjoyment. 'Little policemen ask such questions!'

Buchanan stood up and took Zadig by the arm. 'We're leaving you to yourself,' he said abruptly. 'I hope you'll have come to your senses when we return.'

In the soundproof antechamber he cracked another bottle of whisky with the Chief Scientist, keeping Lampson under surveillance through the one-way mirror and turning up the amplifier in case Lampson gave way to private utterances during their absence.

'Do you think we should have him "done over" by one of the chaps in the basement?' he plaintively asked. 'We don't seem to be getting very far at present.'

'Beezie' considered the question with scientific dispassion, locking his bony figures together and studying them with detachment. 'I doubt that it would help us. It might even disturb his . . . faculties. He has talents. I think PROSPERO could make use of them.'

Through the one-way glass they could see that Lampson had opened his eyes again. He was staring in their direction. Buchanan had the feeling that it was he rather than Lampson under scrutiny.

'What can we offer him?' said Zadig. 'What will make him work with us?' He stood up and began to prowl about the antechamber, stealthy and saturnine. 'He says he has no "motives". But there must be *something* which would interest him.'

'Why do we have to use him at all?' said Buchanan. 'I pulled him in because he was being a nuisance to us. He was seriously upsetting the Russians. And it's clear from what we've picked up from Schultz via the Smith woman that it was Lantern House which has been causing the "bleed-off" of power from Blandfordness in the last few months. We'd like to know *how*, of course. That's why he's here. But is there any further use for him once we've found out?'

Zadig turned his back and crossed his arms. Secretly despising all non-scientific colleagues, he pondered the question of how to get across to this mere administrator – this innumerate, this untrained fool – the harsh technical facts. 'My dear fellow,' he said, picking a word which he knew would make Buchanan uncomfortable (English possessed pecking-order subtleties which not even the Central Bohemian dialect of Prague could altogether match). 'My dear fellow . . .' He waited for the snub to take effect. 'You know as well as I do that Blandfordness is a failure – despite that vast American investment in psycho-electronics. It will never produce more than phantoms. Its little . . . projections will remain as elusive, as vague, as *harmless* as the natural "UFO" phenomenon it's based on.'

'We've some evidence,' said Buchanan defensively, 'that the "natural" thing, as you call it, can sometimes do substantial damage. We've been studying it since the 1950s. It can rip the guts out of cattle. It can melt the surface of an A-class road. Do you remember what happened to that stretch of the A338 in November 1967?'

'I remember.'

'Sometimes, it burns. We've got the hospital records of more than thirty cases on the PROSPERO file. Occasionally, it stops cars.'

'How often? How *predictably*?'

Buchanan was silent.

'What do you think our research has been about?'

He turned to face Buchanan. Buchanan avoided his eye. Through the one-way glass Lampson seemed to be studying them with close attention.

'Blandfordness has got some excellent "machinery",' continued Zadig as patiently as his temper permitted. 'Our American friends are good at "machinery". We've learnt something from them. I've modified much of our equipment at Keisgaig simply by watching what the Americans have imported into Blandfordness. But they've missed the vital factor. Only we – the British – have understood it.' We, the British . . . it seemed to Zadig at this moment that the only talent still retained by the British was a grudging willingness to permit talented foreigners to run their affairs for them. He thought with melancholy anger of the submission of Prague to the Germans in 1938, of the Communist *putsch* of a decade later, of the rolling of Russian tanks across the frontier in 1968. For the time being a dedicated ex-Czech had better place his confidence in these innocent public-schoolboys who – though their democracy was running out – retained a modicum of influence and a sense of fair play derived from cricket. 'The vital factor,' he repeated. 'The *human* factor.'

Buchanan glumly nodded. 'Beezie' had said this kind of thing before.

'Keisgaig is ahead of Blandfordness – ahead of the Russians, ahead of the French – for one reason and one reason only: we have recognized the importance of using individuals with the right . . . gifts alongside the best we can contrive in psycho-electronics.' Zadig paused and turned his small, sharp eyes towards Buchanan. 'I'm bound to say – my dear fellow – that you and MI5 have not yet provided us with a great deal to work with.'

Buchanan uneasily recalled the 'disappearances' he had connived at in recent months. They were all smallish fry who had been picked as much for their 'disappearability' as their talents: an elderly 'white witch' living on the edge of Salford with fifty-seven cats; a Welsh dowser; a 'medium' picked from the Bayswater Circle mainly because his way of life was solitary; some weird girl abducted from St Ives; one or two others like them.

'Lampson is unique – anyway in our present experience,' said Zadig. He came and sat down again, pouring himself a stiff shot of whisky, regretting the purer – the less peaty – spirits of his native Bohemia. 'Lampson – whether or not he quite knows how he did it – gouged out two channels in Tangham Wood last Thursday and killed some animal. He was undoubtedly draining the power from Blandfordness. But he's the most powerful "factor" we've yet come across. I think he could give . . . substance – *real* substance, *predictable* substance – to the PR effect.'

'How would we keep control of him?'

Zadig studied his glass. 'I think we've lost it already,' he said softly. It was the most damaging admission he had yet made. Buchanan, sensing an Achilles' heel, groped for it through a fog of technicalities. He distrusted this foreign technocrat; he loathed the necessity of working with him. The man was a mere Bohemian, after all (geographically speaking). 'What went wrong on the nights of 12 October and 1 November?' said Buchanan, pressing his advantage. When all was said and done, it was he who had authorized the seventh and eighth of Loch Keisgaig's Resonance Operations for these two days. It was he, not 'Beezie' who would have to send in a white sheet to Ministers if the truth came out.

'My dear fellow,' said Zadig, 'it was ingenious of you to lay on those naval vessels to the west of the Faroes for our two little tests. We aimed for them, of course. I only wanted some wheels of phosphorescence and a ball of light. Perhaps a waterspout or two . . .'

'So what went wrong?'

Zadig peered through the amber fluid in his glass. He had come to dislike whisky. It reminded him too much of the peaty shores of Keisgaig. Standing by the monitoring chamber, a hundred feet below the level of the Loch, commanding with a certain gloomy pride the bank upon bank of pyscho-electronic apparatus which ranged the muddy corridors, now partly clad with concrete, which had been hacked into the peaty underworld by Her Majesty's Royal Engineers without the faintest conception of what they were doing, Zadig had seen uncomfortable miracles. Familiar miracles he had grown used to – those propagated under close control by apparatus he understood. There was nothing 'supernatural' about what he was doing; he had merely harnessed, as a good Czech should, something as innocent – though also perhaps as deadly – as the power of thunderstorms. It produced 'phenomena'; useful 'phenomena'; 'phenomena' which could be focused by the weird little people that Buchanan and MI5 had placed at his disposal. Up to the sixth test – a mere Close Encounter of the Second Kind, imposed on a dull and elderly Lancashire couple who happened to be taking an eccentric winter holiday in the Isle of Lewis – all had gone as Zadig had expected. Then came the tests of 12 October and 1 November. They were meant to be a little more dramatic, sufficiently so to be thrust at Her Majesty's Navy, riding the October swell between the Faroes and Iceland, rather than to be offered to mere tourists (who were hardly likely to be armed with geiger-counters or instructed in their use). And then those uncomfortable 'miracles' had taken place: the appearance of some tall, fairish creature in the monitoring chamber, its hair at shoulder length, its eyes wide and blue, accompanied by smaller greenish entities whose lipless mouths had uttered harsh little sounds, like metal grating on metal.

'What went wrong?' said Buchanan again.

The ships riding the swell three hundred miles to the north-west had seen nothing. Vehicles far above them had suffered strange intrusions. On 12 October MICKEY-III had been . . . encumbered. On 1 November MICKEY-III and SOYUZ-27 had been grappled by a net three hundred metres broad.

'It was not our fault,' said Zadig. 'It was the fault of . . . something else.' To the end of his days there would linger with him the memory of some fair-haired creature, its locks at shoulder length. It resembled so closely the Hon. G.M. Lampson that his scientific curiosity was aroused. 'I think we have some evidence that Lampson already knows how to "resonate" with Keisgaig as easily as he does with Blandfordness.' For what reason, though? With what 'motive'? The monitoring chamber had filled a millisecond later with a writhing mass of ropelike worms. Thirty thousand miles above it, at the same instant, according to the record kept by Jodrell Bank, MICKEY-III and SOYUZ-27 had succumbed to greasy tentacles of the same kind. The synchronicity was too good to be untrue. The half-angelic creature which had manifested in the monitoring chamber, that pansified parody of St Michael, had killed fourteen men and triggered the grimmest confrontation between East and West since the Cuban missile crisis of 1962. Later, when the monitoring chamber underwent its routine dowsing down, the stench of sulphur was so powerful that two of Zadig's crew had needed oxygen to bring them round.

They went back in to the interrogation room and made Lampson offers of the kind he had been expecting. Unbinding him from the chair, they proferred sandwiches of good red beef and the best that Fortnum offered in smoked salmon; A's expense account was rarely under scrutiny by the narrow-minded. But to Lampson flesh was disgusting even when ingested. He was at war with the flesh; even his own he often deplored, observing its grubby necessities with amused distaste. He contented himself with drinking the peaty fluid of their Water of Life and making them the lordly gift of some knowledge he possessed which he thought they would find interesting.

'That Lucy Fr . . . That female Lucifer . . . She may be dangerous to you. She and that fleshly fool she couples with.' The pale eyes surveyed them. They glanced aside to avoid their dizzying intrusion. 'You will find them in the Pennines if you send your forces quickly.' He moved his head, causing his angel's hair to tremble like spun glass. He smiled, radiant with some inner mirth. 'Blandfordness and its little lantern-show might be useful to you.'

On the bitter morning of 7 November 1990, a little before sunrise, John Eliot, a fugitive, woke with a two days' growth of beard to find himself in the embrace of the fleshly Lucy Frensham. They lay together, like babes in the wood, in the back of Crowley's 'banger'. Parked a little off the tarmac track which led across the moors to Cumbria, they were sheltered behind a knoll on the lower slopes of Wether Fell, grateful to have found the remnants of the old Roman road which ran between Bainbridge and Ribblehead. Its tough paving had endured for nearly two thousand years to give them something approaching the stable and the horizontal on which to rest for a few freezing hours.

John tenderly dislodged the arm of his mistress-accomplice and climbed out of the back of the van. Across the valley of the minor road below him the peaks of Dodd Fell, already sprinkled with a dusting of winter snow, had begun to catch the sun, hidden somewhere behind him to the east below the skyline of the moors. He crouched on the frozen grass, shuddering with cold, conscious of not having eaten since lunchtime the day before (Lucy had at least had the benefit of some generous American rations at the last meal of the day at the Bentbridge Sick Quarters), and counted the money in his wallet. It was not quite enough to buy them the next tankful of petrol. He looked at his credit cards, his cashpoint card, the other two pieces of plastic of a similar shape and size which allowed him to cash cheques at the rate of fifty pounds a day in several European countries including England, including perhaps also Scotland. But he was growing old in wiliness at a rate which not only surprised him but left him feeling rather pleased with himself. Trading in those slips of plastic to some bank clerk in Appleby or Penrith, or slipping that cashpoint card into the slit of a high-street dispenser, would tell them where he was. Whoever that 'them' might be.

At the corner of his eye he noted, without much curiosity, that a misty cloud was forming above Dodd Peak, a quarter of a mile across the valley. It was lenticular in shape, formed like a lens, rather more domed on its upper surface than below. From moment to moment it came to a more definite shape, black and metallic, sullenly rejecting the sunlight which had already set the snow crystals on the Peak into a pointillist glitter.

He went back into the van and roused the dreaming Lucy. 'I'm frightened,' she said in a small girl's voice, still haunted by the phantoms of an uneasy sleep. It brought out the best in him. He slipped off his Jermyn Street jacket, now grubbied by the accidents of escape, and put it round her shoulders. He would have liked to make her a cup of tea but knew that it would have to wait until they crossed into Cumbria. Money meant for petrol had better buy them rations instead. Petrol would have to be found in some other way.

'Why?' she said, studying her bare feet, pressing his two-day bristle against her cheek. 'What have we done?'

'PROSPERO,' said John. 'Does PROSPERO mean anything to you?' Merely for glimpsing Part Three of a file called PROSPERO, merely for helping a patient to discharge herself from unwanted medical treatment, he had been suspended from duty, fired upon by the United States Air Force, nearly arrested by Royal Air Force guards, pursued across country, given mysterious pointers to a lake called Keisgaig at the northern end of Scotland.

'I think I know the RO bit,' she said, turning her face towards him. ' "Resonance Operations". The Grand Old Man at Jodrell was on about "Resonance Operations" when we had that incident on 12 October. I don't think I was supposed to know. But he'd written it down in his desk diary. "RO. Resonance Operations. Us or them?".' She gazed across his shoulder. 'And I heard him say something like "Resonance Operations" when we were monitoring MICKEY-III the same night.'

He saw her eyes widen. They were looking somewhere beyond him through the back of the van. 'For God's sake?' she said.

He turned and saw it. A dark, dome-shaped 'vehicle', fifty feet across, floating up from the valley below them. It seemed to hover on three bright shafts of light, casting a glow across the Roman road in the pool of early-morning twilight which the sun had not yet dispersed. There was the murmuring buzz of something like a vast beehive. He resonated with the vibrations of it.

'Pinpointed,' said Air Commodore Crowley. 'We've picked them up. I can give you the grid reference.'

At the other end of the scrambler-telephone the voice of Aleister Buchanan squawked and croaked. Beyond Crowley's window the sun had just risen above the easterly sea. Its great orange globe, magnified by the November fog, loomed to the north of the lighthouse. Convection currents caused it to pulsate. It seemed to shed squirming threads of fire towards the water.

Crowley heard Buchanan out, gripping the telephone receiver between chin and collarbone, glumly doodling comic strip UFOs and little aliens on his desk jotter. He allowed Whitehall's squawking anger to trouble his engaged ear without comment.

Was it *his* fault that Eliot had suddenly become a dangerous outlaw? Should he have questioned Eliot's pass (setting aside the slightly awkward matter of the girl's lack of documents)? Eliot had mentioned PROSPERO. It was a name known to perhaps twenty or thirty people. It was the passport to a privileged and private world. Crowley began to frame in his mind the stiff little memorandum he would presently send to Buchanan for the sake of his official position. Immediately, he rested on a comfortable sense of competence. Blandfordness had latched on to Buchanan's 'targets' with amazing ease, guided by nothing more than the word 'Pennines' and his own estimate of how far they might have travelled overnight.

Buchanan croaked into momentary silence. Crowley picked this welcome gap to get his own back. 'You do know that I can't conceal any of this from my American chum?' The silence persisted. 'He'll now know that we're pursuing a couple of fugitive Brits for some weird reason of our own. It's bound to make him suspicious. I'll be surprised if he's not already on the blower to that counterpart of yours in the CIA.'

The distant voice came back to him with tinny force. 'Pass it off as part of Op DISINFORM. For Christ's sake use your initiative! There are fifty or sixty DISINFORM targets. Surely you can bury this bloody couple among that lot!'

Useless, thought Crowley, to remind Buchanan that the DISINFORM targets had already been on-file at Blandfordness for the past seven months and that John Eliot was not among them. On that point his American friend could certainly not be conned. He framed another tart little paragraph in his intended memorandum but bent his present ear to Whitehall's hysteria.

'Give them everything you've got. Clobber them. Hold them up till I can get other forces up there.'

The line cleared. Crowley replaced the receiver. Putting through an internal call to his dual-key counterpart, he found the number engaged. A swift check with his own switchboard confirmed that his USAF friend was calling London. Mr Conrad Friedman now doubtless knew that the Brits had some little local difficulty on their hands. It could only be hoped that it wouldn't point him towards Keisgaig.

Crowley toyed with the thought of phoning Buchanan back and

then dropped it. He had better get on with his present instructions. As a humble serving officer he would do his duty first and make his protest later. He would 'give them everything he'd got', putting out of his mind that he had rather liked John Eliot.

There merely remained the minor puzzle of why the Bland-fordness furies had found John Eliot so swiftly. The DISINFORM targets, destined to receive their messages in the next day or so, were identified by grid references in the Ordnance Survey. In several cases, if MI5 were right, there was already a degree of 'resonance' on the part of target individuals; the PE apparatus would have little difficulty in latching on to them. But what possible 'resonance' could John Eliot possess? What on earth had enabled the plasmoid to come alongside him so swiftly, within minutes of the initial OS probe?

John Eliot slammed shut the back doors of the van and clambered across Lucy into the driving seat. The thing now lay above them, cocooning them in a web of blinding light. Boulders on the moor around them glittered like diamonds. The buzzing vibration had dropped and deepened towards infrasound. His head pounded with it, his clenched teeth sang in resonance, thrusting a sonic probe into the echo-chamber of his skull.

The passenger door was still half ajar. He leaned across, meaning to wrench it shut. But Lucy, climbing across the passenger seat from the back of the van, thrust him aside. She was scrambling on to the footplate, shoving the door wide open, groping her way into the open terror.

He shouted an incoherent warning, half in panic, half in childish anger. The stupid bitch . . .! He scrabbled at her clothing, grasping his own jacket, loosely wrapped about her shoulders. It fell to the ground outside the van, scattering its contents. Coins ran away down hill, sparkling like little catherine-wheels in the weird illumination from above. His wallet tumbled across the frozen grass, flapping open, shedding credit cards and crumpled banknotes, ending for ever whatever connection he had once had with the world of the orderly and solid.

The sound from above had modulated towards thunder. The blazing light had grown to be a torment, thrusting needles of fire across the tender interface between the backs of his eyes and the optical centres of the neo-cortex. His skull screeched with it. He switched on the ignition and stamped his foot on the accelerator. There was a grinding of gears; he had left the damn thing engaged before falling into swinish slumber at half-past two that morning. He let in the clutch and wrenched the lever into first with a trembling hand. The motor petered out. He tried the headlights, but the whole system was now paralysed.

He beat his hands on the steering -wheel, choking back tears of rage and shame. Only that 'thing' above his head had stopped him from driving off in a blind panic across the moor, leaving the one and only 'entity' he now valued to whatever fate had overtaken her. He remembered a moment on the parapet of a lighthouse at Plymouth Hoe. Dreading heights, he had nevertheless taken two small sons of an old friend to the top of that appalling tower. One had leaned over. Paralysis had gripped him. He knew in that instant that nothing – not even the tumbling over into the gravity-well below the lighthouse of the promising life which was now thrusting itself into the risks of abrupt oblivion – would unlock his cowardice. He would let the boy fall, trapped in his own fear. It had been no merit of his own that this stupid child had spun himself back across the hand-rail with a cheerful guffaw, wholly unaware of the agonies he had given rise to.

Cowardly – shaking with abject panic – John groped his way across the passenger seat, placed his foot on the ledge below the metal door, descended to the moor with as much male aplomb as he could now manage. He would bear with him for the rest of time the knowledge that only the failure of an internal-combustion engine had saved him from an act which he would always have trembled to remember. It came to him abruptly that he had 'failed' often before, but must now succeed before too long. He caught a terrifying glimpse down endless corridors of past failure.

Lucy was crouching on the moor. She was peering upwards, wrapped in the common sense of her woollen overcoat. She looked like St Joan, thought John. Like the Maid of Orleans. Like that sixteen-year-old kid, trapped by a plausible St Michael on the outskirts of Domrémy in 1428, given the 'destiny' she must follow, committed already to that bonfire in the Place du Vieux-Marché at Rouen – that little piece of over-radiant energy – on 30 May 1431.

He found that he had been an English soldier on that occasion not much more than nineteen years old, puking in the back ranks around the square as she had shrieked her way into the presence of the all-merciful.

She was looking towards the sky. He followed her gaze. The disc-demon above them had begun to fade. It had grown translucent. It was moderating towards the semi-visible. He could see the sun through it towards the east. It was dissolving into streaks and patches of something insubstantial. Its humming menace had modulated into something as innocent as the sounds of summer, incongruous on that November morning but reminding John Eliot of other days, some while ago, before the world had come between himself and the earth he lived on.

His face felt flushed, as though he had stood too near to a martyr's death. Hers was radiant and peaceful, her eyes wide with something which looked like happiness or wonder. He had the irrational feeling that she had somehow 'dispersed' the semi-tranquil demon which had been sent to haunt them.

The thing had gone, leaving only a wisp or two of some gauzy trace. As he watched it, it winked out of existence. He saw with surprise that the sun had jumped abruptly above the moorland to the east. It was already well into the sky. Glancing at his watch, he found that it had stopped at a little before eight. Lucy's read ten to nine and was still going. Fifty minutes had 'disappeared'.

They got back into the van. The engine functioned immediately. Whatever had interfered with it had now left them. Guided by an obscure instinct, John headed away from the minor road lying between the fells along which they had travelled in the small hours. It would be better – safer – to go in some new direction. He drove towards Bainbridge, four miles ahead along the Roman track laid down by legionary-engineers nearly two millennia before. It ran like a straight-edge across the moors, up hill and down dale with ruthless determination, though now somewhat pitted by time and weather. He hoped the suspension of Crowley's little 'banger' would survive this pot-holed switchback.

'Did you see him?' said Lucy, turning her face.

John kept his eyes to the track, guiding the van on its bumpy odyssey. '*Him*'? What did she mean by 'him'?

'I'd say,' said Lucy, 'if I weren't a rationalist, if I weren't an

111

astro-physicist, and all that . . .' He could feel her eyes upon him but stared studiously ahead. 'I'd say that I'd seen something out of the Heavenly Host?' he felt strangely angered by this womanish nonsense; it cramped his stomach with embarrassment. 'I'd say,' said Lucy, 'that I'd seen something like St Michael . . . Or St Gabriel . . .'

The van bounced slowly ahead at five miles per hour. 'What *I* saw,' said John, not looking at her, 'was . . .' A what, for God's sake? 'A flying saucer,' he said lamely. It hardly seemed much less foolish than Lucy's 'angel'.

'I saw a shining shield,' she said. 'He was carrying it above him in his left hand.' She gathered the woollen overcoat about her.

'It was a damn disc!' said John angrily. 'A fake one, at that!' He groped for terms, remembering something she had recently told him. 'It was a bloody "Resonance Operation". Something they've . . . propagated.' He remembered an orange weirdness at the gates of Blandfordness, a vehicle in Tangham Wood collecting 'evidence', a phoney story about Little Green Men made up by Conrad Friedman and Colonel Hoyt at Bentbridge. PROSPERO flashed across his mind. It began to make some sense. 'PR' might mean 'Propagation'. 'OS' was 'Over Space'. 'PE' remained obscure. 'RO' – it was abundantly clear – stood for 'Resonance Operation'. 'They've invented some new toy, that's all.' He tried to put out of mind the memory of that 'toy', seen not long ago on the slopes of Wether Fell.

'He had wings,' said Lucy dreamily. 'Wonderful great wings.'

John braked, cursing, remembering his jacket and his money, glad of the chance to end these absurdities. He pulled the van to a halt. They were descending a ridge which had risen behind them to conceal the scene of that disturbing but now very nearly intelligible encounter. He wanted time to think about it. It had begun to dwindle towards mere 'electronics'. Perhaps 'electronic' was one of the two words represented by that 'PE' of PROSPERO. Why should they want to kill him for guessing *that*? 'I've got to go back,' he said sullenly, slamming the door of the van behind him.

He trudged back up the hill, came to its top, glanced down into the valley between whose slopes the minor tarmac road twisted its way, then threw himself to the ground, pressing his face against the frozen earth.

Barely three hundred yards away a large, dark car was parked. It was sharply outlined against the frosted slopes of the fell beyond it. Its black-glass windows threw back at him with pinpoint brilliance a reflection of the sun behind his shoulders. Three men in black stood near it. One of them, with an air of casual alertness, began to saunter in his direction, lightly pressing a black-gloved hand to something at his hip.

John slithered back down the slope, ran at a crouched run, came to the van, gabbled harsh messages across its open window. 'Go! For Christ's sake, go! I'll join you. I'll get there.'

'There'? Where? Wherever her mad hallucinations took her!

She looked at him with frightened eyes. She began to protest.

He hammered his fists on the van-door, turning fear into simulated rage. 'Get out, you bitch!'

She clambered across into the driving-seat. Tears were trickling down her face.

'Leave me in peace!' he shouted, agonized with the need of driving her into flight and safety.

The van bounced forward across the ruined pavement, gasped its way up the next slope, tipped over the ridge ahead, vanished from view.

With a pounding heart, stifling a feeling of loneliness and desolation, John Eliot climbed back up the ridge of the hill behind him. Prompted by bad B-movies, he extended his hands above him, showing that he carried nothing lethal, demonstrating beyond doubt that he was totally submissive to whatever destiny might now be impending.

His destiny sauntered across the ridge. A man in black. His revolver was now drawn. It was aimed laconically at John Eliot's heart.

Seeing who it was, Eliot began to laugh. He had supposed that Buchanan, or MI5, or even the special Branch of Scotland Yard – something British, at all events – had come to find him. He hadn't expected aliens!

The web or network in which he was now enmeshed seemed to have gained new dimensions.

6
DISINFORM

A network lay across the United Kingdom. By 1990 it had existed for more than forty years. It consisted of some thousands of individuals, old and young, eccentric and sensible, visionary and down-to-earth. Some were weird, many were wonderful, all were inquisitive, most felt frustrated. Only one thing united them, a belief that something not yet identified, often seen in the sky though sometimes closer at hand, detected as an 'object' but possessing ghostly qualities which no decent object should demonstrate, was haunting the human species. They seemed to have evidence that it had been doing so for hundreds if not thousands of years, perhaps for as long as humanity had existed.

They were frustrated for two reasons. The first was that none of them – nor anybody known to them, not even the friends of friends – had ever found lasting proof that the thing was 'real' (in whatever sense of that troublesome word their quarrelsome debates might point to). True there were sometimes passing traces: Angel's Hair fell from the sky from time to time, other gelatinous things, sometimes a substance which looked like blood, occasionally fish, feathers, ice, pig-iron and other pedestrian objects. A man called Charles Fort had amused himself with making catalogues of these absurdities in the early part of the twentieth century, most of them drawn from highly reputable sources. True there were photographs of things seen in the sky, of beasts glimpsed at a distance, of ectoplasm oozing from mediums in ill-lit rooms, of the fin (maybe) of some pseudo-plesiosaur lurking, sub-aqueous, in the black waters of a loch. True there were circular marks sometimes left in meadows, or the indentation of supposed landing-pods, or the plaster-casts of a gigantic foot. But the photographs were always too fuzzy – or far too precise – to cause more than derision or bilious irritation in people who minded their reputations. Foot-prints and indentations melted with the snow or were ploughed up by farmers, and the casts made of them too often had the look of *objets* not so much *trouvés* as contrived (and not even with the attention to detail which conscientious art students might have brought to them). Lake-monsters evaded the best that sonar could thrust at them. Other creatures shyly vanished as soon as nets, guns or other overtures were offered. Angel's Hair and other perishables swiftly perished. The remaining, more durable, arte-facts silently endured on the shelves of museums and laboratories, leaking away their credibility as time passed.

These truths dismayed the faithful. They *believed* what they believed. They *knew* that something 'real' lay behind these obstinate evasions. And they were not alone in doing so. By 1983 there were far more people in the United States of America – more than half the population, in fact – who believed in 'flying saucers' than could easily remember the name of the President they had had the misfortune, or the misjudgement, or the mere absence of mind, to elect to office. Statistics were not available for the United Soviet Socialist Republics; the British had not bothered to find out; the French were keeping their own figures to themselves . . . But ordinary citizens everywhere were as far apart in this matter from the governments they had chosen to elect or had had imposed upon them as they found themselves on most other questions.

It was the indifference – or apparent indifference, or perhaps downright obfuscation – on the part of these governments that was the other source of frustration to the dedicated few who not only believed that something of great importance was 'going on' but gave their private time to tracking it down – tramping across muddy fields to interview sullen farmers whose cattle had been mutilated, tactfully cross-examining troubled housewives in whose living-rooms had appeared, in a husband's absence, visions as terrible as anything imagined by Hieronymous Bosch, sitting by the bedsides of sturdy truck-drivers who, merely relieving nature on some lonely stretch of road, had come face to face with something which left them nervously unmanned, or marked with the appearance of eczema, or haunted by memories of some desperately close encounter with a silvery female (from Venus? from Orion? from the Pleiades?) whose fascination could never

115

be confessed to any wife or girlfriend. But no government department believed these things – or admitted that it did.

Among the buffs – the UFO-buffs, the Bigfoot-buffs, the mystery-animal-buffs, the poltergeist-buffs, the buffs who prayed for extraterrestrial intervention in the cruel and terrible affairs of *Homo sapiens*, the buffs who feared possession by Lucifer and his dark angels – there was an endless debate about the reasons for this official 'cover-up'. It was conducted with all the loving-fury which possesses those who are united by nothing except their opposition to an existing system of belief and power. It is the fate of all such oppositions to be shattered into fragments by the complacent rock of those who appear to be impregnably in office – until the day comes when the rock succumbs to some great force and those who have been battering at it discover that they have far more in common than their differences. For the weird fringe of those who believed in something ultraworldly that day had not yet come. They fell into two factions: those who believed that 'the authorities' knew nothing (and therefore needed to be jerked out of their somnolence into a greater concern with the public good – before it was too late); and those who were certain that '*they*' knew everything, particularly that the world was on the verge of invasion by ultra-human forces – for good or ill – but were seeing fit to conceal the facts in case ordinary people (whom '*they*' secretly despised) should 'get out of hand' – to the extent, for example, of needing closer attention from the police forces than even the recent and massive investment in police powers would be up to.

On the night 8/9 November 1990 and for several days thereafter (the installation of Blandfordness could only manage a handful of targets at a time, and Air Commodore Crowley's American counterpart was proving awkward about his instructions), the second of these two factions scored its biggest triumph for some years past. They had long cherished the rumour that little green corpses were being held on ice at Wright Patterson Field in the United States; they had recently heard that a French scientist had been shown something similar at a French Air Force base near Paris; but the solid evidence for these things had proved as elusive as the crock of gold at the end of any rainbow. Then suddenly the evidence came to them as abundantly as the shower of shoddy coins which Zeus had scattered over Danaë in the foreknowledge that he would, by this device, beget Perseus upon her before the weekend was over.

There was, to start with, a statement from Downing Street. It was couched in prose which lay somewhere between Churchillian oratory and the cautious constipations of any government circular. It was repeated for twenty-four hours on every sound- and visual-broadcast. The Prime Minister had asked that it should be. Her merest asking had now become a matter of terror to anybody who wished to hang on to his job. It hinted at tremendous events which were now about to come to pass. 'We shall meet them on the beaches,' it said. 'We shall meet them on the landing-grounds. We shall meet them in the fields and in the streets. We shall meet them in the hills. Everywhere, we shall meet them in amity.' There had been an ugly row in the Prime Minister's office over 'amity': there was a school of thought which considered 'friendship' more likely to be understood by the electorate, having in mind the many years of Labour perversion of the education system. For obscure reasons of her own the Prime Minister had preferred 'amity'. It remained uncertain who 'they' might be. The public were merely exhorted to report 'sightings' to any agency of Her Majesty's administration. The Prime Minister ended on a patriotic note. Only the virtues of thrift and self-reliance, recently reinculcated into the electorate by the determined policies of her own govern-ment, had made it possible for the British to be leading the world in this matter. 'This matter' was left unexplained.

Aleister Buchanan was quite pleased with this statement. She had mutilated a good deal of his prose, but the essential message remained intact. Even 'Beezie' seemed content: the statement gave 'Beezie' a basis for the next steps he wanted to take. Buchanan put out of mind the likely consternation of his American chums. Conrad Friedman, late of the CIA (doubtless still acting for them), had gone to earth somewhere. He couldn't even worry himself too much about Eliot and the Frensham woman. Keisgaig would shortly make its 'demonstrations'; the Russians could then be got back to the negotiating table; the British public wouldn't have the faintest idea of what was going on until the PM informed them; the Americans could be told to resume the slightly subordinate position from which they should never have been allowed to escape in 1776; the French would do what they were told. (He had only that morning persuaded the French authorities that a warrant should be issued for the arrest of some scientific maverick called Foucault, or some such.) After that, peace would reign – and the British (no pun intended) would hold its reins. Buchanan was, in his way, a patriot.

Operation DISINFORM went very much to plan. The Prime Minister's statement had excited expectations among the faithful. Bruno Zadig and RAF Blandfordness did the rest.

They stood in a cold field in Lancashire. Three members of the Lancaster Group for Aerial Mysteries. They took what shelter they could from the piercing wind by huddling in a leafless spinney, wrapping their woollies and overcoats about them. They were a dedicated group. Never less than one of them had failed to keep this vigil for the past fifteen years. They knew that this field was a destined place. Strange rings had been found in it in 1975.

A modest housewife among these three was the first to see it. An oval of light, descending like a falling leaf. Its colour was first orange, and then blue, and then finally green. It settled into a far corner of the field with a humming sound. Ambassadors came from it.

The three looked at each other. They had always expected this visitation. Why else should they have spent so many boring nights under the chilly firmament with nothing except meteors and earth-satellites to titillate their wonder? Now that it had come, they felt uncertain what to do.

It was stout, little Beryl who was sent to meet them. She went forward, nervously clutching woollen-gloved hands together in a gesture which she hoped was peaceful. She knew that something was at last about to make sense of her life. She had a spastic son, and a boring husband, and two daughters who really should have done much better in their 'O'-levels, and an elderly, incontinent mother. She reached them and found that they were . . . (how should she later put it to friends and neighbours?) . . . '*shining*'.

She was taken aboard some 'vessel', conducted by these friendly and splendid creatures. (Their companions were not too appealing, she had to admit: one looked like a monkey with clawed feet! But, then, how was *she* to judge what creatures from another world should look like?) She was asked to take everything off under the yellowish gleam of some light which came from the ceiling but seemed to have no bulbs. (Bert had never asked her to do anything like that.) She was 'examined'. Parts of this experience didn't seem too comfortable. Later, they explained that they came from the Constellation of Orion. Mankind must really stop messing about with nuclear weapons and that kind of thing. It seemed to make sense. She took care to remember what they said.

Later on, the sergeant in the local police station was wonderfully helpful. He hadn't been too kind before – for example, when they had told him in 1987, and again in 1989, of a bright light seen in the sky not too far from a neighbouring airfield which was obviously being watched by Them. This time, he even gave them a cup of tea. He said he would tell the Prime Minister. It was the most wonderful night she had ever had.

Lord Lampson, known to his fellow Peers as 'the Suffolk Wonder', shivered in the night air, feeding his winter-quartered peacocks at the bottom of the lawn at Lantern House. His son Gregorius, was not there. Gregorius had gone away, the servants told him, looking at him with a certain cautious reserve which he ascribed to his age and his nobility. But the absence of Gregorius was not surprising. They didn't get on too well together. They had never got on at all, now that he came to think of it. Gregorius was a strange boy (though now thirty-nine); he looked like a 'changeling', something substituted by unknown hands for the real son which the Viscount had always wanted, some sensible fellow, with a feel for horses, who would one day take his appointed place in the House and put down sensible questions about the impending visitation from outer space; and Gregorius had, after all – in a certain sense – murdered his mother. You could hardly blame a boy of four for bringing snakes into the house; it showed a very proper sense of natural history; but an *adder* . . . ? Winnifred, it had to be said, had gone under with not very creditable suddenness; but she came of frail stock, excellent though its pedigree might be. All the same, it was the kind of thing which left a coolness – that, and the lad's unappealing way with small mammals.

119

Viscount Lampson sighed in the darkness. He had, when it came to it, sadly missed his lady-wife. He had never looked for another.

Glancing above his peacocks, he saw the flash of the Ness lighthouse on the Suffolk coast and, a little way to the north of it, some greenish glow from that ugly, military installation whose construction he had vigorously opposed at Westminster. (It had to be said for the democratic process that it permitted every kind of question, even if the answers were usually disappointing.) The glow shaped itself into a bubble. Streamers of light fell from it. It began to move in his direction, sweeping across the marshy fields like a great will-o'-the- wisp. The peacocks shrieked. A horse in the stable whinnied with terror and began to pound its stall with frenzied hooves.

The Viscount looked up in hope, sensing that, at last, he was about to receive an Answer to the great Question he had long been pressing in what the Commons laughingly called 'Another Place'. A voice spoke to him from a greenish cloud above the elms. It was the voice of the dead mother of Gregorius.

But he failed to hear its message. He had fallen face forward on to the muddy grass, scattering a handful of the grain meant for his favourite birds. The shock had killed him. He was – when the facts later came to be examined – one of the only two failures in the whole of the programme of Operation DISINFORM. Putting it another way, Zadig and Buchanan were able to say that the success rate had exceeded ninety-six-point-nine per cent.

The phantoms came to many others. They came to the Para-searchers of Bristol, to the Society of the Friends of Avebury, to the Metaphysicals of Wood Green, to the Pleiades People, to the Sheffield Tibetans for a Better Britain, to an organization called STARWATCH in Newcastle-upon-Tyne, to the Devil Worshippers of Orpington, to the Society for the Propagation of Space Wisdom, to the Buddhists of Orion, to all the others listed in Part Three of the PROSERO file. They also came to many whose credentials were beyond reproach: a network centred in the north-west whose cautious and conscientious approach to the weirdness of the unidentified had struck the Ministry of Defence as making them a prime target for DISINFORM (their voice would be listened to); another group of similar common sense, located in Wiltshire; a lone investigator, living in Beckenham, who had often glimpsed 'vehicles' in the night sky, and who had had the courage or temerity to write a book about that most notorious of modern 'contactees', the ill-famed George Adamski (*his* visitors had come from Venus – somewhat before the time at which the space-probes of the United States and the USSR had made Venus an unlikely place for extra-terrestrials); the redoubtable editors of two learned (though 'fringe') journals; many other sane and sensible citizens in the front line of research; the Honorary President (it hardly needed to be said) of the first and foremost association in the United Kingdom for the investigation of the UFO phenomenon, Major General James McDougal-Planchett (now retired).

Everywhere, the message of the 'visitors' was the same. Zadig intended it; Buchanan had seen to it; the Prime Minister and her tame committee had, with somewhat shaky knowledge, endorsed it. At last, after many years, entities from beyond the Earth were about to declare themselves. Whether they were 'little' or 'green' would have to be left to the perception of their hosts (Blandfordness could only do its best). All that mattered to British propaganda was that 'they' were coming, that and the fact that the British – that thirteenth tribe of Israel – would be the first to receive them.

DISINFORM was, on the whole, hugely successful. Even allowing for the loss of a Viscount, its percentage 'rate of strike' would have approached ninety-eight-point-five had it not been for McDougal-Planchett. The rest of the 'network' was stunned into the expectation of a miracle. They were called upon by Men in Black who, for the first time in their mythology, not only took them seriously but uttered no threats. Their telephones were tapped – but openly and in a friendly manner. The MIBs, chauffered in MI5's expensive vehicles, took a number of them into the protective custody of a comfortable London hotel to await 'work of national importance'. The network came near to feeling flattered – even in those several cases where the phantoms which had visited them had seemed rather more fiendish than extra-terrestrial.

General McDougal-Planchett, too, felt flattered. He would certainly have sent a stiff letter to somebody, the Prime Minister if necessary, if in all that ferment of visitations no emissary had come to the President of the country's most august organization for the explanation of the inexplicable. But he felt not only flattered but suspicious. Somewhere behind the arras he smelt a rat.

The General received his own visitation in the small hours of 10 November. He was standing in the great conservatory of his granite mansion, gazing out across the Minch towards the Butt of Lewis. In this northerly part of Scotland, warmed by the Hebridean outposts of the Gulf Stream, the winter was coming late. It would be some weeks yet before Cape Wrath, ten miles to the north, suffered the first of the great onslaughts which the North Atlantic annually made upon it. Even some freakish rhododendron in the shrubbery had seen fit to put out an absurdly late – or touchingly early – flower-head. It was from behind this anachronistic bush that the General's visitor appeared.

'It' was clad in evening dress. (From the very start, the General felt a curious reluctance to grace it with the name of 'he'.) It swept the leaves aside – or perhaps they were merely repelled by it. It seemed to glide across the lawn without much movement of the feet. It resembled in this respect a djinn which the General had once encountered on the banks of the Euphrates in 1943 while serving as a young subaltern in Mesopotamia (some 'sand-devil' or local 'vortex', whipped up by the desert winds, which had nevertheless blossomed into a mushroom cloud, fifty feet high, possessing eyes, altering for ever a junior Lieutenant's perception of the odd planet he happened, for the time being, to be serving on). It floated forward. It moved its patent-leather shoes in a perfunctory imitation of walking. Only its formal attire gave the General any feeling of confidence – that, and its evident intention of making for the front door.

He wondered whether to get the butler out of bed. Perhaps a visiting-card might be demanded. Perhaps 'it' might be invited to cool its heels in the library (assuming that heels formed part of its accomplishments) while the urgent question was considered of whether the General happened to be 'at home'. But poor McBean was now on the verge of being overworked. He was not only a butler but also most other things which might once have been afforded – and November was proving to be a time for visitors of several kinds. There was, for example, that old fellow, with a somewhat battered pigeon in his pocket, who had turned up the evening before and was now sleeping in the orangery. He had utterly refused to sleep under any larger roof; houses, it seemed, were not a style to which he grown accustomed. McBean had had to walk his supper to him across three hundred yards of the 'wilderness' garden – baked beans on a silver salver, plus a dash of lentils for a pigeon called by the whimsical name of 'Seventeen'. There was also an impending visit by his old acquaintance, Jean-Paul Bien-Aimé. The General fingered Dr Foucault's telegram, lying in the padded pocket of his dressing-gown. McBean would have to get up at five o'clock the following morning, and harness the pony, and drive forty miles to the nearest railhead, and rack his peasant brains for some frenchified mess which might quieten the stomach of this tiresome Gallic physicist (haggis having proved a disaster in '88), and uncork something in the cellar which would appeal to the fellow's nationalist sensibilities. On the whole, McBean had better be left alone.

McDougal-Planchett went to the front door and drew its bolts. His visitor – his visitant – shimmered 'its' way across the threshold. He showed it into the conservatory. At close quarters it resembled a comic-opera version of Mephistopheles.

'I bring you tidings of great joy,' it said.

The General studied its top hat with distaste. The hat was at least two sizes too big. Whatever this thing might be it could at least have picked a decent outfitter. The tall, black cylinder sagged on the creature's face to rather below the level of the cheekbones. Two slits had been hacked out of it. Eyes looked at him from behind them. They seemed to glow with a light of their own.

'Joy,' said the General neutrally.

'We are coming to you. We bring messages of hope.'

'It is good of you to take the trouble,' said the General.

'Your planet is in deadly peril. We wish to save you from the consequences of your folly.'

'What is the price of this remarkable kindness?'

The creature was silent.

McDougal-Planchett turned his back, pretending to occupy himself in repotting cinerarias. He glanced at the book he had recently been reading – the curiosities collected by one, John Aubrey, in the seventeenth century. 'Anno 1670, not far from Cyrencester, was an Apparition,' John Aubrey had written. The General took a covert look at his visitor. It was certainly an 'Apparition': it was partly transparent to the *Hammamelis mollis* now struggling into flower beyond the conservatory windows. 'Being demanded whether a good Spirit or a bad,' continued Aubrey, 'it returned no answer, but disappeared with a curious perfume and most melodious Twang. Mr W. Lilly believes it was a Farie.'

'I think,' said the General, 'that you are probably a fairy.' It was not the sort of thing he would have considered saying to any of the gallant officers or Other Ranks whom it had once been his privilege to command. It went against his grain to say it even to an apparition. But the time had now come for plain speaking.

The creature flickered. It gave a curious shriek from beneath its top hat cylinder. It vanished even more quickly than it had come – not too 'melodiously', it had to be said (two panes in the conservatory roof were shattered by its explosive going), and its 'curious purfume' stank of ozone or sulphur.

A failure was recorded at Blandfordness. The President of UFORA was clearly a dangerous man, even though he did not yet know it himself.

McDougal-Planchett's maverick behaviour was somewhat counter-balanced by help from another quarter. Julius Ben Caesar Schultz turned out to be an unexpected bonus for DISINFORM.

The mere mention of Julie's curious messages to the London number she had given him (it had taken till ten o'clock the following morning to persuade those dim local policemen to let him call it) had produced, within hours, a large black car, three Men in Black, a swift suave journey to the metropolis, and a very friendly interview with two posh limeys in what seemed to be an expensive hotel in Mayfair (except that its windows were barred, not to mention double-glazed with a darkish kind of glass).

' "Men in White",' he explained to them. 'She said she'd been napped by Men in White. Just let me get my hands on those bastards!'

His hosts glanced at each other. He thought he heard one of them say, 'American chums?'. It made him feel kind of at home.

'She had this burn. The shits had done something to her face. Christ, I'd kill them!'

'Lantern-light,' said one of the two men jocularly. 'She was probably too near a lantern.' It seemed like a private joke. Not a very good one, he thought. But it reminded him of what she'd said. 'Yeah, well,' he said, scowling to relieve his temper, 'there *was* some gobbledygook about a "lantern". What the hell did she mean by that?'

They shook their heads, smiling. 'Anything about a "House"?' said one of them. 'A *Lantern* House?' The other chipped in with something about a 'Lamp', or the 'son of a Lamp'. It sounded weird to him. He felt they were getting off the point.

'Where the fuck is she?' he said truculently, passionately. He was missing her terribly. His socks were in a god-awful state. He was *worried* about her. 'She said "aliens",' he said. He took them through the last few frightening minutes of Julie's disappearance near Warminster.

'Aliens? You're sure she said "aliens"?'

'Goddam aliens!' he shouted. Christ, these Brits were thick some days! 'Came in a bloody rocket, I reckon.' He explained about the Warminster Group for Space Contact. He mentioned a dozen other wonderful British organizations he belonged to. He saw them ticking off the names on a piece of paper they had with them. They seemed to have heard of STARWATCH, and UFORA; and the Pleiades People. He began to feel a little better about their common sense.

They left him alone for half an hour, sending up a hamburger and French fries with a heavily built fellow who stayed with him while he ate them.

They came back. 'We think you can help us,' said one of them.

'We want you to talk to your friends,' said the other.

Help them?

They gave him a new visa, valid for six months, and two hundred pounds in used banknotes. 'You're a privileged man, Mr Schultz. You're nearly a contactee. You nearly saw *Them* the other night.' His head spun with it; he seemed to hear angels singing; the money looked good. 'Go and talk to your friends. Prepare them for the Great Day.'

'But don't mention PROSPERO, there's good fellow,' said the other.

He got up to go, and was then overtaken by angry grief. 'Where *is* she?' he shouted. He pounded his fists on their expensive table. He came near to tearing up their banknotes (stuffing the visa prudently into his pocket).

'Oh, you'll find her, Mr Schultz.' They glanced at each other. 'We'll promise you that.'

He found her.

In the downstairs lobby of this weird hotel.

Looking as though she was waiting for him.

They fell into each other's arms. He could hardly stop hugging her. With a wad of notes in his pocket, he took a taxi to the goddam Hilton and hired a goddam apartment for the night, high enough up that costly tower to look down into the grounds of Buckingham Palace. He seemed to see the Queen of England walking about with two small, long dogs. Julie washed his socks. They had an amazing Encounter. And then another. And then another. He quite forgot to ask her about the aliens she'd been spending her time with.

Julie thought about her 'aliens' – first American ones and then Russian. She glanced again at the appealing alien form of Julius, wishing that MI5 had given her some less attractive 'target'. But her instructions were quite clear.

She knew why the Russians had released her – they were hoping for a 'lead'. She had discussed this matter with Mayfair colleagues, ruefully admitting that KGB tactics with a lighted cigar and some electrical apparatus had caused her to let drop the word PROSPERO, though not its meaning. MI5 hadn't seemed too worried. She divined that PROSPERO was on the verge of being declassified.

'What should I do next?' she'd asked. She remained a patriot. She wanted to do what would be helpful to her country.

'Go back to that American chum of yours.'

'Where is he?' she said, keeping her voice to the right level of official neutrality.

'Oh, you'll find him,' they said airily. She knew that she could trust to their 'arrangements'. She tried not to show that it made her happy.

'What then?' she asked.

'Our Russian chums will be following you, of course.'

'Of course.'

'They'll be hoping for a lead to Keisgaig.'

She nodded.

'We're sending you quite close to it. But we think we can take the risk. The main operation will be over in a few days' time.'

She took care not to show that this gave her great relief. She would always be a patriot, but there were times when a girl hankered to get back to a bit of private life.

'Where, then?' she asked.

They gave her the address of the President of UFORA. Some military chap in Scotland. 'Take that American yobbo with you. Talk to the old boy. Make sure he hoists in the DISINFORM cover-story. He's influential with the "freaks" network. The story is LGM. We don't want the public playing up for the time being with any other kind of theory. Your American target is a push-over for what we want. We'll ship him back to the States later on – or dispose of him in some other way. You won't be clobbered with him.'

In the small hours of 11 November, remembering that this was what her parents had called 'Poppy Day' (recalling some occasion three-quarters of a century ago, when millions had died for reasons now largely forgotten), Julie Smith tenderly examined her 'target'. He lay on his back in an expensive bed, thrusting great snores towards a ceiling which was far more costly than anything he should have tried to afford. He would find, tomorrow, that most of his poisoned money would be needed to pay the bill. It was lucky that the Mayfair 'friends' had kitted her up with resources enough to get them to their next 'target'.

She only wished that she didn't *like* the present one.

Or not, at any rate, so much. The sight of his great, coarse socks hanging above the gold taps in the ornate bathroom came near to causing her emotions which the Head of MI5 would have thought unprofessional.

President McClusky spoke to Comrade-Marshal Zinsky on their

lukish-warmish line.

The Oval Office was stuffed from end to end with the highest kind of brass. The Director of the Central Intelligence Agency was jostled by the Chairman of the Joint Chiefs of Staff. Members of the National Security Agency found themselves pressed to the wall by Pentagon scientists whom they half distrusted but mainly feared. A privileged Senator, made privy to this great occasion, thrust forward his handsome profile, obscuring as best he could the platinum hair-do of the Vice-President. (He had always known it was a mistake to appoint a woman.)

The room was breathless. They had been briefing the President for five hours. They could only hope that the old fool had now got it into his showbiz head what he had to do. In an adjoining room a bevy of top-security-cleared operators prepared to record the exchanges with Moscow.

Comrade-Marshal Zinsky cleared his throat. Talking so much in recent days on the hot line had made him husky. He would be seventy-six before too long.

In the great bleak room, lying a little below the onion domes of the Kremlin, the inner core of the Praesidium had come to keep him company: the Comrade-Minister of Defence, the head of the Committee of State Security, the Comrade-Hero of the People's Space Agency, scientific comrades from Plesetsk, the comrade-leaders of the armed forces, Comrade Bulgov, that mere upstart of sixty-seven who, as Marshal Zinzky was well aware, waited in the wings of history to supplant him.

The room kept a Siberian silence. They had been briefing the Comrade-Marshal since yesterday. They hoped that he now knew his historic destiny – all, that is, except Comrade Bulgov, who had his dagger and his apparatchiks at the ready and would be quite content if Comrade Zinsky cocked it up. In an adjoining room an array of tape-recorders, controlled by a comrade-electrician who might well have to be sent to weather out his remaining lifetime in a labour camp when he had performed his historic but risky duties, awaited the privilege of overhearing the exchanges with Washington.

'Greetings, Uncle Sam,' said the Comrade-Marshal. He, too, like Rocky McClusky, was inclined to leave the niceties of diplomatic protocol to his translator.

'Hi there, Ivan.'

Tape-recorders tape-recorded. Earnest young electricians, even those liable to incarceration, adjusted their controls for volume, treble, bass, background hiss, extraneous noise, cosmic particle interruption, unforeseen static, unforeseeable accidents, the wholly foreseeable tremulo in the voices of two old men.

'We have a common cause, comrade.'

'Sure thing,'said Rocky McClusky. He glanced around the Oval Office, hoping that his failure to repudiate 'comrade' would not be reported on Capitol Hill. He gave a bronchitic growl.

'Those allies of yours. . . Those British friends . . .'

'No allies of mine, Ivan. No friends of ours.' McClusky saw that the Director of CIA was nodding vigorously. A note was slipped to him. Somebody called Friedman had picked up somebody called Eliot. (Names, names . . . why the hell should the President of the United States be expected to remember what goddam shit had picked up goddam whom?)

'Those British friends of yours . . .'

McClusky squared his jaw. 'Now see here, Ivan . . .' He saw that this bit of firmness was going down well with the Senator. 'Do you want us to pull out our London Ambassador or something?' He laughed, man to man, stifling a mild spasm of Parkinsonian tremor.

Down in Red Square some scrawny lunatic with a placard inscribed 'PEACE' was being dragged away by the Kremlin guards, his heels trailing on the frosty ground. Zinsky was glad to find that his long-sighted focus remained in working order. Glancing through the lower half of his bifocals, he reread the note recently passed to him by the Head of KGB. Somebody called Birkov had recently picked up a female called Smith and had then released her 'for intelligence purposes'. The Comrade-Marshal twitched his bushy Georgian eyebrows. A Head of State could hardly be expected to trouble himself with this kind of kitchen-work. He smiled in a pleasant, though sinister, manner at Comrade Bulgov. He flicked again through the notes in front of him. 'We have a common cause . . .' No, he had done that bit. 'You and we are the Super-Powers.' The hot-line muttered with approval. 'You and we have discovered a new force.' He took silence for agreement. 'You and we must make the necessary treaty, comrade.' What 'force'? he wondered. There was hardly time to keep up with the technicalities these days; even the SS 25 had somewhat escaped him. But 'treaty' sounded promising; perhaps Bulgov could be sent to Geneva to haggle over the details for the rest of the decade.

The hot line hotted up a little. The President and the Comrade-Marshal shouted at each other from time to time, partly to impress the assembled bureaucracies which they imagined they controlled, partly because they had grown a trifle deaf and the line was bad. In the end they reached the agreement they had always known they would.

'The British must be brought under control . . . Put out of action, if necessary.'

'Sure, sure.'

'The French as well.'

'OK. OK.'

'We must then work for a Limitation Agreement. Just between the two of us, Uncle Sam.'

'Sure thing, Ivan.'

Each of them, as was only proper, kept a fact or two up his sleeve. The President of the United States, sustained by military and intelligence colleagues, failed to disclose the information (he was hardly too well aware of it, himself) that there was now some chance of getting control of a new British facility which would leave the Ruskies not knowing their unmentionables from their expletives deleted. The Comrade-Marshal, for his part, took care not to mention that promising experiments were near to completion at Plesetsk. He would not hesitate to use them (without quite knowing what they were) in the interests of the peace-loving masses of the people's democracies.

They put down their telephones – touchingly old-fashioned instruments for the age they lived in – with comforting sensations of peaceful coexistence. They had found a unity of purpose. Putting the British in their place would give them both some satisfaction. They had been finding the British somewhat tiresome for a while past.

Aleister Buchanan, had he been privy to this conversation between super-powers, might well have felt a glow of uneasy patriotism. To John Eliot patriotism had now ceased to be even a refuge from his cowardice. A mere thirty minutes with Conrad Friedman and his well-trained thugs had dug out of him the likely meaning of PROSPERO and the name of a Scottish loch. He was now being driven northwards in a car with blackened windows. He nursed a desperate sense of failure and what seemed like a broken rib. Not even the flicker of some great light in the sky above Loch Ness (the Aurora Borealis? The glow of some debris falling back from space?) lifted his spirits. It had the look of an approaching storm.

7
Property and Possessions

Lem had a vision of the Earth. It lay some thousands of miles below him, its blue-grey sphere marked with the curlicues of great weather-systems. Unseen energies whipped up its atmosphere into whirlpools and vortices of tremendous force. A winter storm drifted in the North Atlantic not far from the coast of Scotland. It moved as stealthily as any djinn or sand-devil on the banks of the Euphrates. On the face of the globe it sketched a feathery spiral, delicate as the markings on a pigeon's wing, deadly as a thousand megatons.

'What do you see?' said the voice of the political officer by his side.

Lem muttered, incoherent, smiling at a private joke. He was a boy of ten again, picking up some spiral shell on the shores of the Black Sea, tracing his own curves in the sands of a seaside resort with a child's spade, knowing in that instant that the same forces governed both of them, the child and the shell, foreseeing that the tidal energies of the world would presently wash them both away.

'Tell us, comrade,' said the political officer, standing by his left ear.

'He may be too far under,' said the voice of the Comrade-Surgeon, somewhat further off.

Lem giggled, searching for words. Whatever it was that the Comrade-Surgeon had injected into his veins a quarter of an hour ago had sharpened his vision but dulled his speech. His tongue lay in his mouth like an unwelcome morsel, too large and leathery to be chewed and swallowed, too firmly anchored to the back of his throat to be spat out. He extended its tip between parched lips and hissed at them.

Comrade Birkov conferred with the Comrade-Surgeon. Lem

heard them both withdraw to the discreet distance at which a consultant discusses his patient's cancer with his registrar. 'We must restore some sense of responsibility,' he heard Comrade Birkov saying – Comrade Oleg Birkov, recently returned, it seemed, from the little British outpost of Western power. Lem, lying on his back in the grey Ganz-field of the translucent goggles now strapped across his face, remembered the pebble lenses of Comrade Birkov; poor Comrade Birkov seemed unusually short-sighted. 'It must run its course, comrade,' murmured the discreet voice of the Comrade-Surgeon. 'We shall take his present condition into account when we calculate the dose for the next occasion.'

But Lem had lost interest in them. He lay on his back in the white bed, not too uncomfortably thonged, not too inconsiderately drugged. (This stuff was better than Sulfazine.) The planet lay below him at a distance of twenty thousand miles. He watched the endless flicker of new forms in its turbulent atmosphere. The world made and remade itself in successive particles of time. It drew on the substances congealed within it during the clock-tick of its five thousand million years. It played with the five forces available to it, largely indifferent to whether its principal life-form had yet wholly understood them.

Lem peered into the grey mist of the milky, perspex hemispheres which the Comrade-Surgeon had strapped across his main receptors of electro-magnetic radiation. The Comrade-Surgeon had kindly explained that this apparent blinding would help Lem to see more widely, more deeply, more in accordance with the historic destiny of the peace-loving masses. Lem peered. His skin tingled with ancient energies. The world shaped and reshaped itself in multitudinous forms.

Off the coast of Scotland the spiral of the great storm had tightened upon itself like a clock spring wound by unseen hands. Lem looked at it with childish pleasure. He had the feeling that he could, by some tiny flick of the imagination, release its catch, nudge it further south or west, spill the deadly energies of its unwinding on whatever coast he chose. The giddiness of great power possessed him. He teetered on some vertigo of the will.

'Lem!' said the Comrade-Surgeon sharply.

Lem heard the little whirr of a control on the operating console.

A surge of power thrust its way through the electrodes implanted in his shaven skull. His hands trembled in the grip of the electronic manacles shackled about his wrists. He felt himself snatched up – wrenched with terrible roughness from that riverbank of forty years before as the five-foot tidal bore hissed its way across the water to the little boy, paddling in the shallows, who merely wanted to pat the silken skin of that great suave creature. Lem laughed aloud with pleasure at the sheep which lolled and tumbled with closed eyes at the water's crest – then howled with rage and disappointment in the trembling arms of his father. The silken beast passed out of sight forever like a lost friend.

Whimpering, Lem came to himself again. Tears of rage and disappointment had leaked their way under the Ganz-goggles and were running down his cheeks. Snatches of some rapid conversation drifted into his blurred mind.

'Megalomania . . . It's a risk with all of them . . .'

'We expect you to keep control, comrade.' (Birkov's voice.)

Silence. Then words like 'prototype stage . . . far too hasty development . . . we could do with another year, comrade . . .'

'There may only be days.'

'What evidence is there that the Other Side . . .?'

'You can leave such matters to the intelligence services, my friend.'

The Comrade-Surgeon came and stood by him, holding his shackled wrist. 'You are valuable property, comrade,' he said gently. 'You must keep possession of yourself. You must do only what we are training you to do.'

Lem sullenly nodded – to the extent that his clamped skull permitted.

'We shall be giving you certain . . . targets when the time comes. Until then you are to do nothing outside the experimental programme.'

Lem was silent, keeping possession of himself, knowing that he was valuable property. They had already trained him to make plasmoids at a distance of a thousand metres, strictly within the perimeter fence of the establishment. They were training him to lose his regret that the weird scorch-marks gouged into the floor of the animal laboratory by his Ganz-field imagination seemed capable of killing a hundred rats at a blow. He had never much

135

liked rats. To the sad-eyed little Rhesus monkeys, on the other hand, he had tried to send messages of good cheer. He was glad that the Rhesus monkeys did not yet seem to form part of the experimental programme.

They swung him more westerly – Lem was well aware that his political friends were doing it. It cut him down to size; it removed his childish temptation to tamper with hurricanes. He came to rest above Scotland. He was not quite sure whether they spoke English there.

'Listen, comrade,' said Oleg Birkov. 'Listen and attend. Make sure that you do nothing but listen.'

Lem listened, studying the ancient hills, the landlocked lakes, the heather-covered slopes. Some gabble rose up to him. It was couched in English (to his great relief – at his age he boggled at mastering the Gaelic). It came from a woman. He sensed that she was young. She spoke of 'angels'. She was on about 'St Michael' or 'St Gabriel'. He felt mildly embarrassed. His grandmother would certainly have understood, but 'angels' formed no part of Historical Necessity. 'Help us,' she seemed to say. But he could hardly have been brought to Plesetsk to help the forces of bourgeois-imperialism! He was almost relieved to hear some other voice, following hard upon her own.

The Comrade-Surgeon whistled through his teeth. Lem heard Birkov draw in his breath with a sharp gasp and then swear. He guessed that they were standing by the thick glass window of the Komarov chamber at the end of the control room. 'Jesus!' said Comrade Birkov, 'Jesus Christ!' Twitched by rage or fear, Comrade Birkov, senior member of the KGB, could find no better relief for his feelings than forgotten blasphemies drawn from a forbidden opiate of the masses.

Lapped in his own opiates, Lem had no more than a second in which to enjoy this irony. In the Ganz-field of his blinkered vision something had begun to form – a pale-eyed, albino creature, its hair at shoulder length. It resembled some evil St Michael or St Gabriel. It was attended by little greenish entities, half its height, lipless and moving like marionettes. The white eyes flicked across his face, then settled on a point beyond him. Lem felt a chill or mildew groping for his most secret bones – that hidden part of him which would lie in the earth for thousands of years, waiting to be disentombed by the grave-diggers of the thirtieth century (assuming there was one), prepared to lie patiently for aeons beneath the sediment of seas not yet born in order to give evidence to the future of a missing link between *Homo sapiens* and whatever new thing might then have come to being.

He knew that it was evil, whatever 'evil' could now be said to be. He guessed that his comrade-friends were watching it through the sulfide-toughened glass of the Komarov chamber, that safe little 'monitor' named by the Plesetsk authorities (for reasons best known to themselves) after the cosmonaut-hero Vladimir Mikhaylovich Komarov, the first man to die on a space-mission. (He had fallen to his death on 24 April 1967, his re-entry capsule 'entangled in its main parachute' – or so they had put it about before burying his ashes in the walls of the Kremlin.) In that observation chamber, as carefully insulated against the forces to which it gave a peephole as any bubble-chamber or emulsion-plate made available to some French physicist in the bowels of CERN, the comrade-friends would now be seeing what Lem saw. But they would be seeing it through a glass darkly. Lem found that he had to see it face to face.

He listened again for the voice of the young woman. But she was silent. He forced himself to study the face of the pale-eyed entity, grateful to find that it had not yet found the focus of his own pupils. As he watched it, it flickered and grew dim, dwindled to a point, winked out of existence. It left behind it some wailing cry and a cloudy darkness. Lem sweated with relief.

Presently, they unscarfed him, thanked him brusquely, loosened his manacles. Comrade Birkov, his eyes huge behind the pebble glasses, spoke of 'steps of the highest urgency'. The Comrade-Surgeon poured him a sleeping draught.

Lem went back trembling to the prison of his well-appointed quarters, happy to be the property of any State which set itself against that Western monstrosity. He steeled himself to get up again at dawn, to train for twenty hours out of the coming twenty-four, to exercise his talents if need be on the little primates huddled together for warmth in the animal laboratory a thousand metres away.

Viscount Gregorius Mansfield Lampson, his father having now

conveniently left him the title, sat upright and unmoving in the comfortable, powered chair placed at his disposal by Dr Bruno Zadig.

In the control room of the Prospero Unit, a hundred feet below the level of Loch Keisgaig, he forebore to play with the controls of this contraption. The flick of a lever by his left thumb would, if he wished, ease him gently into the horizontal. Another would rotate the chair to whatever new orientation suited his fancies. Above his head a steel skull-cap waited to steady his vertebrae if he felt the need. Soft leather manacles were ready about the chair to shackle his arms and his legs if the flesh proved difficult. But Lampson had come to disdain the flesh as well as the world; he had made his pact with another party. He had no need for Zadig's little restraints and gadgets. He was interested only in Zadig's source of power.

Zadig watched him covertly, avoiding the pale eyes. Lampson picked up his thoughts. They were easy to read. Zadig was wondering how to 'keep control'.

Lampson gave a little mirthless rasp. This bony Czech, wonderously over-developed in his left hemisphere, could think of nothing but 'machines' and 'machinery', 'programs' and 'protocols', 'mechanics' and 'electronics', 'control systems' and soulless 'cybernetics'. (For a moment 'soul' detained Lampson, but it was a word which he tended to find uncomfortable.) Zadig, having stumbled by accident across Lampson's talent, knowing (uneasily) that his gadgetry would be worth little more than Blandfordness without it, was now perplexed by the problem of how to use this talent as a property of the State – without giving its possessor a dangerous degree of independence. To Viscount Lampson, recently ennobled by the fortunate accidents of death, it resembled the little local difficulty on which earlier Lampsons had sometimes harangued Their Lordships in Another Place. Monarchs made standing armies – 'to maintain public order', 'to repel foreign enemies'. But having made them, they viewed them with unceasing dread. They slept uneasily at nights. They awoke at four o'clock each morning, listening for the military convoy at the palace gates, the bright young Colonel with a sten gun, the sounds of a firing-squad marching to a royal assignment.

'What are you afraid of?' said Lampson smiling.

Zadig parried the question. 'You can do nothing without *us*.'

'You know very well that I can do a great deal. Otherwise, I would not be here.'

'With us you can do a great deal more.'

Lampson looked at the monitoring chamber behind Zadig's shoulder. Twenty-four hours before, mistily half congealed within that sphere of toughened glass, had appeared some entity, humanoid in form its skull domed and large, its deep-set eyes anxious and enquiring. Lampson detected another of his own kind, one of those few, gifted creatures who understood the nature of the world more clearly than most of the blind, two-legged fools, and would know how to use it – if he wished. But this other 'talent' had not yet learned to wish . . . Lampson concealed the mirth of this irony, keeping his pale eyes unwinking. There – at some place called 'Plets' or 'Plesk', two thousand miles away on the edge of the Ural mountains – the authorities of the State were striving to overcome what they would doubtless call 'ethical block', that sentimental aberration which sometimes prevented the flesh from making a meal of its own kind, from tormenting its own kind to death, from hunting every other kind of flesh into extinction. Here, at the Keisgaig Station, the authorities of the State (very similar, it seemed, to authorities of the State anywhere) were faced with the reverse problem – how to let off the leash without too much risk to themselves a 'talent' which had no qualms of any kind.

'Why are you drugging my food?' said Lampson. 'Why are you not linking me with more than a fraction of your power?' He swivelled his chair and gazed through the open door at the end of the control room. In the concrete corridor beyond it, bank upon bank of Zadig's 'psycho-electronic multipliers', stacked up to ceiling height, extended as far as the eye could see.

'What would you do with it?' said Zadig, keeping the pupils of his eyes a little out of alignment with Lampson's

'What will *you* do without me?' said Lampson, entertained by Zadig's paradox, foreseeing that Zadig would shortly have to grasp the other of the two horns of his tiresome dilemma.

Above Zadig's head, Keisgaig's warning siren began to ululate. It shrieked its way upwards towards the ultrasonic, fell back to infra-sound, mounted again to electronic hysteria. Once, 'siren' had meant merely the seductive voice of women, drawing towards them, across the intervening waters, the lusty dissatisfactions of men who had been too long at sea. In Zadig's century it had come to mean the wailing, banshee voice which jerked men out of the arms of lovers towards catastrophe.

Zadig ran from the control room, mounted steel companionways towards the upper world, passed the concrete cell in which some Lucy female (some 'female Lucifer', as Lampson called her) was now under interrogation. He came to the surface, comforted to find himself in the company of a score of soldiers, kneeling in the November gale with rifles at the ready.

Above them in the sky, perhaps a mile distant, the rapier-point of a great sword stabbed towards Keisgaig loch, a shaft of light held by a vast and shadowy hand. Broad at its upper end, the beam tapered to the sharpness of a lance at its lower. Its dazzling tip shone with a lambent blue. If this was heat, thought Zadig, it had already passed the level which any metal could withstand. Lead would vaporize, even steel would melt. As though in answer to this thought gouts and globules of a bluish flame began to fall towards the surface of the loch, a hundred yards away. The loch hissed and shrieked with the sounds of water far too quickly turned to steam. A smell of ozone or sulphur was whipped into Zadig's nostrils by the driving wind.

A hundred feet below him, alone in the control room, Lampson laughed aloud. Disdaining to watch these events in the little gadgetry of Zadig's monitoring chamber, he flicked the surgical chair into its horizontal mode and lay face upwards, keeping his eyelids parted by gazing with his inner vision. Zadig's platoon of infantry had begun to fire their rifles. Their harmless leaden slugs – they were not even using the silver bullets which ghouls and werewolves were said to fear! – fell foolishly into the loch and were quietly digested by its freezing waters. Above them, the sword-beam crackled with energy, shedding its drops of ultraviolet blood.

Somewhere within the Keisgaig Station a woman was sobbing. The Lucy-female. The Frensham-fool. She was gabbling into the ear of the suave intelligence officer who sat with her the nonsensical monosyllable of 'Lem'. 'Lem!' she seemed to be shouting as tears ran down her face, 'Lem! Lem!'

Lampson shed this woman's hysteria. He focused his mind on

Zadig's problem. He groped for its source and found it. It seemed to lie within the dome-shaped skull of a dwarfish creature two thousand miles to the east. Its 'ethical block' had been partly overcome. Powers had been given to it by officers of the State.

Lampson lay lazily at ease, knowing that Zadig, too, would shortly have to place his ingenious toys at the disposal of the only talent which knew how to make use of them. Two of Zadig's soldiers were now being carried away on stretchers. It would teach him the necessary lesson.

Presently, Lampson slept. Not even he, partly lodged in the imperatives of the biosphere, could wholly escape the flesh. But he slept with his eyes open. Not even in sleep did he ever close them.

By the waters of the great lake ('loch', was a word unknown to him) Jake lay comfortable on the tarpaulin which a kind lady called Lucy had given him. The heather made a springy mattress beneath it. The lady's gift of rags and blankets, dragged from the back of her quite unladylike van before she had dropped him off near the house of some kind gentleman, had kept him warm and dry. Not quite as warm, it had to be admitted, as the gentleman's garden shack, with its walls of stone and glass, and its stone figures, and its little trees in wooden tubs. But he couldn't have stayed there for long. He knew that he had to go further 'upwards' in the direction of a group of stars which someone had once told him was called 'The Bear' (though to Jake it looked more like one of his mother's copper ladles). It made him uncomfortable, in any case, to be sleeping among so many people with their clothes off.

Jake extended a hand into the freezing November dawn and found the lady's tin-opener, lightly lifted in a Woolworth's on the edge of a place called Inverness – 'stolen', he would have to say if Calvinistically exact. He opened a tin of cold baked beans and munched with satisfaction. The beans, too, had been 'stolen' by the lady, together with a sackful of other tins and a large bag of lentils for Mr Seventeen, from the back of a parked grocery van near a place called Bonar Bridge. This time, she had left a scribbled note and the contents of her handbag – a round, flat silvery thing with pinkish flour in it, a square of silk, the golden top of a fountain pen. To Jake it hadn't looked quite enough; there was probably some degree of 'stealing' in it; his mother would certainly have thrashed him for anything of the kind. But it seemed a kindness on the lady's part, that and the long relief to his travel-weary feet from the Inver place. The Good Lord would probably take it into account when judging the lady. And hadn't the Good Lord once sent ravens to Elijah in the wilderness with gifts of locusts and honey? They, too, had probably been stolen. Jake scattered a handful of lentils to Mr Seventeen and allowed ethical questions to pass him by.

Overnight, the gale had blown itself out. The morning was cold but still. The pale sun, mistily shining from Jake's left, set the waters of the lake into a sombre gleam.

He thought about the strangeness of the night – something like lightning in the sky above him, bangs and hisses all over the place, men shouting, rifles firing, the lake heaving itself into angry billows, the wind howling in from the direction of his right thumb as he looked 'downwards' towards the moon. He had had to tuck Mr Seventeen's anxious head beneath his jacket to keep him calm.

This morning, the lake was peaceful. Jake felt peaceful, too. He would have liked to thank the lady more fully before she had disappeared to some destination of her own. But he had at least managed to press into her hand his most precious possession a large, round, pearly button which gave different 'pictures' according to the angle from which you looked at it. It had rested in his pocket for sixty years. For the kind gentleman he had not been able to do anything except to scrawl 'Ta' on the dusty windowpane of the gentleman's somewhat immodest shack.

Jake munched on cold baked beans and presently helped himself to the extraordinary luxury of tinned rice pudding. He knew that it had been right to tramp those extra footsore miles towards 'The Bear'. He had found what he had come to find. He was not yet quite sure what it was. But something below the still surface of the waters, lying perhaps as deep as the heather-clad mountains around him were high, told him that he was near the end of his journey.

On the night of 15 November 1990, two days after the initial probe at Keisgaig Station, RAF Blandfordness was put out of action.

Globes of light fell from the air towards it. They clung to its forest of aerials, exploding them seawards in pyrotechnic fury. A zig-zag lightning stroke snaked in from three thousand feet above the North Sea, deadly as a hamadryad. It searched out the water-tower of Blandfordness, scalded its contents to something approaching steam, ripped the tank apart, scattered these super-heated waters to the troops below, sent them reeling back to the concrete shell of the main building.

Air Commodore Crowley put in a call to Buchanan. Buchanan received it, chilled and unshaven in his Blackheath residence, shortly before dawn.

'They've got it, they're on to us,' gasped Crowley, choking. Buchanan could almost sniff the stench of sulphur across the telephone wire. 'We chucked back everything we could at them. They scattered our little phantoms like rainclouds.' Buchanan waited as Crowley, clasping a hand across the telephone, concealed as best he could the unappealing spasms of the flesh. 'For God's sake take care of PROSPERO . . .' The line went dead.

Buchanan made a swift call to Zadig and confirmed that Lampson had been put on to something like full power since the probe at Keisgaig two days before. 'Give him everything he needs. Keep a defensive screen. Stand by for a counter-demonstration.' He curtly overrode Zadig's reservations.

Half an hour later the news reached him of the destruction of a French facility in the Hautes Cévennes. Its death-throes had sent a wave of apparitions across the French countryside in those uncannily straight lines which a French ufologist had once called '*orthotenies*' and some called 'leys'. In the hinterland of Suffolk an old Gypsy woman, sleeping under a hedge, had burst into the weird flames of spontaneous human combustion. Two cases of what seemed like mild radiation sickness were reported from Aldeburgh.

Later that morning Buchanan stood by the Prime Minister's elbow in the sub-ground bunker to the west of Downing Street. A little beyond its steel-girt walls lay the War Room of Winston Churchill. Something of the Old Man's spirit, filtering along the intervening corridors, had crept into the Lady's stance. She was approaching her finest hour. Buchanan sensed that she would by now, like her great predecessor, be sporting the steel hat of the

British infantry of 1940 if her hairstyle had permitted. Instead, the great coiffure, piled up like the extremest version of an eighteenth-century wig, gave her the look of William Pitt the Younger, Second Earl of Chatham, Prime Minister of England, announcing to Parliament the victory of Lord Nelson at Trafalgar. It was merely an irony of history that she happened to be talking of disasters.

She spoke on the hot line to the American President, huskily gracious, ironly resolved. 'I and my government, Mr President . . .' (she glanced round the hastily assembled PROSPERO Committee) '. . . will take full responsibility for the defence of the West.' She had borne with very cheerful fortitude the news of the night's incidents: they had left her in charge of the only usable hardware in this new field of glory. This morning, she had used the faintest touch of rouge.

The gleam in her eye hardened towards a glint, her voice edged towards something more strident. 'It's a *British* property, Mr President,' Buchanan heard her say. He guessed that 'fingers on triggers' and 'hands on safety-catches' had raised their ugly heads. She continued the interchanges for several minutes. 'Britain' cropped up repeatedly, together with 'West', 'trust', 'undivided control' and 'closest consultation – time permitting, of course'. (Of course.) She briefly suspended the call and fixed the committee with an iron look. 'I've talked him out of *that* nonsense,' she said. 'All he wants now is an observer at Keisgaig. I'm inclined to let him have it.'

Buchanan vigorously shook his head. If she wanted to keep a single-key at Keisgaig, she had better not let in a locksmith. But the Defence Secretary had got there first, rushing in like a well-tailored angel where fools might at least have had the timidity to consult officials first. 'It will do no harm,' said the Defence Secretary, 'to let the Americans see at first hand the power that we . . . you, that is, Prime Minister . . . now control. It will be a sop to *them* and a likely benefit to *us*.' He saw that he had pleased her. She quelled a half-hearted objection from the Minister Without Portfolio, glanced at Buchanan (who judged it best to keep silent), gave the President her gracious permission, concluded the call. 'He seems to have some senior member of the State Department already in the Scottish area,' she said casually.

She congratulated the Committee on Operation DISINFORM.

It was the first time she had ever thanked them. It would divert the attention of the public for a little longer. She gave crisp instructions for the handling of the media. She announced that she would shortly be making an Historic Broadcast to 'my people'. She would then address 'those UFO persons' at a rally in Wembley Stadium, together with as many of the world's press as could be quickly assembled. The House of Commons need hardly be troubled, she felt.

She made Buchanan kneel on the shabby carpet (bequeathed to No. 10 by a Mrs Chamberlain in 1938) and went through the motions of knighting him. The Person Up The Road would ratify it in due course. She announced a proposed honour for 'that great patriot', the Viscount Lampson. Nothing less than a dukedom would be suitable. 'I shall make him the Duke of Washington,' she told them. 'It will make a very telling point with our American friends.'

'The Duke of Washington, DC, ma'am?' Buchanan ventured to ask, wheezily clambering to his feet again, 'or the Duke of Washington, Washington?' He hoped she remembered that one was the capital of the United States and the other that north-western state in which a certain Mr Arnold had first seen 'flying saucers' in 1947.

'Both if necessary, I suppose,' she said casually.

Buchanan could see that she was already thinking about targets. She was searching out some battleship to sink, some concentration of troops to set on fire, some other little demonstration of the Will. She was clearly going out of her mind, a woman possessed, a woman in the possession of a great new property. He noticed for the first time that her eyes were somewhat pale. They distantly resembled the eyes of the prospective Duke of Washington.

Conrad Friedman received his instructions from the White House on coded telex in the security wing of an American base in eastern Scotland. He had been waiting for them for two days. The loss of Blandfordness had turned out rather well. It had jerked the Old Cowboy into action. It had got him the entrée to Keisgaig.

He stared through the grille of Eliot's cell, studying the haggard face of the sleeping man, wondering whether to dispose of Eliot immediately. He concluded that Eliot might be useful baggage, something to be traded in with the Brits at the right moment. Why waste him at this stage?

Later, he drove rapidly towards the western tip of Scotland along the coast road from Thurso. He was accompanied by two other men in black, one of whom sat by the handcuffed Eliot behind the dark glass of the passenger compartment. Friedman was glad to see that Eliot, though still semi-comatose with the treatment which the 'boys' had given him, was alive enough to be useful property.

McDougal-Planchett switched off the television set and sat silent. He glanced around the library at the faces of his guests, sensing a common emotion. The Prime Minister's broadcast had left them stunned and frightened.

'. . . determined steps against those responsible for these outrages . . .' News had been coming in all day of those weird 'outrages', one of them in England, one in France. (Foucault had talked of flying home, despite the warrant waiting for him.) But *what* 'determined steps'? She had promised terrors but told them nothing.

'She can't mean *nukes*, for chrissake?' said Julius Schultz. A vacant and foolish smile had crept across his face beneath haunted eyes. 'She told us three days ago that *They* were coming. She can't be wanting to nuke *Them* . . .' He looked up towards the ceiling and seemed to see beyond it. 'They're coming to *save* us, man!'

Julie Smith had taken him by the arm. 'You stupid great oaf!' she said, kissing him.

The General saw that tears had gathered in her eyes. He looked away in irritation. The President of UFORA often had to put up with this kind of thing from the UFO 'fringe' – and gladly. (God bless them for their obstinate patience in the face of those oddities which everyone else neglected.) But he could have done without it at the moment. He wondered again why these two had been sent to see him.

'What does this Prime Minister of yours mean by "*British* steps"?' said Foucault stiffly. There had been no mention of France, no mention of the Americans, not even a reference to

NATO. She had spoken of British skill, British ingenuity. 'Britain will not neglect its duty to defend Western values against alien aggression.'

'Alien aggression . . .' thought McDougal-Planchett. He doubted that the Prime Minister meant LGM; she meant the Soviet Union. 'Determined steps . . . British steps . . .' She could only mean a nuclear attack. Somewhere at sea some Polaris submarine had received its orders, waiting only for the final signal. Somewhere on the other side of the Iron Curtain a pre-emptive first strike was probably being prepared, might already have been launched . . .

Chilled to the marrow of his ageing bones, the General gazed bleakly across the sea towards the northern Hebrides, glad that it could hardly be too much longer before he took that final, ancestral journey into the setting sun. He remembered an apparition, sent to haunt him a little while ago. Perhaps it had been a warning that his own little coracle was being prepared by whatever order of beings attended to such matters. Sooner might now be better than later.

'I think your Prime Minister has taken charge of ghosts,' said Foucault behind him.

'Possessed by devils, more likely,' muttered the General bitterly.

'No,' said Foucault seriously. 'I think she commands apparitions. I think she is a witch, that Lady of yours. A witch who is making use of electricity. She is not talking of nuclear weapons but of spectres.'

The General turned to face him, ignoring the hysterical burst of laughter from the foolish girl locked arm in arm with her naïve American boyfriend.

'I think she has discovered a new force,' said Foucault. 'I, too, my friend. . .'

The times were enough to drive most people from their senses, thought McDougal-Planchett. But Foucault . . .? That rational physicist – rational at least on weekdays (on Sundays he went to Mass, and believed in transubstantiation, and prayed to the Holy Trinity). Foucault . . .? The General had spent much of his life pursuing the inexplicable. He had seen a djinn; he had listed tens of thousands of reports of lights in the sky, discs in the sky, 'entities' closer at hand, 'close encounters' between the most ordinary of people and that persistent 'something' which was always weird and sometimes alarming; he had met an apparition in his own living-room not many days before. But Foucault . . .?

'Why is there a warrant for my arrest?' said Foucault angrily. 'Why have they destroyed all copies of my paper in the journal of CERN? Why have they suppressed my article for *Le Figaro*, informing the nation that I, Foucault . . .' (he spluttered with rage) '. . . have been shown a pitiful attempt to convince us that ambassadors from space have come among us?'

Julius began to make a protest. The General quelled him.

'Why has there been so much talk in your own country during the past few days of Men who are Little and Green?'

The General saw that Julie Smith was openly weeping. He frowned, embarrassed. Women tended to have these crises, of course . . . He heard her mutter some word like 'disinform'; it sounded like nonsense.

'Two months ago,' said Foucault, 'I discovered a new principle. Action at a Distance. I found a new particle. I operated upon it. I used the most powerful of the electro-magnetic apparatus which those little *pissoirs* of accountants have permitted us to purchase at CERN. I caused it to take new paths in the photographic emulsion. At the same instant, my friend . . .' He paused for breath, determined to avoid a stroke. 'At the same instant an esteemed colleague – Protestant, it has to be admitted, but competent none the less – detected identical traces in his own apparatus at a distance of seventy kilometres.'

'PROSPERO!' said Julie Smith. She seemed to be sobbing.

The General ignored her. 'So . . .?' he asked.

'So, my friend,' said Foucault, shrugging, suddenly dejected, 'my country . . . my own country . . . the country of St Joan of Arc . . . might well have claimed priority. If petty officials of the State had not suppressed me.' His eyes glistened with anger. 'But now . . .' He raised his arms in a sullen gesture.

' "British skill", "British ingenuity",' said the General, quoting from the Prime Minister's speech. 'You mean that we, too, have got on to this . . . "action at a distance"?' The facts – if facts they were – were far too new to be assimilated. They seemed to have little to do with those persistent oddities which the President of UFORA had spent so much of his life in looking into – and failing to understand.

Julie Smith had gone to pieces. '*British* initiative!' she sobbed hysterically. '*British* skill! He's nothing but a damned Czech!' On the verge of betraying the State to which she had given oaths of secrecy, she was finding the last refuge of her patriotism in a trace of xenophobia.

'A Czech?' said the General, puzzled.

'Zadig. Dr Bruno Zadig.'

'Old "Beezie"? I know him well. He's nearly one of us. I've served with him on committees.'

'PROSPERO!' sobbed Julie Smith. The Calibans of her approaching treachery seemed to be pinching her black and blue. There was no sign yet of any Ariel. She squeezed her sodden handkerchief. ' "Plasmoid Reproduction Over Space" . . .' She broke off.

'Well, that's the PROS bit,' said McDougal-Planchett gently. 'What about PERO?'

She stared solemnly into her lap, holding Julius by the hand. 'PROSPERO. "Plasmoid Reproduction Over Space by Psycho-Electronic Resonance Operations" It's a way of picking up whatever force it is that . . .' She tightened her hand on Julius's. 'Whatever it is that causes that UFO thing, and the sea serpents, and the lake monsters, and Bigfoot, and the "mystery animals", and the poltergeists . . . All that stuff which you and this great slob here and all the rest of you keep trying to find. . .'

Julius embraced her. 'Whoa, girl! Steady, girl!'

'It's nothing worse than lightning,' she said. 'It comes and goes – just like thunderstorms. It's a *natural* thing . . .' She broke off, burying her face in Julius's shoulder.

The General thought of natural things: the catastrophic power of hurricanes, earthquakes, great volcanoes. He thought of Benjamin Franklin, flying his fragile kite into a thunderstorm, collecting its discharge of energy into a little Leyden jar. He thought of one of Franklin's successors, instantly killed when trying the same experiment. 'You mean,' he said – cautiously, pedantically, trying to get into everyday terms what the girl was saying – 'you mean that there's something about the place – the world, the Earth – which . . . produces these things?'

'Yes.'

'And it's as natural as . . . the weather, the Aurora Borealis, a tidal bore, electricity, nuclear power?'

'Yes.'

'But the British government – the British Prime Minister – has got control of it?'

'Yes.'

'Where?'

She shuddered. She wept. The conditioning of MI5 was hard to shrug off.

'Tell us,' said the General gently.

She told them. It pulled her half apart. 'Keisgaig,' she whispered. 'Loch Keisgaig. Ten miles north of here.'

The General stiffly embraced her. 'And you,' he asked gravely, 'where have *you* come from?'

'MI5,' she said, shaking with a kind of ague, turning her head away from Julius.

Julius got up, stumbled backwards in his oversized boots, stared at her with hatred and contempt. 'You fucking Limeys!' he began to shout. 'You bitches! You bastards!' His universe was crumbling. The Shining Ones from Another World had been snatched from him. This little Shining One, here, had been abruptly transfigured to a cheap and sordid tramp of the security services. 'Jesus . . . !' he shouted. (Foucault winced at the blasphemy and crossed himself.) 'Christ Almighty!' Julius stumbled from the room, slamming the door behind him. Outside in the corridor, he could be heard weeping. Through the thick panels of the door the words of his incoherent rage came back to them, muffled and obscured. 'I'll never change my fucking socks again!' he seemed to be shouting.

McDougal-Planchett returned to the window and turned his back. He waited for the girl's storm of tears to weather away into the aftermath of sobs. In the cycle of the ages, in present appalling circumstances, what could this little local tragedy now matter? (Though what else, now that he came to think of it . . .?) He squared his shoulders. 'You have a valid pass to this . . . Keisgaig place?'

'Yes.' She paused. 'But nobody else can use it.'

He would have to make use of *her*, then. . .

The General stared across the sea towards the Isle of Lewis. The misty, November sun was setting. He foresaw journeys which could not now be avoided.

Dr Bruno Zadig stood with his unwelcome guests in the ante-chamber to the control room. Beyond its dark-glass portal the Duke of Washington lay lazily at ease in the surgical chair. Along the corridors on the other side of the antechamber the psycho-electronic multipliers idled at half power.

'The President wants a direct strike at Plesetsk,' said Conrad Friedman, icily polite, menacingly firm. 'I'm sure you guys get the point.' He glanced at the MI5 girl, amused that she was very well known to him but would never remember it. In that truth-drugged sleep in the Bentbridge sick quarters she had given away a great deal to American intelligence. He would almost have been grateful to her if gratitude had formed part of his repertoire.

Zadig uneasily fingered the crumpled instructions in his pocket, recently decoded by his cypher officer. Plesetsk . . . He, too, would have liked an immediate operation against Plesetsk. Intelligence sources were unanimous that Plesetsk was the Russian counterpart of Keisgaig. The disaster at Blandfordness seemed to show beyond doubt that Plesetsk possessed terrifying powers.

He parried, clenching his instructions between damp fingers. 'This is a *British* facility, Mr Friedman.' (Developed, he thought privately, by a very talented Czech.) 'It is the *British* Prime Minister, Mr Friedman, who must take responsibility for the choice of targets.'

'Sure, sure,' said Friedman soothingly, 'but it lies with you guys to give her the right advice.' He slipped a laconic hand into his stylish British jacket. 'The President would take it as a personal favour if you came up with the right decision.'

Zadig sniffed bribery in the wind but knew that he was powerless to make use of it. He wanted, in any case, nothing but the gift of the restored freedom of his own country. It seemed unlikely that this American official, notwithstanding his diplomatic immunity, his secret line to the White House, his apparent influence with the PM and the President, possessed the power to give him the liberty of Bohemia!

'What target *has* she chosen?' said Julie Smith.

Zadig glanced uneasily at her. Whitehall, for reasons best

known to themselves, had saddled him with this 'political officer'. Her pass was entirely in order. He had not even thought it expedient to cross-check her with Buchanan. One had to live with these things. 'Am I at liberty to tell you in the presence of . . . ?' He glanced at Friedman, fervently wishing that a simple scientist could be spared these political embarrassments.

Friedman gave a contemptuous laugh and turned his back. 'In the presence of "*aliens*"?' he shot across his shoulder. 'For God's sake . . . !'

'You can tell us, Dr Zadig,' said the MI5 girl.

Zadig scrunched into a tiny ball the absurd message now lying in his pocket. He went to the dark window which gave on to the control room and stared at the Viscount Lampson, the newly created Duke of Washington. Lampson lay at ease. Zadig envied him. 'Red Square . . .' he murmured, almost beneath hearing.

'Red Square?' said Friedman.

Zadig hunched his shoulders. 'Tomorrow morning,' he said, 'Marshal Zinsky is taking the salute at a march-past of Soviet forces. In Red Square. Outside the Kremlin.'

'So?'

'My instructions are . . .' Could he really tell them? 'My instructions are to make a counter-demonstration. To cause a tank or two to burst into flames. To kill a score or two of infantry. To pick off one or two members of the Politburo . . .'

'While leaving Plesetsk intact?'

Zadig nodded. He dared not tell them that Plesetsk had been ruled out because Lampson refused to 'deal' with it. Lampson claimed to be 'interested' in Plesetsk. Messages had flashed back and forth between Keisgaig and London. ('I can't make him do what he doesn't want to do.' 'What can you make him do, then?')

'Has your Prime Minister hoisted in,' said Friedman, 'that this will trigger the Soviets into massive retaliation? *And* leave them the power to do so?'

'I've had my instructions,' said Zadig mulishly.

Julie Smith intervened. 'There's someone you'd better arrest,' she said curtly. 'The President of UFORA. A dangerous man. He's guessed a great deal too much.'

'Arrest? I've no powers of arrest.'

'I'll cover it.' She paused and stared him into silence. 'Do you want me to ring London?'

Zadig miserably shook his head. His faculty was science. He had not expected to find himself in charge of a prison camp.

Friedman chose this moment to play a card of his own. 'There's another guy I think you'd better pull in. A fellow called Eliot. I'm holding him in my car. Two miles up the road.'

Eliot. Zadig had been warned about John Eliot. He nodded, frowning. (Where the hell could this new captive be stored? He already had some Frensham woman on his hands. And now the President of UFORA . . .)

'And there's some old guy camping out on the banks of the lake,' said Friedman.

But Zadig had had as much as he felt that Keisgaig could take in.

The Duke of Washington rocked his chair idly back and forth, using the control button in its comfortably upholstered arm. The domed ceiling above him, gently illuminated by a source not visible, went forth and back in resonance. It reminded him of those many curved interiors, those hidden chambers at the heart of a multitude of 'vehicles', which humankind had been reporting for some time past. ('They took me up some steps. I was in a sort of capsule. They made me undress. They gave me a medical examination. I was forced to have sexual intercourse against my will.') He gave the mirthless rasp which relieved his flesh of that little tension which humankind called humour.

Dr Zadig had gone away. He seemed to be preparing himself to receive visitors. He had left behind him what he was pleased to call 'instructions' – little quantums of air, vibrated by his vocal chords into particles of man-sense. They had fallen upon the complex (though clumsy) membranes, hammers, bones, nerves, cranial interconnections, aural centres of the neo-cortex, which Lampson was briefly entertained to call his 'sense of hearing'.

Instructions! It was Zadig who took instructions, not the Duke of Washington. Zadig could merely request.

Using quite other faculties than his sense of hearing, Lampson listened to the incessant murmur of the world about him. He felt as though some inner ear was cupped by a great conch. It's

153

labyrinthine channels picked up the energies of a vast sphere which mantled the earth. Lampson floated lazily, luxuriously, in the drifts and eddies of this hyper-zone, masking his inward vision, listening, instead, to the unceasing hiss and crackle of its 'weather-systems'. It resembled, this supersphere, the ocean of air which lapped the terrestrial globe, the oceans of water which lay beneath this atmosphere, the wrinkled and ceaselessly moving skin of the planet itself, the fragile biosphere – that complex and delicate system of all living things – which kept its precarious integrity by an unceasing adjustment to these other forces. Like them, it endlessly shaped and reshaped itself, threw up new forms, created and uncreated prodigies, some as gentle as summer breezes or the lapping of lake water or the flowering of a dandelion, some as terrible as a volcano, a tsunami, a plague of locusts in a country already stricken by famine, some as instantaneous and imper-manent as the blinking of an eye, the flash of a lightning stroke, the tremor of an earthquake, some which endured for the vast clock-tick of a hundred million years like the autocracy of dinosaurs, the slow sedimentation of a Cretaceous sea, the creeping paralysis of a great ice age.

For a moment Lampson was almost possessed by wonder. The power and intricacy of this 'fifth sphere' of the earth, which interpenetrated its other four – the watersphere, the landsphere, the atmosphere, the biosphere – was awesome. It came near to demanding reverence. But 'awe', 'reverence', 'wonder' were – like 'humour' – the mere animal emotions of the little life-form which had, for the moment, come uppermost in the biosphere. Lampson felt no sense of kinship with it.

He became aware that two of these short-lived entities had joined him: the American called Friedman and a female 'political officer' called Smith.

'We've played back the tapes of the Blandfordness . . . incident,' said Friedman curtly.

'Dr Zadig kept a record of them from the monitoring chamber,' said the Smith female.

Lampson wrenched himself reluctantly from the invisible world of the psycho-sphere and stared at his interruptors. He saw that they took care to avoid his eyes.

'Will you do what they've asked you?' said Julie Smith. 'Are you going to play those conjuring tricks in Red Square tomorrow?'

'Those are my . . . instructions,' said Lampson, coming as near to 'humour' as had suited him for some time past.

'What the hell went on at Blandfordness?' said Friedman angrily.

'You tell me you've seen the record,' said Lampson lazily. He closed his eyes again, ending the interview which he had been gracious enough to give them.

They left. He drifted back into the psycho-murmur of the fifth sphere, unmasking vision as well as hearing.

Over the continent of South America, which the sun had not yet reached, the tenuous fluid of the psycho-sphere boiled into tornadoes. Whipped up into local vortices, it whirled saucer-djinns into the innocent lives of a farmer in the Brazilian uplands, a housewife on the ouskirts of Buenos Aires, a couple of vacationing Americans in Venezuela. It had not quite reached the force at which it would turn them into the blue-electric torches of spontaneous combustion. It merely singed their hair, raised purple blotches on their faces, arrested their vehicles, sucked them into saucer visions, gouged up the earth into traces which would remain, for ever, not quite evidential enough for a court of law.

Lampson lazily considered some little intervention of his own which would shape these forces more decisively. He toyed with thoughts of something more entertainingly destructive. But Zadig had left him short of power. Benjamin-Bruno Zadig-Franklin, flying his kite into thunderstorms which he only half understood, was conserving his little witch-technologies for the 'instructions' of his political mistress. The Duke of Washington, likewise, had better wait for that remarkable tomorrow.

Major General McDougal-Planchett (now retired), President of UFORA, was arrested a little before midnight on Friday, 16 November 1990.

Four soldiers, khaki-clad (he was glad to be free of the obsessive mythology of Men in Black), came in an armoured vehicle and took him into custody.

He was nearly apprehended in the full gaze of his butler. But McBean was – mercifully – down in the cellar, searching out new forms of alcoholic solace for Dr Foucault.

Dr Foucault was, alas, rounded up at the same time, together with Julius Ben Caesar Schultz. But the times were difficult. One really couldn't guarantee the immunity of those friends and acquaintances who happened to be with one at the time . . .

On the way to Keisgaig the General, immured with his house-guests in the back of the armour-plated six-wheeler, tried to explain to Julius, by means of the cautious becks and nods which the circumstances made necessary, that his English girlfriend was only doing what the President of UFORA had requested – viz to get him into Keisgaig by whatever device seemed suitable.

But Julius was inconsolable. Civilization was near its end. He had the proof of it in the present state of his most intimate undergarments. The bitch had betrayed him.

Conrad Friedman sent messages to the White House, using the private hot line which the British Prime Minister had been blithe enough to grant him (against the advice of Sir Aleister Buchanan).

Their content was stark and simple.

Blandfordness had not been destroyed by the Russians, it had been destroyed by Viscount Lampson.

Viscount Lampson (as a good American who meant, at all costs, to remain on favourable terms with the Old Cowboy, Friedman had no intention of calling him the Duke of Washington), Viscount Lampson had been given 'powers' by the Brits. His first act had been to attack the USAF installations at RAF Bland-fordness. He had refused to attack Plesetsk. He would probably be causing the Third World War at about 11 a.m. the following morning (Greenwich Mean Time – even the Pentagon would doubtless be able to work out the corresponding times for Moscow and Washington).

Friedman added his strong recommendations for immediate action.

At RAF Bentbridge Colonel Hoyt, judging it inexpedient to consult his British colleague, gave orders for the wheeling out of a serviceable Cruise missile. The President had recently ordered it.

It was relieved of its tarpaulins and cranked up to the right degree of elevation. Squat and bullish as a Minotaur, Hoyt champed on his black cheroot, tilting it skywards at the same proud angle. He gave orders to his crew for the necessary compass bearing. The weapon was swivelled towards the designated target.

A place in Scotland, it seemed. Keisgaig – whatever that might be.

Colonel Hoyt felt grateful that he hadn't been ordered to clobber some English target. Despite those little local difficulties with the farming community, he had grown to be quite fond of the Brits. They had a kind of 'class' which he privately admired. He was glad to be aiming at some remote place which even his vigorous Texan imagination came nowhere near to encompassing.

At 6.27 a.m. Greenwich Mean Time, he pressed the necessary button.

The suave and elegant missile went northwards, hugging the contours of the land. At something a little below supersonic, it would take fifty minutes to get there. It roared across lakes and fells, dipped into valleys, climbed across intervening mountains, causing – to early-morning policemen, Lancashire housewives, hardy fell-walkers, derelict hedge-sleepers – the rumours of an Unidentified Flying Object.

Rocky McClusky, for whom it was still not much past one in the morning, spoke on the hot line to Marshal Zinsky, for whom the day was now well risen.

Marshal Zinsky was being buttoned by attentive aides into the heroic uniform which was tight enough to haul in an old man's paunch, tight enough indeed to come near to strait-jacketing an old man's palsy. In an hour he would be receiving the salute of Soviet forces, held upright by flanking colleagues of the Politburo on the ceremonial platform which overlooked Red Square.

The President reminded the Comrade-Marshal of the cordial *entente* between them. He referred to their recent agreement to stand no nonsense from the British. He implored the Comrade-Marshal to ignore statements made by the British Prime Minister. He assured his old pal Ivan that Uncle Sam was about to blast out of existence a troublesome British facility in the north of Scotland.

Marshal Zinsky could hardly believe his luck. The Americans were about to perform for him – free, gratis and without complaint – a troublesome act which his advisers had recently been pressing: the destruction of the one and only facility in the West which seemed capable of matching Plesetsk. It gave him the confidence to hang shakily about his neck, repudiating the patronizing hand of his private secretary, the great and glittering gewgaw of the Order of Lenin. Conscious of the march of history, he prepared himself to receive the plaudits of the People's armies.

McClusky put down the phone. He had done well. Around the Oval Office there was a groundswell of approval. Tomorrow, he could go back to the ranch, growl his fellow-feeling at the splendid young bullocks now in rut, have another tremulous go at Maisie, leaving behind him the firm smack of a Presidential decision that Plesetsk should receive a hundred megatons of American displeasure as soon as Keisgaig had blossomed into its own magic mushroom of sweet release.

The Duke of Washington lay peacefully in semi-sleep. His eyes were open. His breathing rose and fell, as regularly as the ebb and flow of wavelets on a Pacific shore.

He never dreamed. In a sense, his whole existence was a kind of dreaming. Between dreaming and other states of existence he made no distinction. But there came to him in his open-eyed half-consciousness the shadow show of some other creature, two thousand miles to the east (for whatever 'miles' might matter). It gazed at him with deep-set eyes below a jutting forehead, above prognathous jaws. Its look was mournful; moistures gathered below its optical jellies; it seemed near to weeping. Lampson detected that it had not yet done its duty to the State. A chatter of little monkeys rose up from some experimental menagerie not far from this creature's resting-place; he had not yet killed them. In fact, he had done nothing yet. The death of Blandfordness owed nothing to him; that little exercise had been a playful limbering-up on Lampson's part. He had not even (Lampson now perceived) wielded that electro-magnetic sword above Keisgaig Loch. That and the space disaster of 1 November remained mysterious. But mysteries did not trouble the Duke of Washington; he knew that they were merely minor oddities of which he would presently take the measure.

Across the Grampion Mountains, tilting effortlessly upward to clear their topmost peak, a sleek, suave missile, cheerfully named 'Donald Duck' by the crew which had serviced it, hurtled towards Keisgaig at a speed of Mach Point Nine.

8
The Possessed

Conrad Friedman hammered his fists against the harsh, steel wall of the control room. Hysterical with rage and fear, he left scarlet traces of his haemoglobin on its polished surface. His knuckles were bloody with disillusion.

'Ungrateful bastards!' he whimpered. 'For chrissakes . . .' He choked on his lack of language, glaring with unseeing eyes at the Duke of Washington. Foam flecked his mouth.

'Did you expect *gratitude*?' said Lampson, twitching his pale features into the imitation of a smile.

Friedman groped for words. Something – anything – to enrich the wretched poverty of that 'Sorry, pal . . .' which had squawked down his private line from Washington a quarter of an hour ago.

'Sorry, pal . . .' The tinny yawp of a back-room colonel in the Pentagon. Not even the White House . . . Not even a Chief of Staff . . .

Shakily, Friedman withdrew the gun from his chest-holster, uncertain what target he meant it for. For thirty years he had lied, cheated, plotted, subverted, assisted at a little torture, for the sake of Uncle Sam, for the sake of Democracy. And they couldn't even grace him with a touch of funeral-parlour rhetoric! 'Sorry, pal, it's going skywise in fifteen minutes. Advise you get the hell out.' Christ! He had done a damn sight better for the old hag, his wife's mother, before combusting her in a casket far prettier than Keisgaig! If the President of the United States had been present, Friedman would have shot him. He waved the gun vaguely in Lampson's direction.

' "Ingratitude, thou marble-hearted fiend . . .",' said Lampson, pleased with the sonorities. He turned his inward ear to the megaton of ingratitude now swiftly approaching from the south-east. It would be here within ten minutes.

Friedman held the gun before him, clasping it with both hands to stop it shaking. He pointed it at Lampson's heart, wrenching up the only language now left to him. 'Fuck up that fucking thing! You bleeding know how to do it!' Sweat ran down his forehead, scalding his eyes. 'You fucked up that fucking thing of ours in Suffolk . . . Fuck up that fucking Cruise!' He released the safety-catch. 'I'll fucking kill you if you don't!' He had passed beyond logic into the mere animal appetite of living a little longer.

Lampson ignored him. He searched along the psycho-sphere for the electro-magnetic heart of the approach-death and found it. It delicately ticked away the microseconds, sensing the terrain below it, hunting for the right compass-bearing, adjusting itself from moment to moment to its God-given, Hoyt-given, purposes, preparing to release its detonation system. It was a lowly kind of being, but a being none the less. Its heart was of silicon, not marble. It knew less than Lampson of 'gratitude' and 'ingratitude'. There was nothing more 'fiendish' to it than the programmed intention of a whippet to pursue hares, a spider to spin webs, a shark to sever limbs. But it possessed a modicum of consciousness as well as a superabundance of will; it had a trace of 'mind'. In search of this mind or will, entertained by its sophisticated simplicity, Lampson began to grope with the psycho-threads of his own intention.

Released by Julie, John Eliot and Lucy Frensham raced along corridors, stumbled down companionways, headed in desperate haste for the steel heart of Keisgaig. Thirty feet behind them, McDougal-Planchett struggled to keep up, his heart pounding, his old limbs aching. On an upper level, far above them, Julius Schultz and Dr Foucault restrained Bruno Zadig, gagging him with a strip torn from his own shirt – two aliens in charge of a third: an American and a Frenchman diffidently silencing a Czech.

'Get the power off! Stop Lampson at all costs,' Julie had gabbled at them. 'Red Square!' she had shouted. 'If he does what the Cabinet's told him. . .'

John was armed with a fire axe, wrenched from the wall as they ran. He had thrust Lucy away but found her following him.

They came to a steel-girt corridor, a hundred feet below the surface. Bank upon bank of equipment flanked it on either side.

'That's his power!' shrieked Lucy, reeling from some field of force which thrust at her from the steel-fronted cabinets. She sensed, scarcely a dozen yards beyond the bland surface of these nameless boxes, another tremendous energy, the fifty million gallons of Loch Keisgaig, descending to a thousand feet below them, pressing upon the concrete labyrinth of the station. 'Smash his power!' she shouted.

John swung his axe, dented the steel door of the nearest cabinet, saw that he would have to labour like Hercules to break into it, counted another fifty of these daunting, safelike shells, paused for a fatal moment.

Along a side gallery to their left ran a platoon of soldiers, rifles at the ready. The swift staccato of their left-right, left-right startled the steel tunnels into echoes which fell like hammer blows. 'Run!' shouted Lucy.

They sprinted along the corridor towards doors of blackened glass. Behind them, the General, a commando by training, forgetting the absurdities of age, flung himself to the ground, suffered the onrush of iron-clad boots, felt a rib splinter, repaid it with the savage joy of finding a dozen infantry tumbling into confusion about him, scattering rifles which bounced and clattered on the concrete floor.

John smashed the black-glass doors, thrust himself through, fell into the control room, bleeding from a jagged wound across his cheek.

He came face to face with Friedman.

Bloody face and bloody knuckles confronted each other. Friedman was armed with a gun. Beyond his shoulder stood a weirdish creature which John had not yet met. Its white hair fell to shoulder length, its albino eyes stared through him and beyond him to some other target.

'That's him!' shrieked Lucy.

John stared again at Friedman, keeping the axe behind him. He was ready to die for the sheer satisfaction of cleaving the skull of this commonplace little torturer who had recently tormented him into treason. Lampson meant nothing to him.

'John!' shouted Lucy on a high note of desperation. 'The other one . . . For God's sake, the other one . . .'

Behind them in the corridor the warning siren of the Keisgaig Station was ululating towards hysteria.

John edged past Friedman turning his face into the rictus of a sickly smile. He came to the pale-eyed creature. He raised his axe.

Friedman shot him in the back.

The bullet passed a little above the heart. It would kill him by and by. But not for a while yet.

John Eliot crumpled quietly to the floor. He had done his best, he supposed. His life began to unfold itself before some inward eye – rather slowly and surprisingly peacefully. He found that an 'angel' had taken him about the shoulders. Her tears fell upon his upturned face. He found that they were warm and somewhat salty.

Lampson glanced at the creature lying on the floor. It was certainly out of action; it would cease to function before too long. A female of its species had laid its head in her lap. Water drops ran down her cheeks. She, too, would be harmless enough for a little while.

He stared at the American. But the American had gone to pieces. The American knelt on the floor, monomaniacally muttering some group of phonemes which had to do with the propagation of his species.

Lampson picked up the American's gunpowder-tube, still charged with leaden slugs, and tossed it into the rubbish dispenser. The mindless mechanism gulped it out of existence.

Lampson spared a moment for irony. 'Irony' contained 'humour', which he disdained to understand. But it also encapsulated 'structures' of a more mathematical kind. He was pleased with the symmetry of recent events. Some little group of *Homo sapiens* wanted him out of existence lest he should perform foolish tricks – fatal tricks – in a 'red square' somewhere to their east. Another of their kind was desperate to keep him living – had threatened him with death, indeed, in order to keep him alive! – so that he could use his talents on the megadeath which now lay at a hundred seconds' distance.

Lampson looked into the little 'mind' of the approaching missile. He briefly admired its brutish convolutions; somebody –

some team of somebodies – had spent much ingenuity in designing the complexities of its idiot-soul.

He allowed the hundred seconds to weather into ninety. In a minute and a half Keisgaig would boil skywards.

The minute-and-a-half dwindled towards a minute. Time (for what it was worth) ticked out its remorseless course. Lampson came near to enjoying some idiosyncrasy of the flesh which depended upon postponement.

Sixty seconds became thirty, thirty became fifteen.

Lampson glanced up with his pale eyes through layer upon layer of Keisgaig's earth and steel and concreate. He communed for a moment longer with the entity above him, then flicked it lazily towards another destiny.

Jake, waiting for the November sunrise, saw prodigies above him. A dark angel out of the Pit screeched towards him from the southern mountains, jetting hell-fire, hunching its stubby pinions to its sides. He screwed up his eyes in terror, searching for the memory of whatever sins had come to damn him. He groped for his great bible but could not find it; it lay five hundred miles away in a Suffolk pine wood. He began to pray, half opening his eyes again, waiting for clawed hands to seize him or for the Lord to snatch him into redemption.

A glowing cloud of some stringy substance had suddenly enmeshed the demon. The demon was jerked sideways, tumbled into zig-zag madness, slewed round towards the constellation of The Bear. As Jake watched it, it shrieked away towards the north with the banshee-wail of a Suffolk phantom, riding upwards towards The Bear at a crazy angle.

With trembling hands, not noticing what he was doing, Jake turned the key on a metal box of Pilchards in Tomato Sauce, raking his memory for some guidance from the Book of Revelation. The death of Cat came back to him with unexpected force. A rheumy tear ran down Jake's cheek.

Above him, the glowing cloud pulsated. It was formed of a multitude of snakelike threads, writhing and hissing in the sky. It seemed to rotate upon a hidden centre, suggesting the shape of a great disc or wheel. Then features of a face began to form. Angelic hair to shoulder length, great eyes of staring whiteness, the face of the Great Lord come in Judgement. Jake whimpered, munching pilchards without knowing it, performing some miracle of the fishes without benefit of a loaf. Then, as he watched it, the face softened towards something womanish. A Lady of Mercy began to form. Jake was too good a Presbyterian to suppose that it might be the Blessed Mary. She seemed to smile. Her features resembled those of the kind lady who had thievishly equipped him with a sackful of tinned manna. She carried something in her hands, extending it towards him. It was Cat. Cat somnolent, Cat sleeping, Cat peacefully digesting some celestial meal. In the shadowy resurrection of Cat Jake saw symptoms of his own salvation.

Even by the pre-dawn light he detected that the surface of the lake was now in motion. Wavelets ran across it, intersected, formed troughs and billows, bounced the shining interface into incessant movement like the tremulous skin of a great creature awaiting the onset of an ague.

Lucy cradled the dying head of John Eliot in her lap. She seemed to hear the little murmur of his ebbing life. It came directly into her mind like whispers picked up from the heart of the galaxy by the great dish of Jodrell Bank. Invisible energies surrounded her. She reasonated with them, was enlarged by them, drifted with their tides and currents, was eddied into some new world which lay only a whisker's distance beyond the little nutshell of the ordinary – and was separated from it by walls which the daily grind of the ordinary caused to become as impenetrable as steel.

But the steel walls of Keisgaig had become transparent. Sustained by the energies of the new sphere (*ancient* sphere, sphere as old as the earth itself) into whose weather-systems Bruno Zadig had had the bravado to fly his fragile kite, Lucy Frensham – Lucy Fr . . . 'that female Lucifer', perhaps 'Lucifera', daughter of the morning, inheritor of the radiant – penetrated the impenetrable walls. Beyond them she found other faces, other minds. Minds as simple and innocent as the 'systems-intelligence' of a Titan missile in Colorado waiting for the metal cork of its djinn-bottle to be unstoppered so that it might follow its destiny towards Plesetsk. Minds as strangely peaceful as the mind of a mongoloid baby born

– by the ironies of synchronicity – to a Mongol mother in Outer Mongolia. The minds of murderers. The minds of saints. The mind of some much larger thing . . . (But from this she drew back in fear.) The mind of an old man munching Pilchards in Tomato Sauce on the banks of a loch.

She hunted after other faces, knowing that she must come face-to-face with them – though 'face' was no longer the word she wanted. She found the 'face-mind', 'mind-face', of Lem. His dwarfish, large-skulled countenance was heavy with sorrow. For this sorrow she loved him; his sorrow was a guarantee of a sense of proportion – as much as his sense of humour might have been in other circumstances. (She saw that, in other circumstances, he would have had a Ukrainian sense of humour.) 'Lem,' she murmured, 'do what you must do.' She was not quite sure what he must do; the world was far too complex for any single mind; but she had a feeling that he would soon know.

She came to another mind, another face. Its hair came down to shoulder length, its eyes were pale. She had met it once before. Then, on the road from Domrémy, it had looked like an angel. It had told her – that mere child of sixteen years – that she had a mission and a destiny. She had trusted it – and died a terrible death by fire at Rouen four years later. It was the face of Cro-Magnon man, that cruel and beautiful race of *Homo sapiens* which had trampled out of existence the ugly and gentle Neanderthalers. It was the face of the Duke of Washington.

She saw that Lampson was staring at her. His eyes dizzied her. She was drawn into their pallid depths. His voice reverberated in her head. 'You, too, are gifted . . . You and that other . . . We have a destiny, we three . . . Nothing is impossible to us . . .' Deep within her, Lucy felt the surge of some tremendous force. They were creators, she and this other being. They had come into the possession of a limitless reservoir of power. The same power which 'thought' and 'unthought' all possibilities on the face of the globe. The same vast mind in whose imagination there flickered endlessly the dreams of all possibles and nearly-possibles in the humbler spheres of the material; which had 'thought' the great saurians (and then 'unthought' them); had invented the mammalian; had brought into being Neanderthal and then Cro-Magnon man; had made spiders, tigers, sharks, the duck-billed platypus, the rabies virus, the domestic cat; dreamed endlessly of all potential forms; kept in reserve (and might, in some approaching aeon, thrust into becoming) the shapes of the beautiful and monstrous which haunted the visions of the two-legged life-form to which it had, for the moment, granted a fragile primacy.

'You have a destiny,' said Lampson's voice again. 'You have a mission.'

He had said so once before. She had died by fire. Listening to the thready heartbeat of John's departing life, Lucy found that she preferred it. She remembered a moment of physical ecstasy, lying side by side with him on an August evening in the Sussex Downs, some time before the ordinary had tarnished him. She searched along the psycho-sphere for others of her own kind – an elderly Major General, now in the uncertain custody of soldiers; an American, a Czech, a Frenchman, a girl called Julie Smith whose face had been scorched in a Suffolk mansion by the parlour-dabbling in greater matters by one, Lord Lampson.

She willed these psycho-kin to come and find her, thrusting out of mind the temptations of the tempter-Lampson. From some-where a great way eastwards there came to haunt her the sad face of a Neanderthal man. Under the domed skull and above prognathous jaws the dark and mournful eyes reproached her.

Bruno Zadig came down the companionway into his psycho-electronic corridor of power. Julius Schultz and Dr Foucault flanked him. Julie Smith followed close behind, covering him with a well-concealed revolver. Zadig knew what he must do. He would die if he didn't.

They came level with Zadig's troops, re-forming themselves into soldierly good order in a side gallery, pinioning the old fool who had thrown them into disarray, causing him – with more than minimum force – to assist them with their enquiries.

'Release him!' whispered Julie sharply behind Zadig's back.

Zadig gave curt orders. The General joined them bruised and wheezing, clasping a hand to his damaged ribs. The soldiers came to attention, poised for further orders, possessed by a discipline as mindless as any Titan's.

'Now get the power off,' muttered Foucault, pressing Zadig's elbow, glancing across Zadig's shoulder at his other captor. The steel cabinets flanked them on either side, softly humming with their secret properties.

'I need to start from the control room end,' said Zadig sullenly, his head lowered, his bony fingers nervously interlocked.

They marched him along the corridor towards the smashed doors. Friedman, with the face of a mad dog, abruptly confronted them. Friedman, now locked into endless nightmare, knew that the Bentbridge missile was still approaching. Instant by instant its megadeath drew nearer. He knew nothing of Lampson's conjuring trick. He knew only that Lampson was his one salvation. He would kill to keep it. He groped for his revolver but failed to find it.

Zadig came to the doors of the control room. He pulled out of his pocket the portable mini-safe, slim as a woman's powder-compact, which guarded the key to the control panel. He shakily turned its dial to the succession of numbers which would open it, extracted the key, fumbled it into the lock of the steel door which hid the fifty switches to his banks of multipliers.

Friedman leapt for his throat. They grappled savagely and fell to the floor.

Julie Smith pulled out her gun and aimed it. She had been trained to kill. It was one of the necessities of the patriotic trade she had become apprenticed to. She had shot many bulls-eyes in the back-room shooting-galleries of MI5. ('Not bad for a woman,' they had told her.) She tried to squeeze the trigger but failed to do so. The 'targets' were a bit uncertain . . . They rolled about the floor like rabid animals. Which should she kill . . .? What, in any case, would killing accomplish . . .? If she killed Zadig, which of them would then know what to do with Zadig's equipment? If she killed Friedman . . .?

Friedman seemed, in logic, the right target. She tried again to fire the revolver, and again failed.

The face of another woman gazed out at her through the broken doors – a face encountered when she had been 'casing' Lantern House; encountered again in brief moments of consciousness in the sick quarters of an American base. 'Kill him,' said the voice of this woman, thrusting directly into her mind. 'Stop them . . . At all costs, it must be stopped . . .'

She fired the revolver, aiming for Friedman's ankle, shattering Zadig's femur instead.

Friedman dragged Zadig across the threshold into the control room. Troops thundered down the corridor, knowing their duty. The conspirators were taken into custody.

Presently, they were frog-marched skywards towards a grim little blockhouse on the southern skyline above Loch Keisgaig which did duty as an ammunition store. Lucy Frensham and the dying John Eliot were taken with them. By and by they would be shot to death (a pleasanter fate than burning) – but not until the Director of the Keisgaig Station had given the neccessary orders. These faithful troops would have broken them on the wheel if ordered; or hanged them; or burned them to death. But shooting was administratively more convenient; it was the current fashion in the part of the planet they happened to inhabit. They kept their rifles cocked, awaiting orders.

In the bowels of the Keisgaig Station Lampson, noting that Zadig had been crippled out of action and that Friedman was derelict with madness, prepared himself for his next conjuring trick. Sensing into the psycho-sphere, he found nothing but approval for what he now intended.

9

The Possessor

Lem lay in his cloudy Ganz-field, suffering from 'ethical block' – suffering also from the minor torments with which Birkov had tried to shift it: deprivation of sleep, a short spell on Sulfazine, the deliberate killing of a little Rhesus monkey in his presence to get him used to the idea of killing. Worse things had been threatened – for the sake of Historical Necessity – but the Comrade-Surgeon had been against them: there was a risk of damaging Lem's talent; he needed to be motivated, not mutilated.

Lem would have enjoyed the ironies of the paradox in which the comrades found themselves if he had felt well enough. But he was now feverish and desperately tired. He was also greatly puzzled. That white-haired creature towards the west had done nothing yet to trouble the peace-loving masses. He had merely crippled some Western establishment in Suffolk, then paralysed an American missile. He had sent no phantoms against Plesetsk. And it was now clear to Lem that he had had nothing to do with the disaster to SOYUZ-27 and its American counterpart. (What had? he wondered.)

'Shall we send you back to a mental hospital, comrade?' said Birkov's voice, somewhere behind his head.

Lem nodded, foolishly giggling.

'Or to a labour camp, comrade?' said the Comrade-Surgeon.

Lem thought of the appalling coldness of those northern places, where a man's breath made ice-crystals before his face, froze his tears before there was time to weep them, transformed his urine into rods of ice as it fell to the steel earth. Yet the planet had made such places . . . For reasons of its own . . . and had colonized them with forms invented for its purpose: wolves and great mammoths, fur-clad bears, a snowy panther with sabre teeth, a certain kind of biped, Lem's own kith, who had lived out their gentle and magical lives until some Siberian summer morning, when there came from the south a white-haired, pale-eyed kind of man which had dragged them from their caves and stockades, slaughtered them with left-hemisphere dispassion (disdaining even to rape their womenfolk), stolen their magic to make a kind of science, thrust into oblivion these dwarfish fools who were humbly learning to understand the globe they lived on.

'A prison camp?' said Lem, ancestrally shuddering. Above him, in a sky violet with cold, there shimmered the Aurora Borealis. Its insubstantial pageant flickered with new forms and figures as the seconds passed. Its curtains of electro-magnetic energy streamed in the firmament. He sensed his way into the new globe about him and felt a kinship with it.

'Or shall we attend to your fingernails?' said Birkov.

Lem giggled, knowing that mere pain would be as much a shield as sexual desire against the terrors of the brave new world in which he floated. He almost craved for pain – or pleasure. Any such vigorous stimulation of the senses would protect him from the greater knowledge which pressed upon his mind (whatever 'mind' might be).

He sensed that the two creatures next to him were not yet ready for these illuminations. In a little while they would be – in ten thousand lifetimes, perhaps . . . But not yet, it seemed.

He felt his way along the channels of some new mode of feeling which he called the 'psycho-sphere', a term which came to him from some bourgeois deviation which lay westwards. But its provenance hardly mattered . . .

'His mind is wandering again,' said the Comrade-Surgeon sharply. Lem felt the jab of a hypodermic needle and a surge of fiery ecstasy along his veins. It swept him further into the ocean of the supersphere.

A moment of illumination came, dazzling as a great light. Lem saw with joy and terror a multitude of forms. Types and prototypes; dreams and actualities; the shapes of all things which had ever come into existance or might one day do so. The monstrous and the gentle, the winged and the four-footed, the beautiful and shapely, the grotesque and terrible. Winged lizards and water-lizards, the half-existent denizens of the world's great lakes and oceans, the fully existent saurians and reptiles, were-panthers and panthers-real, the multitude of the two legged, some granted for the moment the mere shadowy semi-life of the wendigo and the yeti, others permitted – for a while – to imbue the brute chemistry of the flesh with temporary form.

'Angels and devils!' said Lem aloud, mumbling thickly through numbed lips. Sounds came to him of some cold and bitter quarrel between Birkov and the Comrade-Surgeon, but he ignored it. Angels and devils had come to haunt him.

There flickered before him two kinds of creature, both walking erect upon two feet, one tall and shapely, seductive to humankind (even to dwarfish folk with black-browed, non-Aryan features), the other squat and greenish, lipless and with pointed ears, repulsive to mammalian flesh. The first had the look of St Gabriel or St Michael. Its hair was long and its eyes pale. Lem knew that this saintly and evil figment of the world's imagination had come into partial existence some tens of thousands of years before. It had wreaked havoc on his own kind, though they had come a little way to domesticating it, partly by magic (when they could escape burning as witches), partly by interbreeding (when marriage laws were not passed against them). The other creature came from much further back. It had never yet – perhaps never would – be granted the precarious 'reality' of *Homo sapiens*. But it had haunted *Homo sapiens* throughout history.

'What do you see?' said Birkov harshly. Lem felt the pudgy little hand of Birkov striking him across the face. Mammalian flesh. Mammalian cruelty. What would those others have been like had they come to being?

Lipless and green.

Large-eyed and pointed-eared.

Never much more than three and a half feet high.

Coming to *Homo sapiens* in the guise of demons.

Lem laughed aloud with the paradox of finding this alien flesh far more congenial to him than the half-Neanderthal squatness of Birkov, the wholly Cro-Magnon and bony blondness of the Comrade-Surgeon.

These greenish little entities were the near-existent progeny of the forgotten saurians. They would have been – if the dispassionate and terrible imagination of the world had permitted – the descendants of some little dinosaur which had learned to walk upon two legs, to sharpen its wits, to cultivate some warmness of the blood, to nurture its young within a body cavity, to hide from *Tyrannosaurus Rex*, to look upwards at the universe. They might have burned fewer witches; might not have tempted a Joan of Arc; might have scraped along with a beetle-browed form of the mammalian biped. Instead, their 'reality' was of the same kind as lake-monsters, trolls, elves, the dragonish inhabitants of the atmosphere, the half-pantherine, half-wolvish monstrosities which degutted cattle on remote farms. They merely flickered on the edge of being, these little greenish ones. They haunted the dreams and nightmares of the other kind of flesh which had supplanted them. From time to time they found a fleeting half-existence when the psycho-sphere whirled itself into the local vortices of globes and saucers. And always they, in turn, were haunted by those saintly entities which grew hair instead of scales and knew far better how to corrupt mankind.

Lem came abruptly face to face with one of those seductive tempters. It hovered among the weather-systems of the psycho-sphere two thousand miles to the west. Its eyes were pale. Its hair came down to shoulder length. There sprouted from its back the gorgeous panoply of feathery white pinions. Searching into its mind, Lem suffered a Siberian coldness. His blood came near to feezing; he had a vision of his own mammalian system of veins and arteries transformed into a tree of scarlet ice. Sensing what Lampson intended, Lem knew that he must stop him.

Little and green. Not quite men. Lampson sensed them all around him. He had made use of them before. He knew how to conjure them. They squeaked and gibbered like little bats, craving for existence.

Lampson unscarfed his local vision and glanced around him. Zadig was whimpering on the floor with a fractured leg. Along the corridor beyond the doors of the control room, Zadig's machines were humming on full power. Friedman had curled up into a foetal position, his eyes closed, his mind suspended.

Lampson soared again into the empyrean of his power. He brushed aside his greenish minions, knowing that he had no further use for them. He focused his mind on the city of Moscow, found the onion domes of the Kremlin, settled towards the tottering Marshal Zinsky, prepared himself to inflict spectral damage.

He spared a moment – almost one of warm-blooded 'humour' – to stall the engines of the aerial pope-mobile in which the British Prime Minister was now descending upon Wembley Stadium. She tumbled the last twenty feet to the indignity of a broken neck, shedding the great coiffure to reveal a head completely bald.

He spared another moment to confirm that a Titan missile had been launched from Colorado and was now at the peak of its strato-spheric arc, prepared to fall upon Plesetsk within half a minute.

The end of the world seemed imminent – or, more accurately, the beginning of a new one. Lampson felt like Lucifer, son of the morning. The world lay in the hollow of his hand. Not even the mournful gaze of some black-browed, crag-faced, non-Aryan creature, lying two thousand miles to the east, could now detain him.

Jake stumbled on elderly legs among the lakeside heather. Mr Seventeen came hard at heel, flapping nervous wings, contriving to look like a very small and very grubby angel. The surface of the lake had heaved itself up into tremendous billows. They broke upon its shores with a sound like thunder, casting spray and spume a hundred feet into the air. Jake no longer liked the look of them.

He wheezed his rheumaticky way upwards, climbing towards a concrete blockhouse. He knew that he would find company there. He had watched half a dozen people, one of them carried on a stretcher, being conveyed there by other kindly people wearing uniforms.

He clambered up the last wheezy slope, grabbing Mr Seventeen with a firm hand, shoving the head of Mr Seventeen beneath his jacket to shut up his nervous chatter.

Behind them, Loch Keisgaig boiled into fury. A vast and shadowy hand burst through its turbulent surface, clasping a lambent sword of crackling energy.

Lem heard death approaching from above. Now in the last

seconds of their vast trajectory across half the world, megatons of power descended. He heard the planet shriek with terror, sensing the fall of this Titan's hammer-blow upon its fragile bones.

Lem was seized with a colossal anger. The long aeons of all that his kind had ever suffered from the left-brain arrogance of Aryan man scorched into fury along his nerves and sinews. He called up every torment and indignity inflicted by black shirts and blond faces and turned them into a fireball of ancestral rage. The fifty thousand years of their appalling tyranny flowed through him in a microsecond, pouring their cruelties like molten metal into the mould of the weapon he was forging.

Around him in the great globe of the psycho-sphere there squeaked and gibbered the psycho-babble of the LGM. He felt them as more than kin.

His exhausted and tormented frame was convulsed with the white heat of his hatred. He knew that it would kill him but felt nothing but a savage joy. There came to him abruptly the pallid eyes of an angelic Aryan, two thousand miles to the west. Lem thrust his lightning into the psycho-sphere.

In his dying moments Dr Bruno Zadig – a conscientious Czech who had done his damnedest for Bohemia – saw that a weird destiny had overcome the Duke of Washington. Lambent flames of an intense bluish colour licked up and down his man-shaped form. His long blond hair went up like tinder. His head shrivelled. A moment later his skull split with a sharp crack. His trunk and limbs crumbled into something as black and oily as burnt molasses, stinking of sulphur. He shrieked his way out of existence, lapped in fire, surrounded by the forms of little, greenish creatures. It might have been called a Spontaneous Human Combustion except that there was nothing too human about the Duke of Washington, and nothing much which could be called 'spontaneous'.

He fell to the floor, a torch ignited by flames which were not too different from those which had sent to her death in 1431 the Maid of Orleans.

A short while after, the waters of Loch Keisgaig thrust the force of their fifty million gallons into the hidden chambers and galleries of the PROSPERO station. They battered down its puny walls and sizzled with a shrieking hiss the impotent little cabinets of Zadig's technology.

A microsecond before the raging waters choked him back into mere potentiality, Zadig glimpsed the vision of a great hand far above him, lifting some emblem to the sky. He saw it, with patriotic fervour, as the hand of certain Bohemian saint which had once promised his countryfolk their liberty.

Property.

Lucy saw that they were property.

Sometimes madness possessed them, but they were possessed for ever by something much larger than mere madness.

She lay with John Eliot in the May sunshine on a hillside above Jodrell Bank, and gently touched the fatal wound, a little above his heart, which had failed to kill him. She, too, had properties. They came to her from that larger thing. She drew on its qualities of mercy, healing a lover. ('I love you,' said John.)

'Property'. A rich word. It meant 'possessions', things owned. ('You're *my* property now, girl,' Julius had said chauvinistically to Julie Smith, catching her on the rebound from the outraged arms of MI5.) It meant the places where people lived and had their being. Houses. Mansions. (' "In my Father's house are many mansions",' Foucault had quoted, primly pious, after they had fled from the terrors of Keisgaig to the General's stony manse.) Houses, even shacks . . . Even some tumble-down, leafy cabin in Rendlesham Forest where an old man foraged for twenty pigeons.

Below them in the Cheshire valley the great eye of Jodrell swivelled in its metal socket, patiently surveying the universe for those few of its properties which it had been trained to see.

Properties . . . some of them as dispassionately terrible as the force of a tempest . . .

The world had not much changed since that November of 1990. A Prime Minister had died; another, not much less over-simple though more securely haired, had taken her place. A cowboy President was preparing himself for re-election with little time to spare except for bullocks and razzamatazz and a casual decision on star-wars weapons. A Comrade-Marshal of the Soviet Union doddered his senile way into total possession by the apparatus which he imagined he controlled. Vast armaments confronted each other across lines drawn on a map. There was again much talk of 'Historical Necessity' and 'Democratic Values'. But an incident or two had taken place which puzzled the back-room planners and caused them, on occasion, to talk to each other on private walks in the woods above Vienna. It was said that a place called Plesetsk was still as deep as a hundred feet in some stringy substance which had smothered a weapon falling upon it, choking to death the whole of its complement of men and monkeys. It was said that this substance closely resembled the thready net which had engulfed SOYUZ-27 and MICKEY-III on the eve of that strange November. There was an uncertain feeling among aides and advisers that some new – or perhaps very ancient – property of the world had declared itself. They were not too sorry to see the destruction of Plesetsk and Keisgaig: those fortunate events had left them free to pursue the game of supremacy by technologies they understood. But there was an uneasiness abroad that other properties existed. And that they were not yet under control. And might prove to be as elusive and alarming as the tendency of the ecosphere to compensate for the mere use of an insecticide in Arizona by imposing a fatal drought in Ethiopia.

Above her in the early-summer dusk Lucy saw a globe of orange light. It was a partially formed event, a mere piece of meteorology, perhaps even a weather-balloon or the planet Venus, shimmered towards the reddish end of the spectrum by the intervening air. As she watched it, it took a more definite shape. Revolving upon itself, it formed a saucer. There was a dome above it, a shallower hemisphere below. It settled towards the ground, casting a beam of brilliant light. Down this shaft of radiance there floated little greenish creatures. 'Help us,' they seemed to say. (The thoughts came directly into her head.) 'Help us to come to being.'

Lucy felt an uneasy kinship with them. She took John Eliot by the arm and went forward to meet them. They seemed to possess – she was certain of it – some secret property of the world which she and her kind could hardly lose by knowing.

Afterword

Spectres are haunting Europe . . . yet everywhere they are in chains.

For nearly forty years – since that first sighting in 1947 of what Kenneth Arnold to our misfortune called 'flying saucers' – not only Europe but the world in general has undergone wave upon wave of what may prove to be the most remarkable visitations in human history. Nobody who takes the trouble to read the literature of this subject (and to winnow out the chaff of its lunatic fringe) can be in any doubt that humankind is a haunted species.

On 24 June 1947 Kenneth Arnold, Acting Deputy United States Marshal and member of an aerial search and rescue organization in the western part of the United States, was searching for a missing aircraft. He was flying near Mount Rainier in the State of Washington, that north-westerly state of the USA which we in the United Kingdom tend to confuse with the Federal capital, DC. In that mountainous region, which recently saw the eruption of St Helen's (perhaps the most daunting exhibition within living memory of the hidden powers of our planet), Kenneth Arnold saw 'saucers'. He reported – doubtless with the same sense of absurdity as grips all of us who come near to such things – that he had seen nine disclike objects travelling at well over a thousand miles per hour. In 1947 no nation on earth possessed *that* kind of technology.

The press were delighted with Arnold's description of these objects. He had called them 'saucers'. 'Saucer' fits very readily into headlines and it has the kind of comfortable cosiness which enables us to domesticate the unknown. It is also convenient as a term of abuse or ridicule if we later wish to repent of our first credulity. 'Little green men' serves the same purpose. 'Little' is a handy means of cutting the marvellous down to size; and 'green' is a form of pigmentation which *all* races can agree to find ridiculous. ('Men' is perhaps a questionable assumption, but doubtless a comforting one.)

Since 1947 several hundred thousand reports have been made of unusual objects seen in the sky or closer at hand. Most can be explained in conventional terms: they are nothing more disturbing than the faulty perception of stars, planets, unusual clouds, meteorological balloons, civil and military aircraft, orbital vehicles, satellite re-entries . . . The twentieth-century sky is rich with debris. But there remains a hard core of sightings (estimated to lie between one thousand and ten thousand in the past forty years) for which no conventional explanation is possible.

These 'high strangeness' sightings have been reported from all countries for which records exist: from China, from the Soviet Union (until the authorities suppressed the non-governmental groups a year or two ago), from Africa, both black and white, from North and South America, from Australasia, from all European countries on both sides of the Iron Curtain. These reports are made by a wide range of people, most of them of obvious competence and common sense, many of them trained observers, including policemen, airline pilots, scientists and other professionals, and very few of them with any obvious motive for inventing the hardly believable stories they have to tell. Indeed, many of them are reluctant to speak, and the cost of doing so is often enough ridicule from friends and family and damage to a career. It is only a tiny minority who gain either money or the dubious prestige of attracting an eccentric and quasi-religious following, and the stories they tell tend to differ markedly from those of the credible (and usually reluctant) witnesses.

From the many whose testimony can hardly be doubted there come stories of lights in the night sky which travel at impossible speeds but can also halt and hover at an instant's notice; of structured 'vehicles' by both day and night, sometimes only hazily defined but often observable in highly material detail; of the occupants of these vehicles; of encounters with vehicles and occupants on the ground, sometimes with terrifying closeness. The reports of these weirdnesses rest – by hundreds, by thousands – in the archives of the many non-governmental groups around the world which study these matters. They never cease to flow; they have not ceased to flow for forty years. It seems probable that events of a similar kind have been occurring for centuries, though we can be far less certain on this point, if only because dedicated groups did not exist to study them.

The volume of hard evidence from the non-governmental groups is overwhelming; there is far too much of it ever to be published in full. We can now add to it the openly available records of the French governmental agency, GEPAN, and the great wealth of documents which have recently been forced out of a reluctant administration in the United States under the American Freedom of Information Act. There is now a Babel Tower of evidence . . . Yet the silence is deafening! Not a single government in the world (with the exception of the French) openly acknowledges that there is even so much as a scientific oddity to be studied, let alone a potential problem of security.

We are a haunted species. The spectres are among us. They continue to come. They rattle their chains. Yet it is we who have, in a certain sense, chained them. There is an astounding public apathy, a climate of uneasy ridicule in the national press when it deigns to give a column-inch to these matters, an air of assumed indifference on the part of government agencies. Only a dedicated fringe of voluntary organizations, struggling with pitifully limited private resources, gives any public attention to the phenomenon.

Yet the phenomenon is undoubtedly under study in at least *some* back rooms . . . That air of governmental indifference *is* an assumed one . . .

From documents released under the Freedom of Information Act in America we have undeniable evidence of a keen interest in the phenomenon on the part of the CIA, the National Security Agency, and other government departments. The facts are meticulously documented in a recent book, *Clear Intent* by Lawrence Fawcett and Barry J. Greenwood (Prentice-Hall, 1984). We know that the French government remains interested: GEPAN continues in existence despite swingeing cuts imposed on many departments by the Mitterrand government a little while ago (though we can only speculate on what use is made of its material by its directing body, the French equivalent of NASA). We know that the Russian Academy of Sciences regularly buys a surprising number of each issue of the most prestigious British journal on the UFO phenomenon (though its importation by ordinary Soviet citizens is forbidden!) We must strongly suspect – to put it no higher – that the British Ministry of Defence is taking a close interest in the phenomenon. As a former Ministry of Defence official, I sincerely hope so! Anything which can enter and leave British airspace with impunity, land on British territory, leave confusing traces in our radar system, interfere with electrical and electronic devices, register itself on film and outmanoeuvre British aircraft (and I think there is evidence for all these things) must surely be of more than passing interest to a government department which is charged with our defence. I hope I shall be thought to compliment rather than criticize my former colleagues and present acquaintances in Whitehall if I ruefully congratulate them on the suave effrontery with which they pretend to be taking no notice of the stranger occurrences reported to them!

It grieves me to add that I think we have some evidence of direct and deliberate misstatement on the part of the Ministry of Defence in at least one important case, the occurrence of strange events on two nights in late December 1980 in a part of Rendlesham Forest adjoining the USAF Base at RAF Woodbridge. We have the evidence for these events in a statement signed on 13 January 1981 by the then Deputy Base Commander, Lt Col (now Colonel) Charles Halt of the United States Air Force. This statement was not made public until 14 June 1983 when – following persistent pressure by the authors of *Clear Intent* (see above) – its release was authorized by the USAF in America under the Freedom of Information Act. Whether this release was an inadvertency at rather low level in the USAF we may never know: despite the Freedom of Information Act, American agencies have proved perfectly capable (and often no doubt with good reason) of sustaining objections in the courts to the release of documents. There is certainly some evidence that Halt was not consulted about the release and that it somewhat dismayed him. Be that as it may, however, the letter of release included the extraordinary statement that the USAF had disposed of its own copy of Halt's report but that: '. . . through diligent inquiry and the gracious consent of Her Majesty's government, the British Ministry of Defence and the Royal Air Force, the US Air Force has provided a copy for you'. The Ministry of Defence have confirmed, in reply to a Parliamentary Question tabled by Major Sir Patrick Wall, MP, that a copy of Halt's report was indeed received by them. Yet we are told in a recent book – *Skycrash* by Brenda Butler, Dot Street and Jenny Randles (Neville Spearman Ltd, 1984) – that the Ministry of Defence had flatly denied any knowledge of supposed events in Rendlesham Forest when inquiries were made to them in 1981, following strong local rumours of an extraordinary occurrence.

The Ministry of Defence may well have good reasons for withholding information about the Rendlesham incidents. As a former Defence official, I would not wish to press questions on any matter touching national security; and in those circumstances I would not be surprised if questions pressed by others were met by a refusal to reply. But I cannot help feeling that it is something of a lapse from the usual standards of a government department to issue a direct misstatement. Concealment is one thing (and is often justified), false denial is quite another.

The RAF Woodbridge case of December 1980 strikes me as one of the most interesting and important of recent years, anyway in this country – perhaps the most significant *military* sighting (or supposed sighting) since the celebrated events of 13/14 August 1956 near RAF Bentwaters and RAF Lakenheath (both of which are, by an entertaining coincidence, quite close to Woodbridge in that much-haunted county of Suffolk). Those who wish to study the Bentwaters/Lakenheath incidents will find descriptions of them in the books mentioned below. The RAF Woodbridge case is described at length in *Skycrash* (see above). It is also to be the subject of several radio and television programmes. Much was said about it in the *News of the World* in 1983, mainly in its issues of 2 and 9 October. Alone in Fleet Street, the then editor, Derek Jameson, decided to give space to Halt's report; and Keith Beabey of the *News of the World* pursued it vigorously in the face of the kind of ridicule which the 'quality' newspapers seem to find it expedient to attach to this mysterious and persistent phenomenon.

It was the Woodbridge case which prompted me to take up a long-shelved intention to write a 'UFO book'. I have chosen, quite deliberately, to cast it as a piece of fiction. Fiction allows the imagination to range widely, and it seems to me that this can sometimes be productive in turning better qualified minds to new aspects of a problem. A false hypothesis can often have as much

183

heuristic value as a good one! It does, at the least, enable serious researchers to consider – and properly test – a new idea, even if only to throw it away when it fails to stand up to scrutiny. I am far from being wedded to the hypothesis on which *A Secret Property* is based. The main object of the book is to entertain, and to do so in the form of a thriller. It most certainly does not reflect any inside knowledge or startling revelation on the part of a former Defence official. (If I had such knowledge, the Official Secrets Act would forbid me to reveal it!)

My 'RAF Bentbridge' must not be taken to represent either RAF Woodbridge or RAF Bentwaters. It merely happens to be situated in Suffolk. And I must add – very firmly – that none of my British, American or French characters is based, even in the most indirect way, on any persons, living or dead, that I have ever known. If I seem critical of the Ministry of Defence or of Whitehall practice, it is simply because I have wanted to point up in dramatic fashion the manner in which bad decisions *can* be taken in unfavourable circumstances; we all know that this sometimes happens. I continue to cherish a very high regard for former colleagues and present acquaintances, and I happen to believe that British civil-service practice is among the best in the world. If at any point in my narrative I seem 'anti-American', this is simply because I see some potential dangers in the methods by which our major ally conducts its military and official business. Some of my best friends are American, and they tend to share my occasional reservations! I must add that Oleg Birkov, my KGB agent, is very closely modelled on a displeasing Russian with whom I once had the misfortune to conduct business. He can sue me if he wishes (assuming he has the insight to recognize himself).

The incident with which my book begins, in the vicinity of 'RAF Bentbridge', bears no resemblance at all to the extraordinary event which, according to Lt-Col Halt's report, took place near RAF Woodbridge in December 1980. I have not wanted to compete in any way with the serious researchers who have written *Skycrash*; and I would not in any case feel competent to do so. I have, instead, followed very closely the details of a bizarre and terrifying encounter experienced by an unfortunate forester on 9 November 1979 near Livingston, West Lothian. A brief summary is given in Hilary Evans's book listed below.

My ufologist friends will recognize that I have somewhat oversimplified the very rich and diverse data they have on file. I have, in particular, picked out the disc-shaped 'vehicle' – the notorious 'saucer' – from the great variety of types which any comprehensive analysis of the reports would have to include; and I have also chosen to give prominence to only two types of 'occupant' – the tall, fair one and the smallish green one. This is mainly for reasons of dramatic simplification. But I think ufologists will agree that the 'saucer' is far and away the commonest vehicle reported; and they will perhaps forgive me my preoccupation with 'little green men', since this is not only a particularly puzzling kind of 'entity' but also the most frequently mentioned when the press wishes to make fun of us. There is something to be said for confronting 'saucers' and 'LGM' head-on (anyway in fiction!)

Those who would like a fuller view of the phenomenon than I have been able to give will find the following books useful. The UFO bibliography is now vast (and a proportion of it is absurd nonsense). But the books listed have been of particular value to me, and they will guide the reader into a far more extensive bibliography if he wishes to find it. (I have already mentioned *Skycrash* and *Clear Intent* and will not repeat them here.)

The Evidence for UFOs	Hilary Evans	The Aquarian Press	1984
UFO Reality	Jenny Randles	Robert Hale	1983
Earthlights	Paul Devereux	Turnstone Press	1982
Operation Trojan Horse	J.A. Keel	Abacus	1973
The UFO Encyclopaedia	Margaret Sachs	Corgi	1981

Scores of others could be listed. The above provide an excellent introduction.

Finally, I would like to acknowledge a number of debts to the people who have tried (successfully or otherwise) to educate me in this extraordinary field or have sustained me in other ways. (None of them has any responsibility for the shortcomings of my narrative or for any inaccuracies in my facts. But I could not have written the book without them.)

First and foremost is Timothy Good, a noted freelance researcher who frequently lectures to learned societies and others on the UFO phenomenon and makes many broadcasts on radio and television. He has also had the courage to publish a book *George*

Adamski: the Untold Story (Ceti Publications, 1983) which re-evaluates the life and character of a man whose very name is sometimes used, alongside 'saucer' and 'LGM', to discredit the whole field. I owe Timothy Good many hours of discussion and an unceasing flow of references and press cuttings.

To Roger F. Dunkley, to whom this book is dedicated, and who has published much and widely in the field of supernatural fiction, I owe endless encouragement and a perceptive fellow-craftsman's reading of the work in progress. Many improvements in the narrative have followed from our discussions.

There are many others and I cannot list them all. In brief, particular thanks to: Paul Devereux from whose book *Earthlights* I lifted that peculiarly evocative expression 'partially formed events' by which I found my imagination fired, even though I differ greatly from him in my interpretation of the phenomenon; Lord Hill-Norton, former Chief of the Defence Staff and currently an active member of the House of Lords Group which studies the UFO phenomenon, for our stimulating correspondence; the authors of *Skycrash* for our several discussions; my close friend, Jean Thorp, for much encouragement, many meals provided at all hours for an author who couldn't be bothered to cook, and sound advice to a non-driver on a suitable choice of motor cars and the technicalities of using and abusing these terrestrial vehicles.

Last but by no means least I owe thanks to: Paul Keegan, formerly of Quartet Books, for commissioning *A Secret Property*; Stephen Pickles of Quartet for accepting it and for making perceptive comments on its text; my agent, Richard Gollner, for timely advice and guidance.

As a concluding afterword I would like to add that I know, quite as well as informed readers, that the 'hot line' does not really operate like an old-fashioned telephone system! Computers and communication satellites and rapid print-out have replaced anything so Edwardian as a hand-held 'voice-box'. But dramatic simplification requires poetic licence. Those who have seen that wonderful and terrifying film *Dr Strangelove* will know what I mean.

Ralph Noyes
London, 1985